here

in the dark, dusty corners of my mind

I feel a strange relief.

I am always welcome here

in my loneliness, in my sadness

in this abyss, there is a rhythm I remember. The steady drop of tears, the temptation to retreat, the shadow of my past

the life I choose to forget has not

will never

ever

forget *me*

BOOKS BY TAHEREH MAFI

Shatter Me: Series One

BOOK 1: *Shatter Me*

BOOK 2: *Unravel Me*

BOOK 3: *Ignite Me*

BOOK 4: *Restore Me*

BOOK 5: *Defy Me*

BOOK 6: *Imagine Me*

Shatter Me: Series One Novellas

BOOK 1.5: *Destroy Me*

BOOK 2.5: *Fracture Me*

BOOK 4.5: *Shadow Me*

BOOK 5.5: *Reveal Me*

BOOK 6.5: *Believe Me*

Shatter Me: Series One Novella Collections

Unite Me

Find Me

Shatter Me: Series Two

BOOK 1: *Watch Me*

BOOK 2: *Release Me*

The Woven Kingdom Series

BOOK 1: *This Woven Kingdom*

BOOK 2: *These Infinite Threads*

BOOK 3: *All This Twisted Glory*

BOOK 4: *Every Spiral of Fate*

An Emotion of Great Delight

A Very Large Expanse of Sea

RESTORE ME

SHATTER ME: SERIES ONE

BOOK FOUR

TAHEREH MAFI

STORYTIDE

An Imprint of HarperCollins*Publishers*

HarperCollins Children's Books,
a division of HarperCollins Publishers,
195 Broadway, New York, NY 10007

HarperCollins Publishers, Macken House,
39/40 Mayor Street Upper, Dublin 1, D01 C9W8, Ireland

Storytide is an imprint of HarperCollins Publishers.

Restore Me

harpercollins.com

Library of Congress Control Number: 2017962481
ISBN 978-0-06-349768-9

Typography by Ray Shappell
26 27 28 29 30 RTLO 10 9 8 7 6 5 4 3 2 1

SPECIAL EDITION, 2026

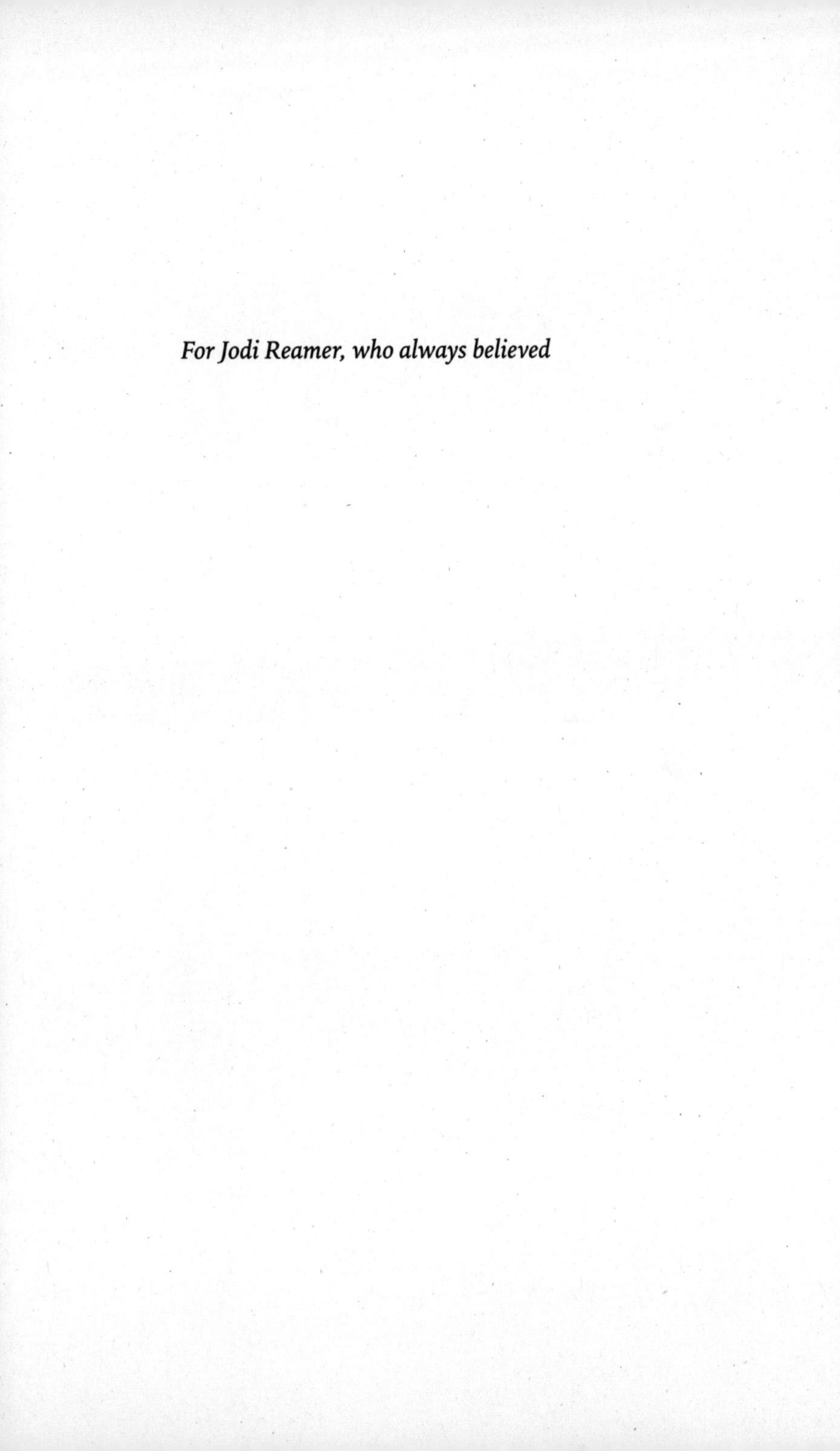

For Jodi Reamer, who always believed

JULIETTE

I don't wake up screaming anymore. I do not feel ill at the sight of blood. I do not flinch before firing a gun.

I will never again apologize for surviving.

And yet—

I'm startled at once by the sound of a door slamming open. I silence a gasp, spin around, and, by force of habit, rest my hand on the hilt of a semiautomatic hung from a holster at my side.

"J, we've got a serious problem."

Kenji is staring at me—eyes narrowed—his hands on his hips, T-shirt taut across his chest. This is angry Kenji. Worried Kenji. It's been sixteen days since we took over Sector 45—since I crowned myself the supreme commander of The Reestablishment—and it's been quiet. Unnervingly so. Every day I wake up, filled with half terror, half exhilaration, anxiously awaiting the inevitable missives from enemy nations who would challenge my authority and wage war against us—and now, finally, it seems that moment has arrived. So I take a deep breath, crack my neck, and look Kenji in the eye.

"Tell me."

He presses his lips together. Looks up at the ceiling. "So,

okay—the first thing you need to know is that this isn't my fault, okay? I was just trying to help."

I falter. Frown. "What?"

"I mean, I knew his punkass was a major drama queen, but this is just beyond ridiculous—"

"I'm sorry—what?" I take my hand off my gun; feel my body unclench. "Kenji, what are you talking about? This isn't about the war?"

"The war? What? J, are you not paying attention? Your boyfriend is having a freaking conniption right now and you need to go handle his ass before I do."

I exhale, irritated. "Are you serious? *Again* with this nonsense? Jesus, Kenji." I unlatch the holster from my back and toss it on the bed behind me. "What did you do this time?"

"See?" Kenji points at me. "See—why are you so quick to judge, huh, princess? Why assume that *I* was the one who did something wrong? Why me?" He crosses his arms against his chest, lowers his voice. "And you know, I've been meaning to talk to you about this for a while, actually, because I really feel that, as supreme commander, you can't be showing preferential treatment like this, but clearly—"

Kenji goes suddenly still.

At the creak of the door Kenji's eyebrows shoot up; a soft click and his eyes widen; a muted rustle of movement and suddenly the barrel of a gun is pressed against the back of his head. Kenji stares at me, his lips making no sound as he mouths the word *psychopath* over and over again.

The psychopath in question winks at me from where

he's standing, smiling like he couldn't possibly be holding a gun to the head of our mutual friend. I manage to suppress a laugh.

"Go on," Warner says, still smiling. "Please tell me exactly how she's failed you as a leader."

"*Hey*—" Kenji's arms fly up in mock surrender. "I never said she failed at anything, okay? And you are clearly over-react—"

Warner knocks Kenji on the side of the head with the weapon. "Idiot."

Kenji spins around. Yanks the gun out of Warner's hand. "What the hell is wrong with you, man? I thought we were cool."

"We were," Warner says icily. "Until you touched my *hair*."

"You asked me to give you a haircut—"

"I said nothing of the sort! I asked you to trim the edges!"

"And that's what I did."

"*This*," Warner says, spinning around so I might inspect the damage, "is not trimming the edges, you incompetent moron—"

I gasp. The back of Warner's head is a jagged mess of uneven hair; entire chunks have been buzzed off.

Kenji cringes as he looks over his handiwork. Clears his throat. "Well," he says, shoving his hands in his pockets. "I mean—whatever, man, beauty is subjective—"

Warner aims another gun at him.

"Hey!" Kenji shouts. "I am not here for this abusive

relationship, okay?" He points at Warner. "I did not sign up for this shit!"

Warner glares at him and Kenji retreats, backing out of the room before Warner has another chance to react; and then, just as I let out a sigh of relief, Kenji pops his head back into the doorway and says

"I think the cut looks cute, actually"

and Warner slams the door in his face.

Welcome to my brand-new life as supreme commander of The Reestablishment.

Warner is still facing the closed door as he exhales, his shoulders losing their tension as he does, and I'm able to see even more clearly the mess Kenji has made. Warner's thick, gorgeous, golden hair—a defining feature of his beauty—chopped up by careless hands.

A disaster.

"Aaron," I say softly.

He hangs his head.

"Come here."

He turns around, looking at me out of the corner of his eye like he's done something to be ashamed of. I clear the guns off the bed and make room for him beside me. He sinks into the mattress with a sad sigh.

"I look hideous," he says quietly.

I shake my head, smiling, and touch his cheek. "Why did you let him cut your hair?"

Warner looks up at me then; his eyes round and green and perplexed. "You told me to spend time with him."

I laugh out loud. "So you let Kenji cut your hair?"

"I didn't let him *cut* my hair," he says, scowling. "It was"—he hesitates—"it was a gesture of camaraderie. It was an act of trust I'd seen practiced among my soldiers. In any case," he says, turning away, "it's not as though I have any experience building friendships."

"Well," I say. "We're friends, aren't we?"

At this, he smiles.

"And?" I nudge him. "That's been good, hasn't it? You're learning to be nicer to people."

"Yes, well, I don't want to be nicer to people. It doesn't suit me."

"I think it suits you beautifully," I say, beaming. "I love it when you're nice."

"You would say that." He almost laughs. "But being kind does not come naturally to me, love. You'll have to be patient with my progress."

I take his hand in mine. "I have no idea what you're talking about. You're perfectly kind to me."

Warner shakes his head. "I know I promised I would make an effort to be nicer to your friends—and I will continue to make that effort—but I hope I've not led you to believe I'm capable of an impossibility."

"What do you mean?"

"Only that I hope I won't disappoint you. I might, if pressed, be able to generate some degree of warmth, but you must know that I have no interest in treating anyone the way I treat you. *This*," he says, touching the air between us, "is an exception to a very hard rule." His eyes are on my lips now; his hand has moved to my neck. "*This*," he says softly, "is very, very unusual."

I stop

stop breathing, talking, thinking—

He's hardly touched me and my heart is racing; memories crash over me, scalding me in waves: the weight of his body against mine; the taste of his skin; the heat of his touch and his sharp gasps for air and the things he's said to me only in the dark.

Butterflies invade my veins, and I force them out.

This is still so new, his touch, his skin, the scent of him, so new, so new and so incredible—

He smiles, tilts his head; I mimic the movement and with one soft intake of air his lips part and I hold still, my lungs flung to the floor, fingers feeling for his shirt and for what comes next when he says

"I'll have to shave my head, you know"

and pulls away.

I blink and he's still not kissing me.

"And it is my very sincere hope," he says, "that you will still love me when I return."

And then he's up up and away and I'm counting on one hand the number of men I've killed and marveling at how little it's done to help me hold it together in Warner's presence.

I nod once as he waves good-bye, collect my good sense from where I left it, and fall backward onto the bed, head spinning, the complications of war and peace heavy on my mind.

I did not think it would be *easy* to be a leader, exactly, but I do think I thought it would be easier than this:

I am racked with doubt in every moment about the decisions I have made. I am infuriatingly surprised every time a soldier follows my lead. And I am growing more terrified that we—that *I*—will have to kill many, many more before this world is settled. Though I think it's the silence, more than anything else, that's left me shaken.

It's been sixteen days.

I've given speeches about what's to come, about our plans for the future; we've held memorials for the lives lost in battle and we're making good on promises to implement change. Castle, true to his word, is already hard at work, trying to address issues with farming, irrigation, and, most urgent, how best to transition the civilians out of the compounds. But this will be work done in stages; it will be a slow and careful build—a fight for the earth that may take a century. I think we all understand that. And if it were only the civilians I had to worry about, I would not worry so much. But I worry because I know too well that nothing can be done to fix this world if we spend the next several decades at war within it.

Even so, I'm prepared to fight.

It's not what I want, but I'll gladly go to war if it's what we need to do to make a change. I just wish it were that simple. Right now, my biggest problem is also the most confusing:

Wars require enemies, and I can't seem to find any.

In the sixteen days since I shot Anderson in the forehead I have faced zero opposition. No one has tried to arrest me. No other supreme commanders have challenged me. Of the 554 remaining sectors on this continent alone, not a single one has defected, declared war, or spoken ill of me. No one has protested; the people have not rioted. For some reason, The Reestablishment is playing along.

Playing pretend.

And it deeply, deeply unnerves me.

We're in a strange stalemate, stuck in neutral when I desperately want to be doing more. More for the people of Sector 45, for North America, and for the world as a whole. But this strange quiet has thrown all of us off-balance. We were so sure that, with Anderson dead, the other supreme commanders would rise up—that they'd command their armies to destroy us—to destroy *me*. Instead, the leaders of the world have made our insignificance clear: they're ignoring us as they would an annoying fly, trapping us under glass where we're free to buzz around, banging broken wings against the walls for only as long as the oxygen lasts. Sector 45 has been left to do as it pleases; we've been allowed autonomy and the authority to revise the infrastructure of our sector with no interference. Everywhere else—and everyone else—is pretending as though nothing in the world has changed. Our revolution occurred in a vacuum. Our subsequent victory has been reduced to something so small it might not even exist.

Mind games.

Castle is always visiting, advising. It was his suggestion that I be proactive—that I take the upper hand. Instead of waiting around, anxious and defensive, I should reach out, he said. I should make my presence known. Stake a claim, he said. Take a seat at the table. And attempt to form alliances before launching assaults. Connect with the five other supreme commanders around the world.

Because I may speak for North America—but what of the rest of the world? What of South America? Europe? Asia? Africa? Oceania?

Host an international conference of leaders, he said.

Talk.

Aim for peace first, he said.

"They must be dying of curiosity," Castle said to me. "A seventeen-year-old girl taking over North America? A teenage girl killing Anderson and declaring herself ruler of this continent? Ms. Ferrars—you must know that you have great leverage at the moment! Use it to your advantage!"

"Me?" I said, stunned. "How do I have leverage?"

Castle sighed. "You certainly are brave for your age, Ms. Ferrars, but I'm sorry to see your youth so inextricably tied to inexperience. I will try to put it plainly: you have superhuman strength, nearly invincible skin, a lethal touch, only seventeen years to your name, and you have single-handedly felled the despot of this nation. And yet you doubt that you might be capable of intimidating the world?"

I cringed.

"Old habits, Castle," I said quietly. "Bad habits. You're right, of course. Of course you're right."

He leveled me with a straight stare. "You must understand that unanimous, collective silence from your enemies is no act of coincidence. They've certainly been in touch with one another—they've certainly agreed to this approach—because they're waiting to see what you do next." He shook his head. "They are awaiting your next move, Ms. Ferrars. I implore you to make it a good one."

So I'm learning.

I did as he suggested and three days ago I sent word through Delalieu and contacted the five other supreme commanders of The Reestablishment. I invited them to join me here, in Sector 45, for a conference of international leaders next month.

Just fifteen minutes before Kenji barged into my room, I'd received my first RSVP.

Oceania said yes.

And I'm not sure what that means.

WARNER

I've not been myself lately.

The truth is I've not been myself for what feels like a long time, so much so that I've begun to wonder whether I ever really knew. I stare, unblinking, into the mirror, the din of buzzing hair clippers echoing through the room. My face is only dimly reflected in my direction, but it's enough for me to see that I've lost weight. My cheeks are hollow; my eyes, wider; my cheekbones more pronounced. My movements are both mournful and mechanical as I shear off my own hair, the remnants of my vanity falling at my feet.

My father is dead.

I close my eyes, steeling myself against the unwelcome strain in my chest, the clippers still humming in my clenched fist.

My father is dead.

It's been just over two weeks since he was killed, shot twice in the forehead by someone I love. She was doing me a kindness by killing him. She was braver than I'd ever been, pulling the trigger when I never could. He was a monster. He deserved worse.

And still—

This pain.

I take in a tight breath and blink open my eyes, grateful for the time to be alone; grateful, somehow, for the opportunity to tear asunder something, anything from my flesh. There's a strange catharsis in this.

My mother is dead, I think, as I drag the electric blade across my skull. *My father is dead,* I think, as the hair falls to the floor. Everything I was, everything I did, everything I am, was forged from the twins of their action and inaction.

Who am I, I wonder, in their absence?

Shorn head, blade switched off, I rest my palms against the edge of the vanity and lean in, still trying to catch a glimpse of the man I've become. I feel old and unsettled, my heart and mind at war. The last words I ever spoke to my father—

"Hey."

My heart speeds up as I spin around; I'm affecting nonchalance in an instant. "Hi," I say, forcing my limbs to slow, to be steady as I dust errant strands of hair from my shoulders.

She's looking at me with big eyes, beautiful and worried.

I remember to smile. "How do I look? Not too horrible, I hope."

"Aaron," she says quietly. "Are you okay?"

"I'm fine," I say, and glance again in the mirror. I run a hand over the soft/spiky half inch of hair I have left and wonder at how the cut manages to makes me look harsher—and colder—than before. "Though I confess I don't really recognize myself," I add aloud, attempting a laugh. I'm standing in the middle of the bathroom wearing nothing but boxer briefs. My body has never been leaner, the sharp lines of muscle never more defined; and the rawness of my body is now paired with the rough cut of my hair in a way that feels almost uncivilized—and so unlike me that I have to look away.

Juliette is now right in front of me.

Her hands settle on my hips and pull me forward; I trip a little as I follow her lead. "What are you doing?" I begin to say, but when I meet her eyes I find tenderness and concern. Something thaws inside of me. My shoulders relax and I reel her in, drawing in a deep breath as I do.

"When will we talk about it?" she says against my chest. "All of it? Everything that's happened—"

I flinch.

"Aaron."

"I'm okay," I lie to her. "It's just hair."

"You know that's not what I'm talking about."

I look away. Stare at nothing. We're both quiet a moment.

It's Juliette who finally breaks the silence.

"Are you upset with me?" she whispers. "For shooting him?"

My body stills.

Her eyes widen.

"No—*no*." I say the words too quickly, but I mean them. "No, of course not. It's not that."

Juliette sighs.

"I'm not sure you're aware of this," she says finally, "but

it's okay to mourn the loss of your father, even if he was a terrible person. You know?" She peers up at me. "You're not a robot."

I swallow back the lump growing in my throat and gently extricate myself from her arms. I kiss her on the cheek and linger there, against her skin, for only a second. "I need to take a shower."

She looks heartbroken and confused, but I don't know what else to do. It's not that I don't love her company, it's just that right now I'm desperate for solitude and I don't know how else to find it.

So I shower. I take baths. I go for long walks.

I tend to do this a lot.

When I finally come to bed she's already asleep.

I want to reach for her, to pull her soft, warm body against my own, but I feel paralyzed. This horrible half-grief has made me feel complicit in darkness. I worry that my sadness will be interpreted as an endorsement of his choices—of his very existence—and in this matter I don't want to be misunderstood, so I cannot admit that I grieve him, that I care at all for the loss of this monstrous man who raised me. And in the absence of healthy action I remain frozen, a sentient stone in the wake of my father's death.

Are you upset with me? For shooting him?

I hated him.

I hated him with a violent intensity I've never since

experienced. But the fire of true hatred, I realize, cannot exist without the oxygen of affection. I would not hurt so much, or hate so much, if I did not care.

And it is this, my unrequited affection for my father, that has always been my greatest weakness. So I lie here, marinating in a sorrow I can never speak of, while regret consumes my heart.

I am an orphan.

"Aaron?" she whispers, and I'm pulled back to the present.

"Yes, love?"

She moves in a sleepy, sideways motion, and nudges my arm with her head. I can't help but smile as I open up to make room for her against me. She fills the void quickly, pressing her face into my neck as she wraps an arm around my waist. My eyes close as if in prayer. My heart restarts.

"I miss you," she says. It's a whisper I almost don't catch.

"I'm right here," I say, gently touching her cheek. "I'm right here, love."

But she shakes her head. Even as I pull her closer, even as she falls back asleep, she shakes her head.

And I wonder if she's not wrong.

JULIETTE

I'm having breakfast by myself this morning—alone, but not lonely.

The breakfast room is full of familiar faces, all of us catching up on something: sleep; work; half-finished conversations. Energy levels in here are always dependent on the amount of caffeine we've had, and right now, things are still pretty quiet.

Brendan, who's been nursing the same cup of coffee all morning, catches my eye and waves. I wave back. He's the only one among us who doesn't actually need caffeine; his gift for creating electricity also works as a backup generator for his whole body. He's exuberance, personified. In fact, his stark-white hair and ice-blue eyes seem to emanate their own kind of energy, even from across the room. I'm starting to think Brendan keeps up appearances with the coffee cup mostly out of solidarity with Winston, who can't seem to survive without it. The two of them are inseparable these days—even if Winston occasionally resents Brendan's natural buoyancy.

They've been through a lot together. We all have.

Brendan and Winston are sitting with Alia, who's got her sketchbook open beside her, no doubt designing something new and amazing to help us in battle. I'm too tired to move, otherwise I'd get up to join their group; instead, I drop my chin in one hand and study the faces of my friends, feeling grateful. But the scars on Brendan's and Winston's faces take me back to a time I'd rather not remember—back to a time when we thought we'd lost them. When we'd lost two others. And suddenly my thoughts are too heavy for breakfast. So I look away. Drum my fingers against the table.

I'm supposed to be meeting Kenji for breakfast—it's how we begin our workdays—which is the only reason I haven't grabbed my own plate of food. Unfortunately, his lateness is beginning to make my stomach grumble. Everyone in the room is cutting into fresh stacks of fluffy pancakes, and they look delicious. All of it is tempting: the mini pitchers of maple syrup; the steaming heaps of breakfast potatoes; the little bowls of freshly cut fruit. If nothing else, killing Anderson and taking over Sector 45 got us much better breakfast options. But I think we might be the only ones who appreciate the upgrades.

Warner never has breakfast with the rest of us. He pretty much never stops working, not even to eat. Breakfast is another meeting for him, and he takes it with Delalieu, just the two of them, and even then I'm not sure he actually eats anything. Warner never appears to take pleasure in food. For him, food is fuel—necessary and, most of the time, annoying—in that his body requires it to function. Once, while he was deeply immersed in some important paperwork at dinner, I put a cookie on a plate in front of him just to see what would happen. He glanced up at me, glanced back at his work, whispered a quiet *thank you,* and ate the cookie with a knife and fork. He didn't even seem to enjoy it. This, needless to say, makes him the polar opposite of Kenji, who loves to eat everything, all the time, and who later told me that watching Warner eat a cookie made him want to cry.

Speaking of Kenji, him flaking on me this morning is more than a little weird, and I'm beginning to worry. I'm just about to glance at the clock for the third time when, suddenly, Adam is standing next to my table, looking uncomfortable.

"Hi," I say, just a little too loudly. "What's, uh, what's up?"

Adam and I have interacted a couple of times in the last two weeks, but it's always been by accident. Suffice it to say that it's unusual for Adam to be standing in front of me on purpose, and I'm so surprised that for a moment I almost miss the obvious:

He looks bad.

Rough. Ragged. More than a little exhausted. In fact, if I didn't know any better, I would've sworn Adam had been crying. Not over our failed relationship, I hope.

Still, old instinct gnaws at me, tugs at ancient heart-strings.

We speak at the same time:

"You okay . . . ?" I ask.

"Castle wants to talk to you," he says.

"Castle sent *you* to come get me?" I say, feelings forgotten.

Adam shrugs. "I was walking past his room at the right time, I guess."

"Um. Okay." I try to smile. Castle is always trying to make nice between me and Adam; he doesn't like the tension. "Did he say he wants to see me right now?"

"Yep." Adam shoves his hands in his pockets. "Right away."

"All right," I say, and the whole thing feels awkward. Adam just stands there as I gather my things, and I want to tell him to go away, to stop staring at me, that this is weird, that we broke up forever ago and it was *weird*, you made it *so weird*, but then I realize he isn't staring at me. He's looking at the floor like he's stuck, lost in his head somewhere.

"Hey—are you okay?" I say again, this time gently.

Adam looks up, startled. "What?" he says. "What, oh—yeah, I'm fine. Hey do you know, uh"—he clears his throat, looks around—"do you, uh—"

"Do I what?"

Adam rocks on his heels, eyes darting around the room. "Warner is never here for breakfast, huh?"

My eyebrows shoot up my forehead. "You're looking for Warner?"

"What? No. I'm just, uh, wondering. He's never here. You know? It's weird."

I stare at him.

He says nothing.

"It's not that weird," I say slowly, studying Adam's face. "Warner doesn't have time for breakfast with us. He's always working."

"Oh," Adam says, and the word seems to deflate him. "That's too bad."

"Is it?" I frown.

But Adam doesn't seem to hear me. He calls for James, who's putting away his breakfast tray, and the two of them meet in the middle of the room and then disappear.

I have no idea what they do all day. I've never asked.

The mystery of Kenji's absence at breakfast is solved the moment I walk up to Castle's door: the two of them are here, heads together.

I knock on the open door as a courtesy. "Hey," I say. "You wanted to see me?"

"Yes, yes, Ms. Ferrars," Castle says eagerly. He gets to his feet and waves me inside. "Please, have a seat. And if you would"—he gestures behind me—"close the door."

I'm nervous in an instant.

I take a tentative step into Castle's makeshift office and glance at Kenji, whose blank face does nothing to allay my fears. "What's going on?" I say. And then, only to Kenji: "Why weren't you at breakfast?"

Castle motions for me to take a seat.

I do.

"Ms. Ferrars," he says urgently. "You have news of Oceania?"

"Excuse me?"

"The RSVP. You received your first RSVP, did you not?"

"Yeah, I did," I say slowly. "But no one is supposed to know about that yet—I was going to tell Kenji about it over breakfast this morning—"

"Nonsense." Castle cuts me off. "Everyone knows. Mr. Warner knows, certainly. And Lieutenant Delalieu knows."

"What?" I glance at Kenji, who shrugs. "How is that possible?"

"Don't be so easily shocked, Ms. Ferrars. Obviously all of your correspondence is monitored."

My eyes widen. "What?"

Castle makes a frustrated motion with his hand. "Time is of the essence, so if you would, I'd really—"

"Time is of *what* essence?" I say, irritated. "How am I supposed to help you when I don't even know what you're talking about?"

Castle pinches the bridge of his nose. "Kenji," he says suddenly. "Will you leave us, please?"

"Yep." Kenji jumps to his feet with a mock salute. He heads toward the door.

"Wait," I say, grabbing his arm. "What's going on?"

"I have no idea, kid." Kenji laughs, shakes his arm free. "This conversation doesn't concern me. Castle called me in here earlier to talk about cows."

"Cows?"

"Yeah, you know." He arches an eyebrow. "Livestock. He's been having me do reconnaissance on several hundreds of acres of farmland that The Reestablishment has been keeping off the radar. Lots and lots of cows."

"Exciting."

"It is, actually." His eyes light up. "The methane makes

it all pretty easy to track. Makes you wonder why they wouldn't do something to preve—"

"*Methane?*" I say, confused. "Isn't that a kind of gas?"

"I take it you don't know much about cow shit."

I ignore that. Instead, I say, "So that's why you weren't at breakfast this morning? Because you were looking at cow poop?"

"Basically."

"Well," I say. "At least that explains the smell."

It takes Kenji a second to catch on, but when he does, he narrows his eyes. Taps me on the forehead with one finger. "You're going straight to hell, you know that?"

I smile, big. "See you later? I still want to go on our morning walk."

He makes a noncommittal grunt.

"C'mon," I say, "it'll be fun this time, I promise."

"Oh yeah, big fun." Kenji rolls his eyes as he turns away, and shoots Castle another two-finger salute. "See you later, sir."

Castle nods his good-bye, a bright smile on his face.

It takes a minute for Kenji to finally walk out the door and shut it behind him, but in that minute Castle's face transforms. His easy smile, his eager eyes: gone. Now that he and I are fully alone, Castle looks a little shaken, a little more serious. Maybe even . . . scared?

And he gets right down to business.

"When the RSVP came through, what did it say? Was there anything memorable about the note?"

"No." I frown. "I don't know. If all my correspondence is being monitored, wouldn't you already know the answer to this question?"

"Of course not. I'm not the one monitoring your mail."

"So who's monitoring my mail? Warner?"

Castle only looks at me. "Ms. Ferrars, there is something deeply unusual about this response." He hesitates. "Especially as it's your first, and thus far, only RSVP."

"Okay," I say, confused. "What's unusual about it?"

Castle looks into his hands. At the wall. "How much do you know about Oceania?"

"Very little."

"How little?"

I shrug. "I can point it out on a map."

"And you've never been there?"

"Are you serious?" I shoot him an incredulous look. "Of course not. I've never been anywhere, remember? My parents pulled me out of school. Passed me through the system. Eventually threw me in an insane asylum."

Castle takes a deep breath. Closes his eyes as he says, very carefully, "Was there anything at all memorable about the note you received from the supreme commander of Oceania?"

"No," I say. "Not really."

"Not really?"

"I guess it was little informal? But I don't thi—"

"Informal, how?"

I look away, remembering. "The message was really

brief," I explain. "It said *Can't wait to see you,* with no sign-off or anything."

"'Can't wait to see you'?" Castle looks suddenly puzzled.

I nod.

"Not can't wait to *meet* you," he says, "but can't wait to *see* you."

I nod again. "Like I said, a little informal. But it was polite, at least. Which I think is a pretty positive sign, all things considered."

Castle sighs heavily as he turns in his chair. He's facing the wall now, his fingers steepled under his chin. I'm studying the sharp angles of his profile as he says quietly,

"Ms. Ferrars, how much has Mr. Warner told you about The Reestablishment?"

WARNER

I'm sitting alone in the conference room, running an absent hand over my new haircut, when Delalieu arrives. He's pulling a small coffee cart in behind him, wearing the tepid, shaky smile I've come to rely upon. Our workdays have been busier than ever lately; thankfully, we've never made time to discuss the uncomfortable details of recent events, and I doubt we ever will.

For this I am forever grateful.

It's a safe space for me here, with Delalieu, where I can pretend that things in my life have changed very little.

I am still chief commander and regent to the soldiers of Sector 45; it's still my duty to organize and lead those who will help us stand against the rest of The Reestablishment. And with that role comes responsibility. We've had a lot of restructuring to do while we coordinate our next moves, and Delalieu has been critical to these efforts.

"Good morning, sir."

I nod a greeting as he pours us both a cup of coffee. A lieutenant such as himself need not pour his own coffee in the morning, but we've come to prefer the privacy.

I take a sip of the black liquid—I've recently learned to enjoy its bitter tang—and lean back in my chair. "Updates?"

Delalieu clears his throat.

"Yes, sir," he says, hastily returning his coffee cup to its saucer, spilling a little as he does. "Quite a few this morning, sir."

I tilt my head at him.

"Construction of the new command station is going well. We're expecting to be done with all the details in the next two weeks, but the private rooms will be move-in ready by tomorrow."

"Good." Our new team, under Juliette's supervision, comprises many people now, with many departments to manage and, with the exception of Castle, who's carved out a small office for himself upstairs, thus far they've all been using my personal training facilities as their central headquarters. And though this had seemed like a practical idea at its inception, my training facilities are accessible only through my personal quarters; and now that the group of them are living freely on base, they're often barging in and out of my rooms, unannounced.

Needless to say, it's driving me insane.

"What else?"

Delalieu checks his list and says, "We've finally managed to secure your father's files, sir. It's taken all this time to locate and retrieve the bulk of it, but I've left the boxes in your room, sir, for you to open at your leisure. I thought"—he clears his throat—"I thought you might like to look through his remaining personal effects before they are inherited by our new supreme commander."

A heavy, cold dread fills my body.

"There's quite a lot of it, I'm afraid," Delalieu is still saying. "All his daily logs. Every report he'd ever filed. We even managed to locate a few of his personal journals." Delalieu hesitates. And then, in a tone only I know how to decipher: "I do hope his notes will be useful to you, somehow."

I look up, meet Delalieu's eyes. There's concern there. Worry.

"Thank you," I say quietly. "I'd nearly forgotten."

An uncomfortable silence settles between us and, for a moment, neither of us knows exactly what to say. We still haven't discussed this, the death of my father. The death of Delalieu's son-in-law. The horrible husband of his late daughter, my mother. We never talk about the fact that Delalieu is my grandfather. That he is the only kind of father I have left in the world.

It's not what we do.

So it's with a halting, unnatural voice that Delalieu attempts to pick up the thread of conversation.

"Oceania, as, as I'm sure you've heard, sir, has said that, that they would attend a meeting organized by our new madam, madam supreme—"

I nod.

"But the others," he says, the words rushing out of him now, "will not respond until they've spoken with you, sir."

At this, my eyes widen perceptibly.

"They're"—Delalieu clears his throat again—"well, sir,

as you know, they're all old friends of the family, and they—well, they—"

"Yes," I whisper. "Of course."

I look away, at the wall. My jaw feels suddenly wired shut with frustration. Secretly, I'd been expecting this. But after two weeks of silence I'd actually begun to hope that maybe they'd continue to play dumb. There's been no communication from these old friends of my father, no offers of condolences, no white roses, no sympathy cards. No correspondence, as was our daily ritual, from the families I'd known as a child, the families responsible for the hellscape we live in now. I thought I'd been happily, mercifully, cut off.

Apparently not.

Apparently treason is not enough of a crime to be left alone. Apparently my father's many daily missives expounding my "grotesque obsession with an experiment" were not reason enough to oust me from the group. He loved complaining aloud, my father, loved sharing his many disgusts and disapprovals with his old friends, the only people alive who knew him face-to-face. And every day he humiliated me in front of the people we knew. He made my world, my thoughts, and my feelings seem small. Pathetic. And every day I'd count the letters piling up in my in-box, screeds from his old friends begging me to see *reason*, as they called it. To remember myself. To stop embarrassing my family. To listen to my father. To grow up, be a man, and stop crying over my sick mother.

No, these ties run too deep.

I squeeze my eyes shut to quell the rush of faces, memories of my childhood, as I say, "Tell them I'll be in touch."

"That won't be necessary, sir," says Delalieu.

"Excuse me?"

"Ibrahim's children are already *en route*."

It happens swiftly: a sudden, brief paralysis of my limbs.

"What do you mean?" I say, only barely managing to stay calm. "*En route* where? Here?"

Delalieu nods.

A wave of heat floods my body so quickly I don't even realize I'm on my feet until I have to grab the table for support. "How *dare* they," I say, somehow still clinging to the edge of composure. "Their complete disregard— To be so unbearably entitled—"

"Yes, sir, I understand, sir," Delalieu says, looking newly terrified, "it's just—as you know—it's the way of the supreme families, sir. A time-honored tradition. A refusal on my part would've been interpreted as an open act of hostility—and Madam Supreme has instructed me to be diplomatic for as long as possible so I thought, I—I thought— Oh, I'm very sorry, sir—"

"She doesn't know who she's dealing with," I say sharply. "There is no diplomacy with these people. Our new supreme commander might have no way of knowing this, but you," I say, more upset than angry now, "you should've known better. War would've been worth avoiding this."

I don't look up to see his face when he says, his voice trembling, "I'm deeply, deeply sorry, sir."

A time-honored tradition, indeed.

The right to come and go was a practice long ago agreed upon. The supreme families were always welcome in each other's lands at any time, no invitations necessary. While the movement was young and the children were young, our families held fast. And now those families—and their children—rule the world.

This was my life for a very long time. On Tuesday, a play-date in Europe; on Friday, a dinner party in South America. Our parents insane, all of them.

The only *friends* I ever knew had families even crazier than mine. I have no wish to see any of them ever again.

And yet—

Good God, I have to warn Juliette.

"As to the, as to the matter of the, of the civilians"—Delalieu is prattling on—"I've been communicating with Castle, per, per your request, sir, on how best to proceed with their transition out of the, out of the compounds—"

But the rest of our morning meeting passes by in a blur.

When I finally manage to loose myself from Delalieu's shadow, I head straight back to my own quarters. Juliette is usually here this time of day, and I'm hoping to catch her, to warn her before it's too late.

Too soon, I'm intercepted.

"Oh, um, hey—"

I look up, distracted, and quickly stop in place. My eyes widen, just a little.

"Kent," I say quietly.

One swift appraisal is all I need to know that he's not okay. In fact, he looks terrible. Thinner than ever; dark circles under his eyes. Thoroughly worn-out.

I wonder whether I look just the same to him.

"I was wondering," he says, and looks away, his face pinched. He clears his throat. "I was, uh"—he clears his throat again—"I was wondering if we could talk."

I feel my chest tighten. I stare at him a moment, cataloging his tense shoulders, his unkempt hair, his deeply bitten fingernails. He sees me staring and quickly shoves his hands into his pockets. He can hardly meet my eyes.

"Talk," I manage to say.

He nods.

I exhale quietly, slowly. We haven't spoken a word to each other since I first found out we were brothers, nearly three weeks ago. I thought the emotional implosion of the evening had ended as well anyone could've hoped, but so much has happened since that night. We haven't had a chance to rip open that wound again. "Talk," I say again. "Of course."

He swallows hard. Stares at the ground. "Cool."

And I'm suddenly compelled to ask a question that unsettles both of us: "Are you all right?"

He looks up, stunned. His blue eyes are round and red-rimmed, bloodshot. His Adam's apple bobs in his throat. "I don't know who else to talk to about this," he whispers. "I don't know anyone else who would even understand—"

And I do. All at once.

I understand.

When his eyes go abruptly glassy with emotion; when his shoulders tremble even as he tries to hold himself still—

I feel my own bones rattle.

“Of course,” I say, surprising myself. “Come with me.”

JULIETTE

It's another cold day today, all silver ruins and snow-covered decay. I wake up every morning hoping for even a slant of sunlight, but the bite in the air remains unforgiving as it sinks hungry teeth into our flesh. We've finally left the worst of winter behind, but even these early weeks of March feel inhumanly frosty. I pull my coat up around my neck and huddle into it.

Kenji and I are on what has become our daily walk around the forgotten stretches of Sector 45. It's been both strange and liberating to be able to walk so freely in the fresh air. Strange, because I can't leave the base without a small troop for protection, and liberating because it's the first time I've been able to acquaint myself with the land. I'd never had a chance to walk calmly through these compounds; I had no way of seeing, firsthand, exactly what'd happened to this world. And now, to be able to roam freely, unquestioned—

Well, sort of.

I glance over my shoulder at the six soldiers shadowing our every move, machine guns held tightly against their chests as they march. No one really knows what to do about me yet; Anderson had a very different system in place as supreme commander—he never showed his face to anyone except those he was about to kill, and never traveled anywhere without his Supreme Guard. But I don't have rules about either and, until I decide exactly how I want to rule, this is my new situation:

I'm to be babysat from the moment I step outside.

I tried to explain that I don't need protection—I tried to remind everyone of my very literal, lethal touch; my superhuman strength; my functional invincibility—

"But it would be very helpful to the soldiers," Warner had explained, "if you would at least go through the motions. We rely on rules, regulation, and constant discipline in the military, and soldiers need a system upon which they might depend, at all times. Do this for them," he said. "Maintain the pretense. We can't change everything all at once, love. It'd be too disorienting."

So here I am.

Being followed.

Warner has been my constant guide these last couple of weeks. He's been teaching me every day about all the many things his dad did and all the things he, himself, is responsible for. There are an infinite number of things Warner needs to do every day just to run this sector—never mind the bizarre (and seemingly endless) list of things I need to do to lead an entire continent.

I'd be lying if I didn't say that, sometimes, it all feels impossible.

I had one day, just one day to exhale and enjoy the relief of overthrowing Anderson and reclaiming Sector 45. One day to sleep, one day to smile, one day to indulge in the luxury of imagining a better world.

It was at the end of Day 2 that I discovered a nervous-looking Delalieu standing behind my door.

He seemed frantic.

"Madam Supreme," he'd said, a crazy smile half hung on his face. "I imagine you must be very overwhelmed lately. So much to do." He looked down. Wrung his hands. "But I fear—that is— I think—"

"What is it?" I'd said to him. "Is something wrong?"

"Well, madam—I haven't wanted to bother you—you've been through so much and you've needed time to adjust—"

He looked at the wall.

I waited.

"Forgive me," he said. "It's just that it's been nearly thirty-six hours since you've taken control of the continent and you haven't been to visit your quarters once," he said in a rush. "And you've already received so much mail that I don't know where to put it anymo—"

"What?"

He froze. Finally met my eyes.

"What do you mean, *my quarters*? I have *quarters*?"

Delalieu blinked, dumbfounded. "Of course you do, madam. The supreme commander has his or her own quarters in every sector on the continent. We have an entire wing here dedicated to your offices. It's where the late supreme commander Anderson used to stay whenever he visited us on base. And as everyone around the world knows that you've made Sector 45 your permanent residence, this is where they've sent all your mail, both physical and digital. It's where your intelligence briefings will be delivered every morning. It's where other sector leaders have been sending their daily reports—"

"You're not serious," I said, stunned.

"Very serious, madam." He looked desperate. "And I worry about the message you might be sending by ignoring all correspondence at this early stage." He looked away. "Forgive me. I don't mean to overstep. I just—I know you'd like to make an effort to strengthen your international relationships—but I worry about the consequences you might face for breaking your many continental accords—"

"No, no, of course. Thank you, Delalieu," I said, head spinning. "Thank you for letting me know. I'm—I'm very grateful to you for intervening. I had no idea"—I clapped a hand to my forehead—"but maybe tomorrow morning?" I said. "Tomorrow morning you could meet me after my morning walk? Show me where these quarters are located?"

"Of course," he said with a slight bow. "It would be my pleasure, Madam Supreme."

"Thank you, Lieutenant."

"Certainly, madam." He looked so relieved. "Have a pleasant evening."

I stumbled then as I said good-bye to him, tripping over my feet in a daze.

Not much has changed.

My shoes scuff on the concrete, my feet knocking into

each other as I startle myself back into the present. I take a more certain step forward, this time bracing myself against another sudden, biting gust. Kenji shoots me a look of concern. I look, but don't really see him. I'm looking beyond him now, eyes narrowed at nothing in particular. My mind continues on its course, whirring in time with the wind.

"You okay, kid?"

I look up, squinting sideways at Kenji. "I'm okay, yeah."

"Convincing."

I manage to smile and frown at the same time.

"So," Kenji says, exhaling the word. "What'd Castle want to talk to you about?"

I turn away, irritated in an instant. "I don't know. Castle is being weird."

That gets Kenji's attention. Castle is like a father to him—and I'm pretty sure if he had to choose, Kenji would choose Castle over me—so it's clear where his loyalties lie when he says, "What do you mean? How is Castle being weird? He seemed fine this morning."

I shrug. "He just seems really paranoid all of a sudden. And he said some things about Warner that just—" I cut myself off. Shake my head. "I don't know."

Kenji stops walking. "Wait, what things did he say about Warner?"

I shrug again, still irritated. "He thinks Warner is hiding stuff from me. Like, not hiding stuff from me, exactly—but that there's a lot I don't know about him? So I was like, 'If you know so much about Warner, why don't *you* tell me what I need to know about him?' and Castle was like, 'No, blah blah, Mr. Warner should tell you himself, blah blah.'" I roll my eyes. "Basically he was telling me it's weird that I don't know that much about Warner's past. But that's not even true," I say, looking at Kenji now. "I know a bunch about Warner's past."

"Like?"

"Like, I don't know—I know all that stuff about his mom."

Kenji laughs. "You don't know shit about his mom."

"Sure I do."

"Whatever, J. You don't even know that lady's name."

At this, I falter. I search my mind for the information, certain he must've mentioned it—

and come up short.

I glance at Kenji, feeling small.

"Her name was Leila," he says. "Leila Warner. And I only know this because Castle does his research. We had files on all persons of interest back at Omega Point. Never knew she had powers that made her sick, though," he says, looking thoughtful. "Anderson did a good job keeping that quiet."

"Oh," is all I manage to say.

"So that's why you thought Castle was being weird?" Kenji says to me. "Because he very correctly pointed out that you know nothing about your boyfriend's life?"

"Don't be mean," I say quietly. "I know some things."

But the truth is, I don't know much.

What Castle said to me this morning hit a nerve. I'd be lying if I said I didn't wonder, all the time, what Warner's life was like before I met him. In fact, I think often of that day—that awful, awful day—in the pretty blue house on Sycamore, the house where Anderson shot me in the chest.

We were all alone, me and Anderson.

I never told Warner what his father said to me that day, but I've never forgotten. Instead, I've tried to ignore it, to convince myself that Anderson was playing games with my mind to confuse and immobilize me. But no matter how many times I've played back the conversation in my head—trying desperately to break it down and dismiss it—I've never been able to shake the feeling that, maybe, just maybe, it wasn't all for show. Maybe Anderson was telling me the truth.

I can still see the smile on his face as he said it. I can still hear the musical lilt in his voice. He was enjoying himself. Tormenting me.

Did he tell you how many other soldiers wanted to be in charge of Sector 45? How many fine candidates we had to choose from? He was only eighteen years old!

Did he ever tell you what he had to do to prove he was worthy?

My heart pounds in my chest as I remember, and I close my eyes, my lungs knotting together—

Did he ever tell you what I made him do to earn it?

No.

I suspect he didn't want to mention that part, did he? I bet he didn't want to include that part of his past, did he?

No.

He never did. And I've never asked.

I think I never want to know.

"Don't worry," Anderson said to me then. *"I won't spoil it for you. Best to let him share those details with you himself."*

And now, this morning—I get the same line from Castle:

"No, Ms. Ferrars," Castle had said, refusing to look me in the eye. "No, no, it's not my place to tell. Mr. Warner needs to be the one to tell you the stories about his life. Not I."

"I don't understand," I said, frustrated. "How is this even relevant? Why do you suddenly care about Warner's past? And what does any of that have to do with Oceania's RSVP?"

"Warner knows these other commanders," Castle said. "He knows the other supreme families. He knows how The Reestablishment operates from within. And there's still a great deal he needs to tell you." He shook his head. "Oceania's response is deeply unusual, Ms. Ferrars, for the simple reason that it is the only response you've received. I feel very certain that the moves made by these commanders are not only coordinated but also intentional, and I'm beginning to feel more worried by the moment that there is an entirely *other* message here—one that I'm still trying to translate."

I could feel it then, could feel my temperature rising, my jaw tensing as anger surged through me. "But you're the one who told me to reach out to all the supreme commanders! This was your idea! And now you're terrified that someone actually reached out? What do y—"

And then, all at once, I understood.

My words were soft and stunned when I said, "Oh my God, you didn't think I'd get any responses, did you?"

Castle swallowed hard. Said nothing.

"You didn't think anyone would respond?" I said, my voice rising in pitch.

"Ms. Ferrars, you must understand—"

"Why are you playing games with me, Castle?" My fists clenched. "What are you doing?"

"I'm not playing games with you," he said, the words coming out in a rush. "I just—I thought—" he said, gesticulating wildly. "It was an exercise. An experiment—"

I felt flashes of heat spark behind my eyes. Anger welled in my throat, vibrated along my spine. I could feel the rage building inside me and it took everything I had to clamp it down. "I am no longer anyone's experiment," I said. "And I need to know what the hell is going on."

"You must speak with Mr. Warner," he said. "He will explain everything. There's still so much you need to know about this world—and The Reestablishment—and time is of the essence," he said. He met my eyes. "You must be prepared for whatever comes next. You need to know more, and you need to know now. Before things escalate."

I looked away, my hands shaking from the surge of unspent energy. I wanted to—needed to—break something. Anything. Instead, I said, "This is bullshit, Castle. Complete bullshit."

And he looked like the saddest man in the world when he said—

"I know."

I've been walking around with a splitting headache ever since.

So it doesn't make me feel any better when Kenji pokes me in the shoulder, startling me back to life, and says,

"I've said it before and I'll say it again: You guys have a weird relationship."

"No, we don't," I say, and the words are reflexive, petulant.

"Yes," Kenji says. "You do." And he saunters off, leaving me alone in the abandoned streets, tipping an imaginary hat as he walks away.

I throw my shoe at him.

The effort, however, is fruitless; Kenji catches my shoe midair. He's now waiting for me, ten steps ahead, holding my tennis shoe in his hand as I hop awkwardly in his direction. I don't have to turn around to see the smirks on the soldiers' faces some distance behind us. I'm pretty sure everyone thinks I'm a joke of a supreme commander. And why wouldn't they?

It's been over two weeks and I still feel lost.

Half paralyzed.

I'm not proud of my inability to get it together, not proud of the revelation that, as it turns out, I'm not smart enough, fast enough, or shrewd enough to rule the world. I'm not proud that, at my lowest moments, I look around at all that I have to do in a single day and wonder, in awe, at how organized Anderson was. How accomplished. How very, very talented.

I'm not proud that I've thought that.

Or that, in the quietest, loneliest hours of the morning I lie awake next to the son Anderson tortured nearly to death and wish that Anderson would return from the dead and take back the burden I stole from his shoulders.

And then there's this thought, all the time, all the time:

That maybe I made a mistake.

"Uh, hello? Earth to princess?"

I look up, confused. Lost in my mind today. "Did you say something?"

Kenji shakes his head as he hands me my shoe. I'm struggling to put it on when he says, "So you forced me to take a stroll through this nasty, frozen shitland just to ignore me?"

I raise a single eyebrow at him.

He raises both, waiting, expectant. "What's the deal, J? *This,*" he says, gesturing at my face, "is more than whatever weirdness you got from Castle this morning." He tilts his head at me, and I read genuine concern in his eyes when he says, "So what's going on?"

I sigh; the exhalation withers my body.

You must speak with Mr. Warner. He will explain everything.

But Warner isn't known for his communication skills. He doesn't make small talk. He doesn't share details about himself. He doesn't do *personal*. I know he loves me—I can feel, in our every interaction, how deeply he cares for me—but even so, he's only ever offered me the vaguest information about his life. He is a vault to which I'm only occasionally granted access, and I often wonder how much I have left to learn about him. Sometimes it scares me.

"I'm just—I don't know," I finally say. "I'm really tired. I've got a lot on my mind."

"Rough night?"

I peer up at Kenji, shading my eyes against the cold sunlight. "You know, I don't really sleep anymore," I say to him. "I'm up at four in the morning every day, and I still haven't gotten through *last week's* mail. Isn't that crazy?"

Kenji shoots me a sideways glance, surprised.

"And I have to, like, approve a million things every day? Approve this, approve that. Not even, like, big things," I say to him. "It's stupid stuff, like, like"—I pull a crumpled sheet of paper out of my pocket and shake it at the sky—"like this nonsense: Sector 418 wants to extend their soldiers' lunch hour by an additional three minutes, and they need my approval. Three minutes? *Who cares?*"

Kenji fights back a smile; shoves his hands in his pockets.

"Every day. All day. I can't get anything *real* done. I thought I'd be doing something big, you know? I thought I'd be able to, like, unify the sectors and broker peace or something, and instead I spend all day trying to avoid Delalieu, who's in my face every five minutes because he needs me to sign something. *And that's just the mail.*"

I can't seem to stop talking now, finally confessing to

Kenji all the things I feel I can never say to Warner, for fear of disappointing him. It's liberating, but then, suddenly, it also feels dangerous. Like maybe I shouldn't be telling *anyone* that I feel this way, not even Kenji.

So I hesitate, wait for a sign.

Kenji isn't looking at me anymore, but he still appears to be listening. His head is cocked to the side, his mouth playing at a smile when he says, after a moment, "Is that all?"

And I shake my head, hard, relieved and grateful to keep complaining. "I have to log everything, all the time. I have to fill out reports, read reports, file reports. There are five hundred and fifty-four other sectors in North America, Kenji. *Five hundred and fifty-four.*" I stare at him. "That means I have to read five hundred and fifty-four reports, every single day."

Kenji stares back, unmoved.

"Five hundred and fifty-four!"

He crosses his arms.

"The reports are ten pages long!"

"Uh-huh."

"Can I tell you a secret?" I say.

"Hit me."

"This job blows."

Now Kenji laughs, out loud. Still, he says nothing.

"What?" I say. "What are you thinking?"

He musses my hair and says, "Aww, J."

I jerk my head away from his hand. "That's all I get? Just an *'Aww, J,'* and that's it?"

Kenji shrugs.

"*What?*" I demand.

"I mean, I don't know," he says, cringing a little as he says it. "Did you think this was going to be . . . easy?"

"No," I say quietly. "I just thought it would be better than this."

"Better, how?"

"I guess, I mean, I thought it would be . . . cooler?"

"Like, you thought you'd be killing a bunch of bad dudes by now? High-kicking your way through politics? Like you could just kill Anderson and all of a sudden, *bam*, world peace?"

And now I can't bring myself to look at him, because I'm lying, lying through my teeth when I say,

"No, of course not. I didn't think it would be like that."

Kenji sighs. "This is why Castle was always so apprehensive, you know? With Omega Point it was always about being slow and steady. Waiting for the right moment. Knowing our strengths—and our weaknesses. We had a lot going for us, but we always knew—Castle always said—that we could never take out Anderson until we were ready to lead. It's why I didn't kill him when I had the chance. Not even when he was half dead already and standing right in front of me." A pause. "It just wasn't the right moment."

"So—you think I made a mistake?"

Kenji frowns, almost. Looks away. Looks back, smiles a little, but only with one side of his mouth. "I mean, I think you're great."

"But you think I made a mistake."

He shrugs in a slow, exaggerated way. "Nah, I didn't say that. I just think you need a little more training, you know? I'm guessing the insane asylum didn't prep you for this gig."

I narrow my eyes at him.

He laughs.

"Listen, you're good with the people. You talk pretty. But this job comes with a lot of paperwork, and it comes with a lot of bullshit, too. Lots of playing nice. Lots of ass-kissing. I mean, what are we trying to do right now? We're trying to be cool. Right? We're trying to, like, take over but, like, not cause absolute anarchy. We're trying *not* to go to war right now, right?"

I don't respond quickly enough and he pokes me in the shoulder.

"Right?" he says. "Isn't that the goal? Maintain the peace for now? Attempt diplomacy before we start blowing shit up?"

"Yes, right," I say quickly. "Yeah. Prevent war. Avoid casualties. Play nice."

"Okay then," he says, and looks away. "So you have to keep it together, kid. Because if you start losing it now? The Reestablishment is going to eat you alive. It's what they want. In fact, it's probably what they're expecting—they're waiting for you to self-destruct all this shit for them. So you can't let them see this. You can't let these cracks show."

I stare at him, feeling suddenly scared.

He wraps one arm around my shoulder. "You can't be getting stressed out like this. Over some paperwork?" He shakes his head. "Everyone is watching you now. Everyone is waiting to see what happens next. We either go to war with the other sectors—hell, with the rest of the world—or we manage to be cool and negotiate. And you have to be *chill,* J. Just be chill."

And I don't know what to say.

Because the truth is, he's right. I'm so far in over my head I don't even know where to start. I didn't even graduate from high school. And now I'm supposed to have a lifetime's worth of knowledge about international relations?

Warner was designed for this life. Everything he does, is, breathes—

He was built to lead.

But me?

What on earth, I think, *have I gotten myself into?*

Why did I think I'd be capable of running an entire continent? How did I allow myself to imagine that a supernatural ability to kill things with my skin would suddenly grant me a comprehensive understanding of political science?

I clench my fists too hard and—

pain, fresh pain

—as my fingernails pierce the flesh.

How did I think people ruled the world? Did I really imagine it would be so simple? That I might control the fabric of society from the comfort of my boyfriend's bedroom?

I'm only now beginning to understand the breadth of this delicate, intricately developed spiderweb of people, positions, and power already in place. I said I was up for the task. Me, a seventeen-year-old nobody with very little life experience; I volunteered for this position. And now—basically overnight—I have to keep up. And I have no *idea* what I'm doing.

But if I don't learn how to manage these many relationships? If I don't at least pretend to have even the slightest idea of how I'm going to rule?

The rest of the world could so easily destroy me.

And sometimes I'm not sure I'll make it out of this alive.

WARNER

"How's James?"

I'm the first to break the silence. It's a strange feeling. New for me.

Kent nods his head in response, his eyes focused on the hands he's clasped in front of him. We're on the roof, surrounded by cold and concrete, sitting next to each other in a quiet corner to which I sometimes retreat. I can see the whole sector from here. The ocean far off in the distance. The sun making its sluggish, midday approach. Civilians like toy soldiers marching to and fro.

"He's good," Kent finally says. His voice is tight. He's wearing nothing but a T-shirt and doesn't seem to be bothered by the blistering cold. He takes in a deep breath. "I mean—he's great, you know? He's so great. Doing great."

I nod.

Kent looks up, laughs a short, nervous sort of laugh and looks away. "Is this crazy?" he says. "Are we crazy?"

We're both silent a minute, the wind whistling harder than before.

"I don't know," I finally say.

Kent pounds a fist against his leg. Exhales through his nose. "You know, I never said this to you. Before." He looks up, but doesn't look at me. "That night. I never said it, but I wanted you to know that it meant a lot to me. What you said."

I squint into the distance.

It's an impossible thing to do, really, to apologize for attempting to kill someone. Even so, I tried. I told him I understood him then. His pain. His anger. His actions. I told him that he'd survived the upbringing of our father to become a much better person than I'd ever be.

"I meant it," I say to him.

Kent now taps his closed fist against his mouth. Clears his throat. "I'm sorry, too, you know." His voice is hoarse. "Things got so screwed up. Everything. It's such a mess."

"Yes," I say. "It is."

"So what do we do now?" He finally turns to look at me, but I'm still not ready to meet his eyes. "How—how do we fix this? Can we even fix this? Is it too far gone?"

I run a hand over my newly shorn hair. "I don't know," I say, too quietly. "But I'd like to fix it."

"Yeah?"

I nod.

Kent nods several times beside me. "I'm not ready to tell James yet."

I falter, surprised. "Oh."

"Not because of you," he says quickly. "It's not you I'm worried about. I just—explaining *you* means explaining something so much bigger. And I don't know how to tell him his dad was a monster. Not yet. I really thought he'd never have to know."

At this, I look up. "James doesn't know? Anything?"

Kent shakes his head. "He was so little when our mom died, and I always managed to keep him out of sight when our dad came around. He thinks our parents died in a plane crash."

"Impressive," I hear myself say. "That was very generous of you."

I hear Kent's voice crack when he next speaks. "God, why am I so messed up over him? Why do I *care*?"

"I don't know," I say, shaking my head. "I'm having the same problem."

"Yeah?"

I nod.

Kent drops his head in his hands. "He really screwed us up, man."

"Yes. He did."

I hear Kent sniff twice, two sharp attempts at keeping his emotions in check, and even so, I envy him his ability to be this open with his feelings. I pull a handkerchief from the inside pocket of my jacket and hand it to him.

"Thanks," he says tightly.

Another nod.

"So, um—what's up with your hair?"

I'm so caught off guard by the question I almost flinch. I actually consider telling Kent the whole story, but I'm worried he'll ask me why I'd ever let Kenji touch my hair, and then I'd have to explain Juliette's many, many requests that

I befriend the idiot. And I don't think she's a safe topic for us yet. So instead I say, "A little mishap."

Kent raises his eyebrows. Laughs. "Uh-huh."

I glance in his direction, surprised.

He says, "It's okay, you know."

"What is?"

Kent is sitting up straighter now, staring into the sunlight. I'm beginning to see shades of my father in his face. Shades of myself. "You and Juliette," he says.

I freeze.

He glances at me. "Really. It's okay."

I can't help it when I say, stunned, "I'm not sure it would've been okay with me, had our roles been reversed."

Kent smiles, but it looks sad. "I was a real dick to her at the end," he says. "So I guess I got what I deserved. But it wasn't actually about her, you know? All of that. It wasn't about her." He looks up at me out of the corner of his eye. "I'd been drowning for a while, actually. I was just really unhappy, and really stressed, and then"—he shrugs, turns away—"honestly, finding out you were my brother nearly killed me."

I blink. Surprised once more.

"Yeah." He laughs, shaking his head. "I know it seems weird now, but at the time I just—I don't know, man, I thought you were a sociopath. I was so worried you'd figure out we were related and then, I mean—I don't know, I thought you'd try to murder me or something."

He hesitates. Looks at me.

Waits.

It's only then that I realize—surprised, yet again—that he wants me to deny this. To say it wasn't so.

But I can understand his concern. So I say, "Well. I did try to kill you once, didn't I?"

Kent's eyes go wide. "It's too soon for that, man. That shit is still not funny."

I look away as I say, "I wasn't making a joke."

I can feel Kent looking at me, studying me, trying, I assume, to make some sense of me or my words. Perhaps both. But it's hard to know what he's thinking. It's frustrating to have a supernatural ability that allows me to know everyone's emotions, except for his. It makes me feel off-kilter around him. Like I've lost my eyesight.

Finally, Kent sighs.

I seem to have passed a test.

"Anyway," he says, but he sounds a bit uncertain now, "I was pretty sure you would come after me. And all I could think was that if I died, James would die. I'm his whole world, you know? You kill me, you kill him." He looks into his hands. "I stopped sleeping at night. Stopped eating. I was losing my mind. I couldn't handle it, any of it—and you were, like, living with us? And then everything with Juliette—I just—I don't know." He sighs, long and loud. Shaky. "I was an asshole. I took everything out on her. Blamed her for everything. For walking away from what I thought was one of the few sure things in my life. It's my own fault, really. My own baggage. I've still got a lot of shit to work out," he says finally. "I've got issues with people leaving me behind."

For a moment, I'm rendered speechless.

I'd never thought of Kent as capable of complex thought. My ability to sense emotions and his ability to extinguish preternatural gifts has made for a strange pairing—I'd always been forced to conclude that he was devoid of all thought and feeling. It turns out he's quite a bit more emotionally adept than I'd expected. Vocal, too.

But it's strange to see someone with my shared DNA speak so freely. To admit aloud his fears and shortcomings. It's too raw, like looking directly at the sun. I have to look away.

Ultimately, I say only, "I understand."

Kent clears his throat.

"So. Yeah," he says. "I guess I just wanted to say that Juliette was right. In the end, she and I grew apart. All of this"—he makes a gesture between us—"made me realize a lot of things. And she was right. I've always been so desperate for something, some kind of love, or affection, or *something.* I don't know," he says, shaking his head. "I guess I wanted to believe she and I had something we didn't. I was in a different place then. Hell, I was a different person. But I know my priorities now."

I look at him then, a question in my eyes.

"My family," he says, meeting my gaze. "That's all I care about now."

JULIETTE

We're making our way slowly back to base.

I'm in no hurry to find Warner only to have what will probably be a difficult, stressful conversation, so I take my time. I pick my way through the detritus of war, winding through the gray wreckage of the compounds as we leave behind unregulated territory and the smudged remnants of what used to be. I'm always sorry when our walk is nearly at an end; I feel great nostalgia for the cookie-cutter homes, the picket fences, the small, boarded-up shops and old, abandoned banks and buildings that make up the streets of unregulated turf. I'd like to find a way to bring it all back again.

I take a deep breath and enjoy the rush of crisp, icy air as it burns through my lungs. Wind wraps around me, pulling and pushing and dancing, whipping my hair into a frenzy, and I lean into it, get lost in it, open my mouth to inhale it. I'm about to smile when Kenji shoots me a dark look and I cringe, apologizing with my eyes.

My halfhearted apology does little to placate him.

I forced Kenji to take another detour down to the ocean, which is often my favorite part of our walk. Kenji, on the other hand, really hates it—and so do his boots, one of which got stuck in the muck that now clings to what used to be clean sand.

"I still can't believe you like staring at that nasty, piss-infested—"

"It's not infested, exactly," I point out. "Castle says it's definitely more water than pee."

Kenji only glares at me.

He's still muttering under his breath, complaining about his shoes being soaked in "piss water," as he likes to call it, as we make our way up the main road. I'm happy to ignore him, determined to enjoy the last of this peaceful hour, as it's one of the only hours I have for myself these days. I linger and look back at the cracked sidewalks and caving roofs of our old world, trying—and occasionally succeeding—to remember a time when things weren't so bleak.

"Do you ever miss it?" I ask Kenji. "The way things used to be?"

Kenji is standing on one foot, shaking some kind of sludge from one leather boot, when he looks up and frowns. "I don't know what you think you remember, J, but the way things used to be wasn't much better than the way they are now."

"What do you mean?" I ask, leaning against the pole of an old street sign.

"What do *you* mean?" he counters. "How can you miss anything about your old life? I thought you hated your life with your parents. I thought you said they were horrible and abusive."

"They were," I say, turning away. "And we didn't have much. But there were some things I like to remember—some nice moments—back before The Reestablishment was in power. I guess I just miss the small things that used to make me happy." I look back at him and smile. "You know?"

He raises an eyebrow.

"Like—the sound of the ice cream truck in the afternoons," I say to him. "Or the mailman making his rounds. I used to sit by the window and watch people come home from work in the evenings." I look away, remembering. "It was nice."

"Hm."

"You don't think so?"

Kenji's lips quirk up into an unhappy smile as he inspects his boot, now free of sludge. "I don't know, kid. Those ice cream trucks never came into my neighborhood. The world I remember was tired and racist and volatile as hell, ripe for a hostile takeover by a shit regime. We were already divided. The conquering was easy." He takes a deep breath. Blows it out as he says, "Anyway, I ran away from an orphanage when I was eight, so I don't remember much of that cutesy shit, regardless."

I freeze, stunned. It takes me a second to find my voice. "You lived in an orphanage?"

Kenji nods before offering me a short, humorless laugh. "Yep. I'd been living on the streets for a year, hitchhiking my way across the state—you know, before we had sectors—until Castle found me."

"What?" My body goes rigid. "Why have you never told me this story? All this time—and you never said—"

He shrugs.

"Did you ever know your parents?"

He nods but doesn't look at me.

I feel my blood run cold. "What happened to them?"

"It doesn't matter."

"Of course it matters," I say, and touch his elbow. *"Kenji—"*

"It's not important," he says, breaking away. "We've all got problems. We've all got baggage. No need to dwell on it."

"This isn't about dwelling on the past," I say. "I just want to know. Your life—your past—it matters to me." And for a moment I'm reminded again of Castle—his eyes, his urgency—and his insistence that there's more I need to know about Warner's past, too.

There's so much left to learn about the people I care about.

Kenji finally smiles, but it makes him look tired. Eventually, he sighs. He jogs up a few cracked steps leading to the entrance of an old library and sits down on the cold concrete. Our armed guards are waiting for us, just out of sight.

Kenji pats the place next to him.

I scramble up the steps to join him.

We're staring out at an ancient intersection, old stoplights and electric lines smashed and tangled on the pavement, when he says,

"So, you know I'm Japanese, right?"

I nod.

"Well. Where I grew up, people weren't used to seeing faces like mine. My parents weren't born here; they spoke Japanese and broken English. Some people didn't like that. Anyway, we lived in a rough area," he explains, "with a lot of ignorant people. And just before The Reestablishment started campaigning, promising to solve all our people problems by obliterating cultures and languages and religions and whatever, race relations were at their worst. There was a lot of violence, all across the continent. Communities clashing. Killing each other. If you were the wrong color at the wrong time"—he makes a finger gun, shoots it into the air—"people would make you disappear. We avoided it, mostly. The Asian communities never had it as bad as the black communities, for example. The black communities had it the worst—Castle can tell you all about that," he says. "Castle's got the craziest stories. But the worst that ever happened to my family, usually, was people would talk shit when we were out together. I remember my mom never wanted to leave the house."

I feel my body tense.

"Anyhow." He shrugs. "My dad just—you know—he couldn't just stand there and let people say stupid, foul shit about his family, right? So he'd get mad. It wasn't like this was always happening or whatever—but when it *did* happen, sometimes the altercation would end in an argument, and sometimes nothing. It didn't seem like the end of the world. But my mom was always begging my dad to let it go, and he couldn't." His face darkens. "And I don't blame him.

"One day," Kenji says, "it ended really badly. Everyone had guns in those days, remember? *Civilians* had guns. Crazy to imagine now, under The Reestablishment, but back then, everyone was armed, out for themselves." A short pause. "My dad bought a gun, too. He said we needed it, just in case. For our own protection." Kenji isn't looking at me when he says, "And the next time some stupid shit went down, my dad got a little too brave. They used his own gun against him. Dad got shot. Mom got shot trying to make it stop. I was seven."

"You were there?" I gasp.

He nods. "Saw the whole thing go down."

I cover my mouth with both hands. My eyes sting with unshed tears.

"I've never told anyone that story," he says, his forehead creasing. "Not even Castle."

"What?" I drop my hands. My eyes widen. "Why not?"

He shakes his head. "I don't know," he says quietly, and stares off into the distance. "When I met Castle everything was still so fresh, you know? Still too real. When he wanted to know my story, I told him I didn't want to talk about it. Ever." Kenji glances over at me. "Eventually, he just stopped asking."

I can only stare at him, stunned. Speechless.

Kenji looks away. He's almost talking to himself when he says, "It feels so weird to have said all of that out loud." He takes a sudden, sharp breath, jumps to his feet, and turns his head so I can't see his face. I hear him sniff hard, twice. And then he stuffs his hands in his pockets and says, "You know, I think I might be the only one of us who doesn't have daddy issues. I loved the *shit* out of my dad."

I'm still thinking about Kenji's story—and how much more there is to know about him, about Warner, about everyone I've come to call a friend—when Winston's voice startles me back to the present.

"We're still figuring out exactly how to divvy up the rooms," he's saying, "but it's coming together nicely. In fact, we're a little ahead of schedule on the bedrooms," he says. "Warner fast-tracked the work on the east wing, so we can actually start moving in tomorrow."

There's a brief round of applause. Someone cheers.

We're taking a brief tour of our new headquarters.

The majority of the space is still under construction, so, for the most part, what we're staring at is a loud, dusty mess, but I'm excited to see the progress. Our group has desperately needed more bedrooms, more bathrooms, desks and studios. And we need to set up a real command center from which we can get work done. This will, hopefully, be the beginning of that new world. The world wherein I'm the supreme commander.

Crazy.

For now, the details of what I do and control are still unfolding. We won't be challenging other sectors or their leaders until we have a better idea of who our allies might be, and that means we'll need a little more time. "The destruction of the world didn't happen overnight, and neither will saving it," Castle likes to say, and I think he's right. We need to make thoughtful decisions as we move forward—and making an effort to be diplomatic might be the difference between life and death. It would be far easier to make global progress, for example, if we weren't the only ones with the vision for change.

We need to forge alliances.

But Castle's conversation with me this morning has left me a little rattled. I'm not sure how to feel anymore—or what to hope for. I only know that, despite the brave face I put on for the civilians, I don't *want* to jump from one war to another; I don't *want* to have to slaughter everyone who stands in my way. The people of Sector 45 are trusting me with their loved ones—with their children and spouses who've become my soldiers—and I don't want to risk any more of their lives unless absolutely necessary. I'm hoping to ease into this. I'm hoping that there's a chance—even the smallest chance—that the semicooperation of my fellow sectors and the five other supreme commanders could mean good things for the future. I'm wondering if we might be able to come together without more bloodshed.

"That's ridiculous. And *naive,*" Kenji says.

I look up at the sound of his voice, look around. He's talking to Ian. Ian Sanchez—tall, lanky guy with a bit of an attitude but a good heart. The only one of us with no superpowers, though. Not that it matters.

Ian is standing tall, arms crossed against his chest, head turned to the side, eyes up at the ceiling. "I don't care what you think—"

"Well, I do." I hear Castle cut in. "I care what Kenji thinks," he's saying.

"But—"

"I care what you think, too, Ian," Castle says, "But you have to see that Kenji is right in this instance. We have to approach everything with a great deal of caution. We can't know for certain what will happen next."

Ian sighs, exasperated. "That's not what I'm saying. What I'm saying is I don't understand why we need all this space. It's unnecessary."

"Wait—what's the issue here?" I ask, looking around. And then, to Ian: "Why don't you like the new space?"

Lily puts an arm around Ian's shoulders. "Ian is just sad," she says, smiling. "He doesn't want to break up the slumber party."

"What?" I frown.

Kenji laughs.

Ian scowls. "I just think we're fine where we are," he says. "I don't know why we need to move up into all *this*," he says, his arms wide as he scans the cavernous space. "It feels like tempting fate. Doesn't anyone remember what happened the last time we built a huge hideout?"

I watch Castle flinch.

I think we all do.

Omega Point, destroyed. Bombed into nothingness.

Decades of hard work obliterated in a moment.

"That's not going to happen again," I say firmly. "Besides, we're more protected here than we ever were before. We have an entire army behind us now. We're safer in this building than we would be anywhere else."

My words are met with an immediate chorus of support, but still I bristle, because I know that what I've said is only partly true.

I have no way of knowing what's going to happen to us or how long we'll last here. What I *do* know is that we need the new space—and we need to set up shop while we still have the funds. No one has tried to cut us off or shut us down yet; no sanctions have been imposed by fellow continents or commanders. Not yet, anyway. Which means we need to rebuild while we still have the means to do so.

But this—

This enormous space dedicated only to our efforts?

This was all Warner's doing.

He was able to empty out an entire floor for us—the top floor, the fifteenth story—of Sector 45 headquarters. It took an enormous amount of effort to transfer and distribute a whole floor's worth of people, work, and furnishings to other departments, but somehow, he managed it. Now the level is being refitted specifically for our needs.

Once it's all done we'll have state-of-the-art technology that will allow us not only the access to the research and surveillance we'll need, but the necessary tools for Winston and Alia to continue building any devices, gadgets, and uniforms we might require. And even though Sector 45 already has its own medical wing, we'll need a secure area for Sonya and Sara to work, from where they'll be able to continue developing antidotes and serums that might one day save our lives.

I'm just about to point this out when Delalieu walks into the room.

"Supreme," he says, with a nod in my direction.

At the sound of his voice, we all spin around.

"Yes, Lieutenant?"

There's a slight quiver in his words when he says, "You have a visitor, madam. He's requesting ten minutes of your time."

"A visitor?" I turn instinctively, finding Kenji with my eyes. He looks just as confused as I am.

"Yes, madam," says Delalieu. "He's waiting downstairs in the main reception room."

"But who is this person?" I ask, concerned. "Where did he come from?"

"His name is Haider Ibrahim. He's the son of the supreme commander of Asia."

I feel my body lock in sudden apprehension. I'm not sure I'm any good at hiding the panic that jolts through me as I say, *"The son of the supreme commander of Asia?* Did he say why he was here?"

Delalieu shakes his head. "I'm sorry to say that he refused to answer any of my more detailed questions, madam."

I'm breathing hard, head spinning. Suddenly all I can

think about is Castle's concern over Oceania this morning. The fear in his eyes. The many questions he refused to answer.

"What shall I tell him, madam?" Delalieu again.

I feel my heart pick up. I close my eyes. *You are a supreme commander,* I say to myself. *Act like it.*

"Madam?"

"Yes, of course, tell him I'll be right th—"

"Ms. Ferrars." Castle's sharp voice pierces the fog of my mind.

I look in his direction.

"Ms. Ferrars," he says again, a warning in his eyes. "Perhaps you should wait."

"Wait?" I say. "Wait for what?"

"Wait to meet with him until Mr. Warner can be there, too."

My confusion bleeds into anger. "I appreciate your concern, Castle, but I can do this on my own, thank you."

"Ms. Ferrars, I would beg you to reconsider. Please," he says, more urgently now, "you must understand—this is no small thing. The son of a supreme commander—it could mean so much—"

"As I said, thank you for your concern." I cut him off, my cheeks inflamed. Lately, I've been feeling like Castle has no faith in me—like he isn't rooting for me at all—and it makes me think back to this morning's conversation. It makes me wonder if I can trust anything he says. What kind of ally would stand here and point out my ineptitude in front of everyone? It's all I can do not to shout at him when I say, "I can assure you, I'll be fine."

And then, to Delalieu:

"Lieutenant, please tell our visitor that I'll be down in a moment."

"Yes, madam." Another nod, and Delalieu's gone.

Unfortunately, my bravado walks out the door with him.

I ignore Castle as I search the room for Kenji's face; for all my big talk, I don't actually want to do this alone. And Kenji knows me well.

"Hey—I'm right here." He's crossed the room in just a few strides, by my side in seconds.

"You're coming with me, right?" I whisper, tugging at his sleeve like a child.

Kenji laughs. "I'll be wherever you need me to be, kid."

WARNER

I have a great fear of drowning in the ocean of my own silence.

In the steady thrum that accompanies quiet, my mind is unkind to me. I think too much. I feel, perhaps, far more than I should. It would be only a slight exaggeration to say that my goal in life is to outrun my mind, my memories.

So I have to keep moving.

I used to retreat belowground when I wanted a distraction. I used to find comfort in our simulation chambers, in the programs designed to prepare soldiers for combat. But as we've recently moved a team of soldiers underground in all the chaos of the new construction, I'm without reprieve. I've no choice now but to go up.

I enter the hangar at a brisk pace, my footsteps echoing in the vast space as I move, almost instinctively, toward the army choppers parked in the far right wing. Soldiers see me and jump quickly out of my way, their eyes betraying their confusion even as they salute me. I nod only once in their direction, offering no explanation as I climb up and into the aircraft. I place the headphones over my head and speak quietly into the radio, alerting our air-traffic controllers of my intent to take flight, and strap myself into the front seat.

The retinal scanner takes my identification automatically. Preflight checks are clear. I turn on the engine and the roar is deafening, even through the noise-canceling headphones. I feel my body begin to unclench.

Soon, I'm in the air.

My father taught me to shoot a gun when I was nine years old. When I was ten he sliced open the back of my leg and showed me how to suture my own wounds. At eleven he broke my arm and abandoned me in the wild for two weeks. At age twelve I was taught to build and defuse my own bombs. He began teaching me how to fly planes when I was thirteen.

He never did teach me how to ride a bike. I figured that out on my own.

From thousands of feet above the ground, Sector 45 looks like a half-assembled board game. Distance makes the world feel small and surmountable, a pill easily swallowed. But I know the deceit too well, and it is here, above the clouds, that I finally understand Icarus. I, too, am tempted to fly too close to the sun. It is only my inability to be impractical that keeps me tethered to the earth. So I take a steadying breath, and get back to work.

I'm making my aerial rounds a bit earlier than usual, so the sights below are different from the ones I've begun to expect every day. On an average day I'm up here in the late afternoon, checking in on civilians as they leave work to exchange their REST dollars at local Supply Centers. They usually scurry back to their compounds shortly thereafter, weighted down with newly purchased necessities and the disheartening realization that they'll have to do it all again the following day. Right now, everyone is still at work, leaving the land empty of its worker ants. The landscape is bizarre and beautiful from afar, the ocean vast, blue, and breathtaking. But I know only too well our world's pockmarked surface.

This strange, sad reality my father helped create.

I squeeze my eyes shut, my hand clutching the throttle. There's simply too much to contend with today.

First, the disarming realization that I have a brother whose heart is as complicated and flawed as my own.

Second, and perhaps most offensive: the impending, anxiety-inducing arrival of my past.

I still haven't talked to Juliette about the imminent arrival of our guests, and, if I'm being honest, I'm no longer sure I want to. I've never discussed much of my life with her. I've never told her stories of my childhood friends, their parents, the history of The Reestablishment and my role within it. There's never been time. Never the right moment. If Juliette has been supreme commander for seventeen days now, she and I have only been in a relationship for two days longer than that.

We've both been busy.

And we've only just overcome so much—all the complications between us, all the distance and confusion, the misunderstandings. She's mistrusted me for so long. I know

I have only myself to blame for what's transpired between us, but I worry that the past ugliness has inspired in her an instinct to doubt me; it's likely a well-developed muscle now. And I feel certain that telling her more about my ignoble life will only make things worse at the onset of a relationship I want desperately to preserve. To protect.

So how do I begin? Where do I start?

The year I turned sixteen, our parents, the supreme commanders, decided we should all take turns shooting each other. Not to kill, merely to disable. They wanted us to know what a bullet wound felt like. They wanted us to be able to understand the recovery process. Most of all, they wanted us to know that even our friends might one day turn on us.

I feel my mouth twist into an unhappy smile.

I suppose it was a worthwhile lesson. After all, my father is now six feet under the ground and his old friends don't seem to care. But the problem that day was that I'd been taught by my father, a master marksman. Worse, I'd already been practicing every day for five years—two years earlier than the others—and, as a result, I was faster, sharper, and crueler than my peers. I didn't hesitate. I'd shot all my friends before they'd even picked up their weapons.

That was the first day I felt, with certainty, that my father was proud of me. I'd spent so long desperately seeking his approval and that day, I finally had it. He looked at me the way I'd always hoped he would: like he cared for me. Like a father who saw a bit of himself in his son. The realization sent me into the forest, where I promptly threw up in the bushes.

I've only been struck by a bullet once.

The memory still mortifies me, but I don't regret it. I deserved it. For misunderstanding her, for mistreating her, for being lost and confused. But I've been trying so hard to be a different man; to be, if not kinder, then at the very least, *better.* I don't want to lose the love I've come to cherish.

And I don't want Juliette to know my past.

I don't want to share stories from my life that only disgust and revolt me, stories that would color her impression of me. I don't want her to know how I spent my time as a child. She doesn't need to know how many times my father forced me to watch him skin dead animals, how I can still feel the vibrations of his screams in my ear as he kicked me, over and over again, when I dared to look away. I'd rather not remember the hours I spent shackled in a dark room, compelled to listen to the manufactured sounds of women and children screaming for help. It was all supposed to make me strong, he'd said. It was supposed to help me survive.

Instead, life with my father only made me wish for death.

I don't want to tell Juliette how I'd always known my father was unfaithful, that he'd abandoned my mother long, long ago, that I'd always wanted to murder him, that I'd dreamt of it, planned for it, hoped to one day break his neck using the very skills he'd given me.

How I failed. Every time.

Because I am weak.

I don't miss him. I don't miss his life. I don't want his friends or his footprint on my soul. But for some reason, his old comrades won't let me go.

They're coming to collect their pound of flesh, and I fear that this time—as I have every time—I will end up paying with my heart.

JULIETTE

Kenji and I are in Warner's room—what's become my room—and we're standing in the middle of the closet while I fling clothes at him, trying to figure out what to wear.

"What about this?" I say to him, throwing something glittery in his direction. "Or this?" I toss another ball of fabric at him.

"You don't know shit about clothes, do you?"

I turn around, tilt my head. "I'm sorry, when was I supposed to learn about fashion, Kenji? When I was growing up alone and tortured by my horrible parents? Or maybe when I was festering in an insane asylum?"

That shuts him up.

"So?" I say, nodding with my chin. "Which one?"

He picks up the two pieces I threw at him and frowns. "You're making me choose between a short, shiny dress and a pair of pajama bottoms? I mean—I guess I choose the dress? But I don't think it'll go well with those ratty tennis shoes you're always wearing."

"Oh." I glance down at my shoes. "Well, I don't know. Warner picked this stuff out for me a long time ago—before he even met me. It's all I have," I say, looking up. "These clothes are left over from when I first got to Sector 45."

"Why don't you just wear your suit?" Kenji says, leaning against the wall. "The new one Alia and Winston made for you?"

I shake my head. "They haven't finished fixing it yet. And it's still got bloodstains from when I shot Warner's dad. Besides," I say, taking a deep breath, "that was a different me. I wore those head-to-toe suits when I thought I had to protect people from my skin. But I'm different now. I can turn my power off. I can be . . . normal." I try to smile. "So I want to dress like a normal person."

"But you're not a normal person."

"I know that." A frustrating flush of heat warms my cheeks. "I just . . . I think I'd like to dress like one. Maybe for a little while? I've never been able to act my age and I just want to feel a little bit—"

"I get it," Kenji says, cutting me off with one hand. He looks me up and down. Says, "Well, I mean, if that's the look you're going for, I think you look like a normal person right now. This'll work." He waves in the general direction of my body.

I'm wearing jeans and a pink sweater. My hair is pulled up into a high ponytail. I feel comfortable and normal—but I also feel like an unaccomplished seventeen-year-old playing pretend.

"But I'm supposed to be the supreme commander of North America," I say. "Do you think it's okay if I'm dressed like this? Warner is always wearing fancy suits, you know? Or just, like, really nice clothes. He always looks so poised—so intimidating—"

"Where is he, by the way?" Kenji cuts me off. "I mean, I know you don't want to hear this, but I agree with Castle. Warner should be here for this meeting."

I take a deep breath. Try to be calm. "I know that Warner knows everything, okay? I know he's the best at basically everything, that he was born for this life. His father was grooming him to lead the world. In another life, another reality? This was supposed to be his role. I know that. I do."

"But?"

"But it's *not* Warner's job, is it?" I say angrily. "It's mine. And I'm trying not to rely on him all the time. I want to try to do some things on my own now. To take charge."

Kenji doesn't seem convinced. "I don't know, J. I think maybe this is one of those times when you should still be relying on him. He knows this world way better than we do—and, bonus, he'd be able to tell you what you should be wearing." Kenji shrugs. "Fashion really isn't my area of expertise."

I pick up the short, shiny dress and examine it.

Just over two weeks ago I single-handedly fought off hundreds of soldiers. I crushed a man's throat in my fist. I put two bullets through Anderson's forehead with no hesitation or regret. But here, staring at an armoire full of clothes, I'm intimidated.

"Maybe I *should* call Warner," I say, peeking over my shoulder at Kenji.

"Yep." He points at me. "Good idea."

But then,

"No—never mind," I say. "It's okay. I'll be okay, right? I mean what's the big deal? He's just a kid, right? Just the *son* of a supreme commander. Not an actual supreme commander. Right?"

"Uhhh—all of it is a big deal, J. The kids of the commanders are all, like, other Warners. They're basically mercenaries. And they've all been prepped to take their parents' places—"

"Yeah, no, I should definitely do this on my own." I'm looking in a mirror now, pulling my ponytail tight. "Right?"

Kenji is shaking his head.

"Yes. Exactly." I nod.

"Uh-uh. No. I think this is a bad idea."

"I'm capable of doing *some* things on my own, Kenji," I snap. "I'm not totally clueless."

Kenji sighs. "Whatever you say, princess."

WARNER

"Mr. Warner—please, Mr. Warner, slow down, son—"

I stop too suddenly, pivoting sharply on my heel. Castle is chasing me down the hall, waving a frantic hand in my direction. I meet his eyes with a mild expression.

"Can I help you?"

"Where have you been?" he says, obviously out of breath. "I've been looking for you everywhere."

I raise an eyebrow, fighting back the urge to tell him that my whereabouts are none of his business. "I had a few aerial rounds to make."

Castle frowns. "Don't you usually do that later in the afternoon?"

At this, I almost smile. "You've been watching me."

"Let's not play games. You've been watching me, too."

Now I actually smile. "Have I?"

"You think so little of my intelligence."

"I don't know what to think of you, Castle."

He laughs out loud. "Goodness, you're an excellent liar."

I look away. "What do you need?"

"He's here. He's here right now and she's with him and I tried to stop her but she wouldn't listen to me—"

I turn back, alarmed. "Who's here?"

For the first time, I see actual anger flicker in Castle's eyes. "Now is not the time to play dumb with me, son. Haider Ibrahim is here. Right now. And Juliette is meeting with him alone, completely unprepared."

Shock renders me, for a moment, speechless.

"Did you hear what I said?" Castle is nearly shouting. "She's meeting with him *now*."

"How?" I say, coming back to myself. "How is he here already? Did he arrive alone?"

"Mr. Warner, please listen to me. You have to talk to her. You have to explain and you have to do it now," he says, grabbing my shoulders. "They're coming back for h—"

Castle is thrown backward, hard.

He cries out as he catches himself, his arms and legs splayed out in front of him as if caught in a gust of wind. He remains in that impossible position, hovering several inches off the ground, and stares at me, chest heaving. Slowly, he steadies. His feet finally touch the floor.

"You would use my own powers against me?" he says, breathing hard. "I am your *ally*—"

"Never," I say sharply, "ever put your hands on me, Castle. Or next time I might accidentally kill you."

Castle blinks. And then I feel it—I can sense it, close my fingers around it: his pity. It's everywhere. Awful. Suffocating.

"Don't you dare feel sorry for me," I say.

"My apologies," he says quietly. "I didn't mean to invade your personal space. But you must understand the urgency here. First, the RSVP—and now, Haider's arrival? This is just the beginning," he says, lowering his voice. "They are mobilizing."

"You are overthinking this," I say, my voice clipped. "Haider's arrival today is about *me*. Sector 45's inevitable infestation by a swarm of supreme commanders is about *me*. I've committed treason, remember?" I shake my head, begin walking away. "They're just a little . . . angry."

"Stop," he says. "Listen to me—"

"You don't need to concern yourself with this, Castle. I'll handle it."

"Why aren't you listening to me?" He's chasing after me now. "They're coming to take her back, son! We can't let that happen!"

I freeze.

I turn to face him. My movements are slow, deliberate. "What are you talking about? Take her back where?"

Castle doesn't respond. Instead, his face goes slack. He stares, confused, in my direction.

"I have a thousand things to do," I say, impatient now, "so if you would please make this quick and tell me what on earth you're talking about—"

"He never told you, did he?"

"Who? Told me what?"

"Your father," he says. "He never told you." Castle runs a hand down the length of his face. He looks abruptly ancient, about to expire. "My God. He never told you."

"What do you mean? What did he never tell me?"

"The truth," he says. "About Ms. Ferrars."

I stare at him, my chest constricting in fear.

Castle shakes his head as he says, "He never told you where she really came from, did he? He never told you the truth about her parents."

JULIETTE

"Stop squirming, J."

We're in the glass elevator, making our way down to one of the main reception areas, and I can't stop fidgeting.

My eyes are squeezed shut. I keep saying, "Oh my God, I *am* totally clueless, aren't I? What am I doing? I don't look professional at all—"

"You know what? Who cares what you're wearing?" Kenji says. "It's all in the attitude, anyway. It's about how you carry yourself."

I look up at him, feeling the height difference between us more acutely than ever. "But I'm so short."

"Napoleon was short, too."

"Napoleon was horrible," I point out.

"Napoleon got shit done, didn't he?"

I frown.

Kenji nudges me with his elbow. "You might want to spit the gum out, though."

"Kenji," I say, only half hearing him, "I've just realized I've never met any foreign officials before."

"I know, right? Me neither," he says, mussing my hair. "But it'll be okay. You just need to calm down. Anyway, you look cute. You'll do great."

I slap his hand away. "I may not know much about being a supreme commander yet, but I do know that I'm not supposed to be *cute*."

Just then, the elevator dings open.

"Who says you can't be cute and kick ass at the same time?" Kenji winks at me. "I do it every day."

"Oh, man—you know what? Never mind," is the first thing Kenji says to me.

He's cringing, shooting me a sidelong glance as he says, "Maybe you really *should* work on your wardrobe?"

I might die of embarrassment.

Whoever this guy is, whatever his intentions are, Haider Ibrahim is dressed unlike anyone I've ever seen before. He *looks* like no one I've ever seen before.

He stands up as we enter the room—tall, very tall—and I'm instantly struck by the sight of him. He's wearing a dark gray leather jacket over what I can only assume is meant to be a shirt, but is actually a series of tightly woven chains strung across his body. His skin is heavily tanned and half exposed, his upper body only barely concealed by his chain-link shirt. His closely tapered black pants disappear into shin-high combat boots, and his light brown eyes—a startling contrast to his brown skin—are rimmed in a flutter of thick black lashes.

I tug at my pink sweater and nervously swallow my gum.

"Hi," I say, and begin to wave, but Kenji is kind enough to push down my hand. I clear my throat. "I'm Juliette."

Haider steps forward cautiously, his eyes drawn together in what looks like confusion as he appraises my appearance. I feel uncomfortably self-conscious. Wildly underprepared. And I suddenly really need to use the bathroom.

"Hello," he finally says, but it sounds more like a question.

"Can we help you?" I say.

"Tehcheen Arabi?"

"Oh." I glance at Kenji, then at Haider. "Um, you don't speak English?"

Haider raises a single eyebrow. "Do you only speak English?"

"Yes?" I say, feeling now more nervous than ever.

"That's too bad." He sighs. Looks around. "I'm here to see the supreme commander." He has a rich, deep voice but speaks with a slight accent.

"Yep, hi, that's me," I say, and smile.

His eyes widen with ill-concealed confusion. "You are"—he frowns—"the supreme?"

"Mm-hm." I paste on a brighter smile. Diplomacy, I tell myself. *Diplomacy.*

"But we were told that the new supreme was wild, lethal—terrifying—"

I nod. Feel my face warm. "Yes. That's me. I'm Juliette Ferrars."

Haider tilts his head, his eyes scanning my body. "But you're so small." And I'm still trying to figure out how to respond to that when he shakes his head and says, "I apologize, I meant to say—that you are so young. But then, also, very small."

My smile is beginning to hurt.

"So it was you," he says, still confused, "who killed Supreme Anderson?"

I nod. Shrug.

"But—"

"I'm sorry," Kenji interjects. "Did you have a reason for being here?"

Haider looks taken aback by the question. He glances at Kenji. "Who is this?"

"He's my second-in-command," I say. "And you should feel free to respond to him when he speaks to you."

"Oh, I see," Haider says, understanding in his eyes. He nods at Kenji. "A member of your Supreme Guard."

"I don't have a Supr—"

"That's right," Kenji says, throwing a swift *shut up* elbow in my ribs. "You'll have to forgive me for being a little over-protective." He smiles. "I'm sure you know how it is."

"Yes, of course," Haider says, looking sympathetic.

"Should we all sit down?" I say, gesturing to the couches across the room. We're still standing in the entryway and it's starting to get awkward.

"Certainly." Haider offers me his arm in anticipation of the fifteen-foot journey to the couches, and I shoot Kenji a quick look of confusion.

He shrugs.

The three of us settle into our seats; Kenji and I sit across from Haider. There's a long, wooden coffee table between us, and Kenji presses the slim button underneath to call for a tea and coffee service.

Haider won't stop staring at me. His gaze is neither flattering nor threatening—he looks genuinely confused—and I'm surprised to find that it's *this* reaction I find most unsettling. If his eyes were angry or objectifying, I might better know how to react. Instead, he seems mild and pleasant, but—surprised. And I'm not sure what to do with it. Kenji was right—I wish more than ever that Warner were here; his ability to sense emotions would give me a clearer idea of how to respond.

I finally break the silence between us.

"It's really very nice to meet you," I say, hoping I sound kinder than I feel, "but I'd love to know what brings you here. You've come such a long way."

Haider smiles then. The action adds a necessary warmth to his face that makes him look younger than he first appeared. "Curiosity," he says simply.

I do my best to mask my anxiety.

It's becoming more obvious by the moment that he was sent here to do some kind of reconnaissance for his father. Castle's theory was right—the supreme commanders must be dying to know who I am. And I'm beginning to wonder if this is only the first of several visits I'll soon receive from prying eyes.

Just then, the tea and coffee service arrives.

The ladies and gentlemen who work in Sector 45—here,

and in the compounds—are peppier than ever these days. There's an infusion of hope in our sector that doesn't exist anywhere else on the continent, and the two older ladies who hurry into our room with the food cart are no exception to the effects of recent events. They flash big, bright smiles in my direction, and arrange the china with an exuberance that does not go unnoticed. I see Haider watching our interaction closely, examining the ladies' faces and the comfortable way in which they move in my presence. I thank them for their work and Haider is visibly stunned. Eyebrows raised, he sits back in his seat, hands clasped in his lap like the perfect gentleman, silent as salt until the moment they leave.

"I will impose upon your kindness for a few weeks," Haider says suddenly. "That is—if that's all right."

I frown, begin to protest, and Kenji cuts me off.

"Of course," he says, smiling wide. "Stay as long as you like. The son of a supreme commander is always welcome here."

"You are very kind," he says with a simple bow of his head. And then he hesitates, touches something at his wrist, and our room is swarmed in an instant by what appear to be members of his personal staff.

Haider stands up so swiftly I almost miss it.

Kenji and I hurry to our feet.

"It was a pleasure meeting you, Supreme Commander Ferrars," Haider says, stepping forward to reach for my hand, and I'm surprised by his boldness. Despite the many rumors

I know he's heard about me, he doesn't seem to mind being near my skin. Not that it really matters, of course—I've now learned how to turn my powers on and off at will—but not everyone knows that yet.

Either way, he presses a brief kiss to the back of my hand, smiles, and bows his head very slightly.

I manage an awkward smile and a small nod.

"If you tell me how many people are in your party," Kenji says, "I can begin to arrange accommodations for y—"

Haider laughs out loud, surprised. "Oh, that won't be necessary," he says. "I've brought my own residence."

"You've brought"—Kenji frowns—"you brought your own *residence*?"

Haider nods without looking at Kenji. When he next speaks he speaks only to me. "I look forward to seeing you and the rest of your guard at dinner tonight."

"Dinner," I say, blinking fast. "Tonight?"

"Of course," Kenji says swiftly. "We look forward to it."

Haider nods. "Please send my warmest regards to your Regent Warner. It's been several months since our last visit, but I look forward to catching up with him. He has mentioned me, of course?" A bright smile. "We've known each other since our infancy."

Stunned, I nod slowly, realization overcoming my confusion. "Yes. Right. Of course. I'm sure he'll be thrilled to see you again."

Another nod, and Haider's gone.

Kenji and I are alone.

"What the f—"

"Oh"—Haider pops his head back in the room—"and please tell your chef that I do not eat meat."

"For sure," Kenji says, nodding and smiling. "Yep. You got it."

WARNER

I'm sitting in the dark with my back to the bedroom door when I hear it open. It's only midafternoon, but I've been sitting here, staring at these unopened boxes for so long that even the sun, it seems, has grown tired of staring.

Castle's revelation left me in a daze.

I still don't trust Castle—don't trust that he has any idea what he's talking about—but at the end of our conversation I couldn't shake a terrible, frightening feeling in my gut begging for verification. I needed time to process the possibilities. To be alone with my thoughts. And when I expressed as much to Castle, he said, "Process all you like, son, but don't let this distract you. Juliette should not be meeting with Haider on her own. Something doesn't feel right here, Mr. Warner, and you have to go to them. Now. Show her how to navigate your world."

But I couldn't bring myself to do it.

Despite my every instinct to protect her, I won't undermine her like that. She didn't ask for my help today. She made a choice to not tell me what was happening. My abrupt and unwelcome interruption would only make her think that I agreed with Castle—that I didn't trust her to do the job on her own. And I *don't* agree with Castle; I think he's an idiot for underestimating her. So I returned here, instead, to these rooms, to think. To stare at my father's unopened secrets. To await her arrival.

And now—

The first thing Juliette does is turn on the light.

"Hey," she says carefully. "What's going on?"

I take a deep breath and turn around. "These are my father's old files," I say, gesturing with one hand. "Delalieu had them collected for me. I thought I should take a look, see if there's anything here that might be useful."

"Oh, wow," she says, her eyes alight with recognition. "I was wondering what those were for." She crosses the room to crouch beside the stacks, carefully running her fingers along the unmarked boxes. "Do you need help moving these into your office?"

I shake my head.

"Would you like me to help you sort through them?" she says, glancing at me over her shoulder. "I'd be happy t—"

"No," I say too quickly. I get to my feet, make an effort to appear calm. "No, that won't be necessary."

She raises her eyebrows.

I try to smile. "I think I'd like the time alone with them."

At this, she nods, misunderstanding all at once, and her sympathetic smile makes my chest tighten. I feel an indistinct, icy feeling stab at somewhere inside of me. She thinks I want space to deal with my grief. That going through my father's things will be difficult for me.

She doesn't know. I wish I didn't.

"So," she says, walking toward the bed, the boxes forgotten. "It's been an . . . interesting day."

The pressure in my chest intensifies. "Has it?"

"I just met an old friend of yours," she says, and flops backward onto the mattress. She reaches behind her head to pull her hair free of its ponytail, and sighs.

"An old friend of mine?" I say. But I can only stare at her as she speaks, study the shape of her face. I can't, at the present moment, know with perfect certainty whether or not what Castle told me is true; but I do know that I'll find the answers I seek in my father's files—in the boxes stacked inside this room.

Even so, I haven't yet gathered the courage to look.

"Hey," she says, waving a hand at me from the bed. "You in there?"

"Yes," I say reflexively. I take in a sharp breath. "Yes, love."

"So . . . do you remember him?" she says. "Haider Ibrahim?"

"Haider." I nod. "Yes, of course. He's the eldest son of the supreme commander of Asia. He has a sister," I say, but I say it robotically.

"Well, I don't know about his sister," she says. "But Haider is here. And he's staying for a few weeks. We're all having dinner with him tonight."

"At his behest, I'm sure."

"Yeah." She laughs. "How'd you know?"

I smile. Vaguely. "I remember Haider very well."

She's silent a moment. Then: "He said you'd known each other since your infancy."

And I feel, but do not acknowledge, the sudden tension in the room. I merely nod.

"That's a long time," she says.

"Yes. A very long time."

She sits up. Drops her chin in one hand and stares at me. "I thought you said you never had any friends."

At this, I laugh, but the sound is hollow. "I don't know that I would call us friends, exactly."

"No?"

"No."

"And you don't care to expand on that?"

"There's little to say."

"Well—if you're not friends, exactly, then why is he here?"

"I have my suspicions."

She sighs. Says, "Me too," and bites the inside of her cheek. "I guess this is where it starts, huh? Everyone wants to take a look at the freak show. At what we've done—at who I am. And we have to play along."

But I'm only half listening.

Instead, I'm staring at the many boxes looming behind her, Castle's words still settling in my mind. I remember I should say something, anything, to appear engaged in the conversation. So I try to smile as I say, "You didn't tell me he'd arrived earlier. I wish I could've been there to assist somehow."

Her cheeks, suddenly pink with embarrassment, tell one story; her lips tell another. "I didn't think I needed to tell you everything, all the time. I can handle some things on my own."

Her sharp tone is so surprising it forces my mind to focus. I meet her eyes to find she's staring straight through me now, bright with both hurt and anger.

"That's not at all what I meant," I say. "You know I think you can do anything, love. But I could've been a help to you. I know these people."

Her face is now pinker, somehow. She can't meet my eyes.

"I know," she says quietly. "I know. I've just been feeling a little overwhelmed lately. And I had a talk with Castle this morning that kind of messed with my head." She sighs. "I'm in a weird place today."

My heart starts beating too fast. "You had a talk with Castle?"

She nods.

I forget to breathe.

"He said I need to talk to you about something?" She looks up at me. "Like, there's more about The Reestablishment that you haven't told me?"

"More about The Reestablishment?"

"Yeah, like, there's something you need to tell me?"

"Something I need to tell you."

"Um, are you just going to keep repeating what I'm saying to you?" she says, and laughs.

I feel my chest unclench. A little.

"No, no, of course not," I say. "I just—I'm sorry, love. I confess I'm also a bit distracted today." I nod at the boxes laid out across the room. "It seems there's a lot left to discover about my father."

She shakes her head, her eyes big and sad. "I'm so sorry. It must be awful to have to go through all his stuff like this."

I exhale, and say, mostly to myself, "You have no idea," before looking away. I'm still staring at the floor, my head heavy with the day and its demands, when she reaches out, tentatively, with a single word.

"Aaron?"

And I can feel it then, can feel the change, the fear, the pain in her voice. My heart still beats too hard, but now it's for an entirely different reason.

"What's wrong?" I say, looking up at once. I take a seat next to her on the bed, study her eyes. "What's happened?"

She shakes her head. Stares into her open hands. Whispers the words when she says, "I think I made a mistake."

My eyes widen as I watch her. Her face pulls together. Her feelings pinwheel out of control, assaulting me with their wildness. She's afraid. She's angry. She's angry with herself for being afraid.

"You and I are so different," she says. "Meeting Haider today, I just"—she sighs—"I remembered how different we are. How differently we grew up."

I'm frozen. Confused. I can feel her fear and apprehension, but I don't know where she's going with this. What she's trying to say.

"So you think you've made a mistake?" I say. "About—*us*?"

Panic, suddenly, as she understands. "No, oh my God, no, not about us," she says quickly. "No, I just—"

Relief floods through me.

"—I still have so much to learn," she says. "I don't know anything about ruling . . . anything." She makes an impatient, angry sound. She can hardly get the words out. "I had no idea what I was signing up for. And every day I feel so incompetent," she says. "Sometimes I'm just not sure I can keep up with you. With any of this." She hesitates. And then, quietly, "This job should've been yours, you know. Not mine."

"No."

"Yes," she says, nodding. She can no longer look at me. "Everyone's thinking it, even if they don't say it. Castle. Kenji. I bet even the soldiers think so."

"Everyone can go to hell."

She smiles, only a little. "I think they might be right."

"People are idiots, love. Their opinions are worthless."

"Aaron," she says, frowning. "I appreciate you being angry on my behalf, I really do, but not *all* people are idio—"

"If they think you incapable it is because they are idiots. Idiots who've already forgotten that you were able to accomplish in a matter of *months* what they had been trying to do for decades. They are forgetting where you started, what you've overcome, how quickly you found the courage to fight when they could hardly stand."

She looks up, looks defeated. "But I don't know anything about politics."

"You are inexperienced," I say to her, "that is true. But you can learn these things. There's still time. And I will help you." I take her hand. "Sweetheart, you inspired the people of this sector to follow you into *battle*. They put their lives on the line—they sacrificed their loved ones—because they believed in you. In your strength. And you didn't let them down. You can never forget the enormity of what you've done," I say. "Don't allow anyone to take that away from you."

She stares at me, her eyes wide, shining. She blinks as she looks away, wiping quickly at a tear escaping down the side of her face.

"The world tried to crush you," I say, gently now, "and you refused to be shattered. You've recovered from every setback a stronger person, rising from the ashes only to astonish everyone around you. And you will continue to surprise and confuse those who underestimate you. It is an inevitability," I say. "A foregone conclusion.

"But you should know now that being a leader is a thankless occupation. Few will ever be grateful for what you do or for the changes you implement. Their memories will be short, convenient. Your every success will be scrutinized. Your accomplishments will be brushed aside, breeding only greater expectations from those around you. Your power will push you further away from your friends." I look away, shake my head. "You will be made to feel lonely. Lost. You will long for validation from those you once admired, agonizing between pleasing old friends and doing what is right."

I look up. I feel my heart swell with pride as I stare at her. "But you must never, ever let the idiots into your head. They will only lead you astray."

Her eyes are bright with unshed tears. "But how?" she says, her voice breaking on the word. "How do I get them out of my head?"

"Set them on fire."

Her eyes go wide.

"In your mind," I say, attempting a smile. "Let them fuel the fire that keeps you striving." I reach out, touch my fingers to her cheek. "Idiots are highly flammable, love. Let them all burn in hell."

She closes her eyes. Turns her face into my hand.

And I pull her in, press my forehead to hers. "Those who do not understand you," I say softly, "will always doubt you."

She leans back, just an inch. Looks up.

"And I," I say, "I have never doubted you."

"Never?"

I shake my head. "Not once."

She looks away. Wipes her eyes. I press a kiss against her cheek, taste the salt of her tears.

She turns toward me.

I can feel it, as she looks at me; I can feel her fears disappearing, can feel her emotions becoming something else. Her cheeks flush. Her skin is suddenly hot, electric, under my hands. My heart beats faster, harder, and she doesn't have to say a word. I can feel the temperature change between us.

"Hey," she says. But she's staring at my mouth.

"Hi."

She touches her nose to mine and something inside me jolts to life. I hear my breath catch. My eyes close, unbidden.

"I love you," she says.

The words do something to me every time I hear them. They change me. Build something new inside of me. I swallow, hard. Fire consumes my mind.

"You know," I whisper, "I never get tired of hearing you say that."

She smiles. Her nose brushes the line of my jaw as she turns, presses her lips against my throat. I'm holding my breath, terrified to move, to leave this moment.

"I love you," she says again.

Heat fills my veins. I can feel her in my blood, her whispers overwhelming my senses. And for a sudden, desperate second I think I might be dreaming.

"Aaron," she says.

I'm losing a battle. We have so much to do, so much to take care of. I know I should move, should snap out of this, but I can't. I can't think.

And then she climbs into my lap and I take a quick, desperate breath, fighting against a sudden rush of pleasure and pain. There's no pretending anything when she's this close to me; I know she can feel me, can feel how badly I want her.

I can feel her, too.

Her heat. Her desire. She makes no secret of what she wants from me. What she wants me to do to her. And knowing this makes my torment only more acute.

She kisses me once, softly, her hands slipping under my sweater, and wraps her arms around me. I pull her in and she shifts forward, adjusting herself in my lap, and I take another painful, anguished breath. My every muscle tightens. I try not to move.

"I know it's late," she says. "I know we have a bunch of things to do. But I miss you." She reaches down, her fingers trailing along the zipper of my pants, and the movement sears through me. My vision goes white. For a moment I hear nothing but my heart, pounding in my head.

"You are trying to kill me," I say.

"Aaron." I can feel her smile as she whispers the word in my ear. She's unbuttoning my pants. "Please."

And I, I am gone.

My hand is suddenly behind her neck, the other wrapped around her waist, and I kiss her, melting into her, falling backward onto the bed and pulling her down with me. I used to dream about this—times like this—what it would be like to unzip her jeans, to run my fingers along her bare skin, to feel her, hot and soft against my body.

I stop, suddenly. Break away. I want to see her, to study her. To remind myself that she's really here, really mine. That she wants me just as much I want her. And when I meet her eyes the feeling overwhelms me, threatens to drown me. And then she's kissing me, even as I fight to catch my breath, and every thing, every thought and worry is wicked away, replaced by the feel of her mouth against my skin. Her hands, claiming my body.

God, it's an impossible drug.

She's kissing me like she knew. Like she knows—knows how desperately I need this, need her, need this comfort and release.

Like she needs it, too.

I wrap my arms around her, flip her over so quickly she actually squeaks in surprise. I kiss her nose, her cheeks, her lips. The lines of our bodies are welded together. I feel myself dissolving, becoming pure emotion as she parts her lips, tastes me, moans into my mouth.

"I love you," I say, gasping the words. *"I love you."*

It's interesting, really, how quickly I've become the kind of person who takes late-afternoon naps. The person I used to be would never have wasted so much time sleeping. Then again, that person never knew how to relax. Sleep was brutal, elusive. But this—

I close my eyes, press my face to the back of her neck and breathe.

She stirs almost imperceptibly against me.

Her naked body is flush against the length of mine, my arms wrapped entirely around her. It's six o'clock, I have a thousand things to do, and I never, ever want to move.

I kiss the top of her shoulder and she arches her back, exhales, and turns to face me. I pull her closer.

She smiles. Kisses me.

I shut my eyes, my skin still hot with the memory of her. My hands search the shape of her body, her warmth. I'm always stunned by how soft she is. Her curves are gentle and smooth. I feel my muscles tighten with longing and I surprise myself with how much I want her.

Again.

So soon.

"We'd better get dressed," she says softly. "I still need to meet with Kenji to talk about tonight."

All at once I recoil.

"Wow," I whisper, turning away. "That was not at all what I was hoping you'd say."

She laughs. Out loud. "Hmm. Kenji is a big turnoff for you. Got it."

I frown, feeling petty.

She kisses my nose. "I really wish you two could be friends."

"He's a walking disaster," I say. "Look what he did to my hair."

"But he's my best friend," she says, still smiling. "And I don't want to have to choose between the two of you all the time."

I look at her out of the corner of my eye. She's sitting up now, wearing nothing but the bedsheet. Her brown hair is long and tousled, her cheeks pinked, her eyes big and round and still a little sleepy.

I'm not sure I could ever say no to her.

"Please be nice to him," she says, and crawls over to me, the bedsheet catching under her knee and undoing her composure. I yank the rest of the sheet away from her and she gasps, surprised by the sight of her own naked body, and I can't help but take advantage of the moment, tucking her underneath me all over again.

"Why," I say, kissing her neck, "are you always so attached to that bedsheet?"

She looks away and blushes, and I'm lost again, kissing her.

"Aaron," she gasps, breathless, "I really—I have to go."

"Don't," I whisper, leaving light kisses along her collarbone. "Don't go." Her face is flushed, her lips bright red. Her eyes are closed in pleasure.

"I don't want to," she says, her breath hitching as I catch her bottom lip between my teeth, "I really don't, but Kenji—"

I groan and fall backward, pulling a pillow over my head.

JULIETTE

"Where the hell have you been?"

"What? Nothing," I say, heat flashing through my body. "I just—"

"What do you mean, nothing?" Kenji says, nearly stepping on my heels as I attempt to outpace him. "I've been waiting down here for almost two hours."

"I know—I'm sorry—"

He grabs my shoulder. Spins me around. Takes one look at my face and—

"Oh, gross, J, what the *hell*—"

"What?" I widen my eyes, all innocence, even as my face inflames.

Kenji glares at me.

I clear my throat.

"I told you to ask him a *question*."

"I did!"

"Jesus Christ." Kenji rubs an agitated hand across his forehead. "Do time and place mean nothing to you?"

"Hmm?"

He narrows his eyes at me.

I smile.

"You guys are terrible."

"Kenji," I say, reaching out.

"Ew, don't touch me—"

"Fine." I frown, crossing my arms.

He shakes his head, looks away. Makes a face and says, "You know what? Whatever," and sighs. "Did he at least tell you anything useful before you—uh, changed the subject?"

We've just walked back into the reception area where we first met with Haider.

"Yes he did," I say, determined. "He knew exactly who I was talking about."

"And?"

We sit down on the couches—Kenji choosing to sit across from me this time—and I clear my throat. I wonder aloud if we should order more tea.

"No tea." Kenji leans back, legs crossed, right ankle propped up on his left knee. "What did Warner say about Haider?"

Kenji's gaze is so focused and unforgiving I'm not sure what to do with myself. I still feel weirdly embarrassed; I wish I'd remembered to tie my hair back again. I have to keep pushing it out of my face.

I sit up straighter. Pull myself together. "He said they were never really friends."

Kenji snorts. "No surprise there."

"But he remembered him," I say, pointing at nothing in particular.

"And? What does he remember?"

"Oh. Um." I scratch an imaginary itch behind my ear. "I don't know."

"You didn't ask?"

"I . . . forgot?"

Kenji rolls his eyes. "Shit, man, I knew I should've gone myself."

I sit on my hands and try to smile. "Do you want to order some tea?"

"No tea." Kenji shoots me a look. He taps the side of his leg, thinking.

"Do you want t—"

"Where is Warner now?" Kenji cuts me off.

"I don't know," I say. "I think he's still in his room. He had a bunch of boxes he wanted to sort through—"

Kenji is on his feet in an instant. He holds up one finger. "I'll be right back."

"Wait! Kenji—I don't think that's a good idea—"

But he's already gone.

I slump into the couch and sigh.

As I suspected. Not a good idea.

Warner is standing stiffly beside my couch, hardly looking at Kenji. I think he still hasn't forgiven him for the terrible haircut, and I can't say I blame him. Warner looks different without his golden hair—not bad, no—but different. His hair is barely half an inch long, one uniform length throughout, a shade of blond that registers only dimly as a color now. But the most interesting change in his face is that he's got a soft, subtle shadow of stubble—as though he's forgotten to shave lately—and I'm surprised to find that it doesn't bother me. He's too naturally good-looking to have his genetics undone by a simple haircut and, the truth is, I kind of like it. I'd hesitate to say this to Warner, as I don't know whether he'd appreciate the unorthodox compliment, but there's something nice about the change. He looks a little coarser now; a little rougher around the edges. He's less beautiful but somehow, impossibly—

Sexier.

Short, uncomplicated hair; a five o'clock shadow; a deeply, deeply serious face.

It works for him.

He's wearing a soft, navy-blue sweater—the sleeves, as always, pushed up his forearms—and slim black pants tucked into shiny black ankle boots. It's an effortless look. And right now he's leaning against a column, his arms crossed against his chest, feet crossed at the ankles, looking more sullen than usual, and I'm really kind of enjoying the view.

Kenji, however, is not.

The two of them look more irritated than ever, and I realize I'm to blame for the tension. I keep trying to force them to spend time together. I keep hoping that, with enough experience, Kenji will come to see what I love about Warner, and that Warner will learn to admire Kenji the way that I do—but it doesn't seem to be working. Forcing them to spend time together is beginning to backfire.

"*So,*" I say, clapping my hands together. "Should we talk?"

"Sure," Kenji says, but he's staring at the wall. "Let's talk."

No one talks.

I tap Warner's knee. When he looks at me, I gesture for him to sit down.

He does.

"Please," I whisper.

Warner frowns.

Finally, reluctantly, he sighs. "You said you had questions for me."

"Yeah, first question: Why are you such a dick?"

Warner stands up. "Sweetheart," he says quietly, "I hope you will forgive me for what I'm about to do to his face."

"Hey, asshole, I can still hear you."

"Okay, seriously, this has to stop." I'm tugging on Warner's arm, trying to get him to sit down, and he won't budge. My superhuman strength is totally useless on Warner; he just absorbs my power. "Please, sit down. Everyone. And you," I say, pointing at Kenji, "you need to stop instigating fights."

Kenji throws a hand in the air, makes a sound of disbelief. "Oh, so it's always my fault, huh? Whatever."

"No," I say heavily. "It's not your fault. This is my fault."

Kenji and Warner turn to look at me at the same time, surprised.

"This?" I say, gesturing between them. "I caused this. I'm sorry I ever asked you guys to be friends. You don't have to be friends. You don't even have to like each other. Forget I said anything."

Warner drops his crossed arms.

Kenji raises his eyebrows.

"I promise," I say. "No more forced hangout sessions. No more spending time alone without me. Okay?"

"You swear?" Kenji says.

"I swear."

"Thank God," Warner says.

"*Same,* bro. Same."

And I roll my eyes, irritated. This is the first thing they've managed to agree on in over a week: their mutual hatred of my hopes for their friendship.

But at least Kenji is finally smiling. He sits down on the couch and seems to relax. Warner takes the seat next to me—still composed, but far less tense.

And that's it. That's all it takes. The tension is gone. Now that they're free to hate each other, they seem perfectly friendly. I don't understand them at all.

"So—you have questions for me, Kishimoto?" Warner says.

Kenji nods, leans forward. "Yeah—yeah, I want to know everything you remember about the Ibrahim family. We've got to be prepared for whatever Haider throws at us at dinner tonight, which"—Kenji looks at his watch, frowns—"is in, like, twenty minutes, no thanks to you guys, but anyway I'm wondering if you can tell us anything about his possible motivations. I'd like to be one step ahead of this dude."

Warner nods. "Haider's family will take more time to unpack. As a whole, they're intimidating. But Haider himself is far less complex. In fact, he's a strange choice for this situation. I'm surprised Ibrahim didn't send his daughter instead."

"Why?"

Warner shrugs. "Haider is less competent. He's self-righteous. Spoiled. Arrogant."

"Wait—are we describing you or Haider?"

Warner doesn't seem to mind the gibe. "You are misunderstanding a key difference between us," he says. "It's true that I am confident. But Haider is arrogant. We are not the same."

"Sounds like the same thing to me."

Warner clasps his hands and sighs, looking for all the world like he's trying to be patient with a difficult child. "Arrogance is false confidence," he says. "It is born from insecurity. Haider pretends to be unafraid. He pretends to be crueler than he is. He lies easily. That makes him unpredictable and, in some ways, a more dangerous opponent. But the majority of the time his actions are inspired by fear." Warner looks up, looks Kenji in the eye. "And that makes him weak."

"Huh. Okay." Kenji sinks further into the couch, processing. "Anything particularly interesting about him? Anything we should be aware of?"

"Not really. Haider is mediocre at most things. He excels only occasionally. He's obsessed mainly with his physique, and most talented with a sniper rifle."

Kenji's head pops up. "Obsessed with his physique, huh? You sure you two aren't related?"

At this, Warner's face sours. "I am *not* obsessed with m—"

"Okay, okay, calm down." Kenji waves his hands around. "No need to worry your pretty little face about it."

"I detest you."

"I love that we feel the same way about each other."

"All right, guys," I say loudly. "Focus. We're having dinner with Haider in like five minutes, and I seem to be the only one worried about this revelation that he's a super-talented sniper."

"Yeah, maybe he's here for some, you know"—Kenji makes a finger gun motion at Warner, and then at himself—"target practice."

Warner shakes his head, still a little annoyed. "Haider is all show. I wouldn't worry about him. As I said, I would only worry if his sister were here—which means we should probably plan to worry very soon." He exhales. "She will almost certainly be arriving next."

At this, I raise my eyebrows. "Is she really scary?"

Warner tilts his head. "Not scary, exactly," he says to me. "She's very cerebral."

"So she's . . . what?" says Kenji. "Psycho?"

"Not at all. But I've always been able to get a sense of people and their emotions, and I could never get a good read on her. I think her mind moves too quickly. There's something kind of . . . flighty about the way she thinks. Like a hummingbird." He sighs. Looks up. "Anyhow, I haven't seen her in several months, at least, but I doubt much about her has changed."

"Like a *hummingbird?*" says Kenji. "So, is she, like, a fast talker?"

"No," says Warner. "She's usually very quiet."

"Hmm. Okay, well, I'm glad she's not here," Kenji says. "Sounds boring."

Warner almost smiles. "She would disembowel you."

Kenji rolls his eyes.

And I'm just about to ask another question when a sudden, harsh ring interrupts the conversation.

Delalieu has come to collect us for dinner.

WARNER

I genuinely dislike being hugged.

There are very few exceptions to this rule, and Haider is not one of them. Even so, every time I see him, he insists on hugging me. He kisses the air on either side of my face, clamps his hands around my shoulders, and smiles at me like I am actually his friend.

"Hela habibi shlonak? It's so good to see you."

I attempt a smile. *"Ani zeyn, shukran."* I nod at the table. "Please, have a seat."

"Sure, sure," he says, and looks around. *"Wenha Nazeera . . . ?"*

"Oh," I say, surprised. "I thought you came alone."

"La, habibi," he says as he sits down. *"Heeya shwaya mitakhira.* But she should be here any minute now. She was very excited to see you."

"I highly doubt that."

"Um, I'm sorry, but am I the only one here who didn't know you speak Arabic?" Kenji is staring at me, wide-eyed.

Haider laughs, eyes bright as he analyzes my face. "Your new friends know so little about you." And then, to Kenji, "Your Regent Warner speaks seven languages."

“You speak *seven* languages?” Juliette says, touching my arm.

“Sometimes,” I say quietly.

It’s a small group of us for dinner tonight; Juliette is sitting at the head of the table. I’m seated to her right; Kenji sits to the right of me.

Across from me now sits Haider Ibrahim.

Across from Kenji is an empty chair.

“So,” says Haider, clapping his hands together. “This is your new life? So much has changed since I saw you last.”

I pick up my fork. “What are you doing here, Haider?”

“*Wallah*,” he says, clutching his chest, “I thought you’d be happy to see me. I wanted to meet all your new friends. And of course, I had to meet your new supreme commander.” He appraises Juliette out of the corner of his eye; the movement is so quick I almost miss it. And then he picks up his napkin, drapes it carefully across his lap, and says, very softly, “*Heeya jidan helwa*.”

My chest tightens.

“And is that enough for you?” He leans forward suddenly, speaking so quietly only I can hear him. “A pretty face? And you so easily betray your friends?”

“If you’ve come here to fight,” I say, “please, let’s not bother eating dinner.”

Haider laughs out loud. Picks up his water glass. “Not yet, *habibi*.” He takes a drink. Sits back. “There’s always time for dinner.”

“Where is your sister?” I say, turning away. “Why didn’t you arrive together?”

"Why don't you ask her yourself?"

I look up, surprised to find Nazeera standing at the door. She studies the room, her eyes lingering on Juliette's face just a second longer than everyone else's, and takes her seat without a word.

"Everyone, this is Nazeera," Haider says, jumping to his feet with a wide smile. He wraps an arm around his sister's shoulder even as she ignores him. "She'll be here for the duration of my stay. I hope you will welcome her as warmly as you've welcomed me."

Nazeera does not say hello.

Haider's face is open, an exaggeration of happiness. Nazeera, however, wears no expression at all. Her eyes are blank, her jaw solemn. The only similarities in these siblings are physical: she bears a remarkable resemblance to her brother. She has his warm brown skin, his light brown eyes, and the same long, dark eyelashes that shutter shut her expression from the rest of us. But she's grown up quite a bit since I last saw her. Her eyes are bigger, deeper than Haider's, and she has a small, diamond piercing centered just underneath her bottom lip. Two more diamonds above her right eyebrow. The only other marked distinction between them is that I cannot see her hair.

She wears a silk shawl around her head.

And I can't help but be quietly shocked. This is new. The Nazeera I remember did not cover her hair—and why would she? Her head scarf is a relic; a part of our past life. It's an artifact of a religion and culture that no longer exists under The Reestablishment. Our movement long ago expunged all symbols and practices of faith or culture in an effort at resetting identities and allegiances; so much so that places of worship were among the first institutions around the world to be destroyed. Civilians, it was said, were to bow before The Reestablishment and nothing else. Crosses, crescents, Stars of David—turbans and yarmulkes, head scarves and nun's habits—

They're all illegal.

And Nazeera Ibrahim—the daughter of a supreme commander—has a staggering amount of nerve. Because this simple scarf, an otherwise insubstantial detail, is nothing less than an open act of rebellion. And I'm so stunned I almost can't help what I say next.

"You cover your hair now?"

At this, she looks up, meets my eyes. She takes a long sip of her tea and studies me. And then, finally—

Says nothing.

I feel my face about to register surprise and I have to force myself to be still. Clearly, she has no interest in discussing the subject. I decide to move on. I'm about to say something to Haider, when,

"So you don't think anyone will notice? That you cover your hair?" It's Kenji, speaking and chewing at the same time. I touch my fingers to my lips and look away, fighting to hide my revulsion.

Nazeera stabs at a piece of lettuce on her plate. Eats it.

"I mean you have to know," Kenji says to her, still chewing, "that what you're wearing is an offense punishable by imprisonment."

She seems surprised to find Kenji still pursuing the subject, her eyes appraising him like he might be an idiot. "I'm sorry," she says softly, putting down her fork, "but who are you, exactly?"

"*Nazeera,*" Haider says, trying to smile as he shoots her a careful, sidelong glance. "Please remember that we are guests—"

"I didn't realize there was a dress code here."

"Oh—well, I guess we don't have a dress code *here,*" Kenji says between bites, oblivious to the tension. "But that's only because we have a new supreme commander who's not a psychopath. But it's illegal to dress like that," he says, gesturing at her face with his spoon, "like, literally everywhere else. Right?" He looks around, but no one responds. "Isn't it?" he says to me, eager for confirmation.

I nod. Slowly.

Nazeera takes another long drink of her tea, careful to replace the cup in its saucer before she leans back, looks us both in the eye and says, "What makes you think I care?"

"I mean"—Kenji frowns—"don't you have to care? Your dad is a supreme commander. Does he even know that you wear that thing"—another abstract gesture at her head—"in public? Won't he be pissed?"

This is not going well.

Nazeera, who'd just picked up her fork again to spear some bit of food on her plate, puts down her fork and sighs. Unlike her brother, she speaks perfectly unaccented English.

She's looking only at Kenji when she says, "This *thing*?"

"Sorry," he says sheepishly, "I don't know what it's called."

She smiles at him, but there's no warmth in it. Only a warning. "Men," she says, "are always so baffled by women's clothing. So many opinions about a body that does not belong to them. Cover up, don't cover up"—she waves a hand—"no one can seem to decide."

"But—that's not what I—" Kenji tries to say.

"You know what I think," she says, still smiling, "about someone telling me what's legal and illegal about the way I dress?"

She holds up two middle fingers.

Kenji chokes.

"Go ahead," she says, her eyes flashing angrily as she picks up her fork again. "Tell my dad. Alert the armies. I don't give a shit."

"Nazeera—"

"Shut up, Haider."

"Whoa—hey—I'm sorry," Kenji says suddenly, looking panicked. "I didn't mean—"

"Whatever," she says, rolling her eyes. "I'm not hungry." She stands up suddenly. Elegantly. There's something interesting about her anger. Her unsubtle protest. And she's more impressive standing up.

She has the same long legs and lean frame as her brother, and she carries herself with great pride, like someone who was born into position and privilege. She wears a gray tunic cut from fine, heavy fabric; skintight leather pants; heavy boots; and a set of glittering gold knuckles on both hands.

And I'm not the only one staring.

Juliette, who's been watching quietly this whole time, is looking up, amazed. I can practically see her thought process as she suddenly stiffens, glances down at her own outfit, and crosses her arms over her chest as if to hide her pink sweater from view. She's tugging at her sleeves as though she might tear them off.

It's so adorable I almost kiss her right then.

A heavy, uncomfortable silence settles between us after Nazeera's gone.

We'd all been expecting an in-depth interrogation from Haider tonight; instead, he pokes quietly at his food, looking tired and embarrassed. No amount of money or prestige can save any of us from the agony of awkward family dinners.

"Why'd you have to say anything?" Kenji elbows me, and I flinch, surprised.

"Excuse me?"

"This is your fault," he hisses, low and anxious. "You shouldn't have said anything about her scarf."

"I asked *one* question," I say stiffly. "*You're* the one who kept pushing—"

"Yeah, but you started it! Why'd you even have to say anything?"

"She's the daughter of a supreme commander," I say, fighting to keep my voice down. "She knows better than anyone else that what she's wearing is illegal under the laws of The Reestablishment—"

"Oh my God," Kenji says, shaking his head. "Just—just stop, okay?"

"How dare you—"

"What are you two whispering about?" Juliette says, leaning in.

"Just that your boyfriend doesn't know when to shut his mouth," Kenji says, scooping up another spoonful of food.

"*You're* the one who can't keep his mouth shut." I turn away. "You can't even manage it while you're eating a bite of food. Of all the disgusting things—"

"Shut up, man. I'm hungry."

"I think I'll retire for the evening also," Haider says suddenly. He stands.

We all look up.

"Of course," I say. I get to my feet to bid him a proper good night.

"*Ani aasef,*" Haider says, looking down at his half-eaten dinner. "I was hoping to have a more productive conversation with all of you this evening, but I'm afraid my sister is unhappy to be here; she didn't want to leave home." He sighs. "But you know Baba," he says to me. "He gave her no choice." Haider shrugs. Attempts a smile. "She doesn't understand yet that what we do—the way we live now"—he hesitates—"it's the life we are given. None of us has a choice."

And for the first time tonight he surprises me; I see something in his eyes I recognize. A flicker of pain. The weight of responsibility. Expectation.

I know too well what it is to be the son of a supreme commander of the Reestablishment—and dare to disagree.

"Of course," I say to him. "I understand."

I really do.

JULIETTE

Warner escorts Haider back to his residence, and soon after they're gone, the rest of our party breaks apart. It was a weird, too-short dinner with a lot of surprises, and my head hurts. I'm ready for bed. Kenji and I are making our way to Warner's rooms in silence, both of us lost in thought.

It's Kenji who speaks first.

"So—you were pretty quiet tonight," he says.

"Yeah." I laugh, but there's no life in it. "I'm exhausted, Kenji. It was a weird day. An even weirder night."

"Weird how?"

"Um, I don't know, how about we start with the fact that Warner speaks *seven languages*?" I look up, meet his eyes. "I mean, what the hell? Sometimes I think I know him so well, and then something like this happens and it just"—I shake my head—"blows my mind. You were right," I say. "I still know nothing about him. Plus, what am I even doing anymore? I didn't say anything at dinner because I have no idea what to say."

Kenji blows out a breath. "Yeah. Well. Seven languages is pretty crazy. But, I mean, you have to remember that he was born into this, you know? Warner's had schooling you've never had."

"That's exactly my point."

"Hey, you'll be okay," Kenji says, squeezing my shoulder. "It's going to be okay."

"I was just starting to feel like maybe I could do this," I say to him. "I just had this whole talk with Warner today that actually made me feel better. And now I can't even remember why." I sigh. Close my eyes. "I feel so stupid, Kenji. Every day I feel stupider."

"Maybe you're just getting old. Senile." He taps his head. "You know."

"Shut up."

"So, uh"—he laughs—"I know it was a weird night and everything, but—what'd you think? Overall?"

"Of what?" I glance at him.

"Of Haider and Nazeera," he says. "Thoughts? Feelings? Sociopaths, yes or no?"

"Oh." I frown. "I mean, they're so different from each other. Haider is so loud. And Nazeera is . . . I don't know. I've never met anyone like her before. I guess I respect that she's standing up to her dad and The Reestablishment, but I have no idea what her real motivations are, so I'm not sure I should give her too much credit." I sigh. "Anyway, she seems really . . . angry."

And really beautiful. And really intimidating.

The painful truth is that I'd never felt so intimidated by another girl before, and I don't know how to admit that out loud. All day—and for the last couple of weeks—I've felt like an imposter. A child. I hate how easily I fade in and out of confidence, how I waver between who I was and who I could be. My past still clings to me, skeleton hands holding me back even as I push forward into the light. And I can't help but wonder how different I'd be today if I'd ever had someone to encourage me when I was growing up. I never had strong female role models. Meeting Nazeera tonight—seeing how tall and brave she was—made me wonder where she learned to be that way.

It made me wish I'd had a sister. Or a mother. Someone to learn from and lean on. A woman to teach me how to be brave in this body, among these men.

I've never had that.

Instead, I was raised on a steady diet of taunts and jeers, jabs at my heart, slaps in the face. Told repeatedly I was worthless. A monster.

Never loved. Never protected from the world.

Nazeera doesn't seem to care at all what other people think, and I wish so much that I had her confidence. I know I've changed a lot—that I've come a long way from who I used to be—but I want more than anything to just *be* confident and unapologetic about who I am and how I feel, and not have to try so hard all the time. I'm still working on that part of myself.

"Right," Kenji is saying. "Yeah. Pretty angry. But—"

"Excuse me?"

At the sound of her voice we both spin around.

"Speak of the devil," Kenji says under his breath.

"I'm sorry—I think I'm lost," Nazeera says. "I thought I

knew this building pretty well, but there's a bunch of construction going on and it's . . . throwing me off. Can either of you tell me how to get outside?"

She almost smiles.

"Oh, sure," I say, and almost smile back. "Actually"—I pause—"I think you might be on the wrong side of the building. Do you remember which entrance you came in from?"

She stops to think. "I think we're staying on the south side," she says, and flashes me a full, real smile for the first time. Then falters. "Wait. I *think* it was the south side. I'm sorry," she says, frowning. "I just arrived a couple of hours ago—Haider got here before me—"

"I totally understand," I say, cutting her off with a wave. "Don't worry—it took me a while to navigate the construction, too. Actually, you know what? Kenji knows his way around even better than I do. This is Kenji, by the way—I don't think you guys were formally introduced tonight—"

"Yeah, hi," she says, her smile gone in an instant. "I remember."

Kenji is staring at her like an idiot. Eyes wide, blinking. Lips parted ever so slightly. I poke his arm and he yelps, startled, but comes back to life. "Oh, right," he says quickly. "Hi. Hi—yeah, hi, um, sorry about dinner."

She raises an eyebrow at him.

And for the first time in all the time I've known him, Kenji actually blushes. *Blushes*. "No, really," he says. "I, uh, I think your—scarf—is, um, really cool."

"Uh-huh."

"What's it made of?" he says, reaching forward to touch her head. "It looks so soft—"

She slaps his hand away, recoiling visibly even in this dim light. "What the hell? Are you serious right now?"

"What?" Kenji blinks, confused. "What'd I do?"

Nazeera laughs, her expression a mixture of confusion and vague disgust. "How are you *so* bad at this?"

Kenji freezes in place, his mouth agape. "I don't, um—I just don't know, like, what the rules are? Like, can I call you sometime or—"

I laugh suddenly, loud and awkward, and pinch Kenji in the arm.

Kenji swears out loud. Shoots me an angry look.

I plant a bright smile on my face and speak only to Nazeera. "So, yeah, um, if you want to get to the south exit," I say quickly, "your best bet is to go back down the hall and make three lefts. You'll see the double doors on your right—just ask one of the soldiers to take you from there."

"Thanks," Nazeera says, returning my smile before shooting a weird look in Kenji's direction. He's still massaging his injured shoulder as he waves her a weak good-bye.

It's only after she's gone again that I finally spin around, hiss, "What the hell is wrong with you?" and Kenji grabs my arm, goes weak in the knees, and says,

"Oh my God, J, I think I'm in love."

I ignore him.

"No, seriously," he says, "like, is this what that is?

Because I've never been in love before, so I don't know if this is love or if I just have, like, food poisoning?"

"You don't even know her," I say, rolling my eyes, "so I'm guessing it's probably food poisoning."

"You think so?"

I glance up at him, eyes narrowed, but one look is all it takes to lose my thread of anger. His expression is so weird and silly—so slap-happy—I almost feel bad for him.

I sigh, shoving him forward. He keeps stopping in place for no reason. "I don't know. I think maybe you're just, you know—attracted to her? God, Kenji, you gave me so much crap for acting like this over Adam and Warner and now here you are, being all hormonal—"

"Whatever. You owe me."

I frown at him.

He shrugs, still beaming. "I mean, I know she's probably a sociopath. And, like, would definitely murder me in my sleep. But damn she's, wow," he says. "She's, like, batshit pretty. The kind of pretty that makes a man think getting murdered in his sleep might not be a bad way to go."

"Yeah," I say, but I say it quietly.

"Right?"

"I guess."

"What do you mean, *you guess*? I wasn't asking a question. That girl is objectively beautiful."

"Sure."

Kenji stops, takes my shoulders in his hands. "What is your deal, J?"

"I don't know what you're—"

"Oh my God," he says, stunned. "Are you jealous?"

"*No,*" I say, but I practically yell the word at him.

He's laughing now. "That's crazy. Why are you jealous?"

I shrug, mumble something.

"Wait, what's that?" He cups his hand over his ear. "You're worried I'm going to leave you for another woman?"

"Shut up, Kenji. I'm not jealous."

"Aw, J."

"I'm not. I swear. I'm not jealous. I'm just—I'm just . . ."

I'm having a hard time.

But I never have a chance to say the words. Kenji suddenly picks me up, spins me around and says, "Aw, you're so cute when you're jealous—"

And I kick him in the knee. Hard.

He drops me to the floor, grabs his leg, and shouts words so foul I don't even recognize half of them. I sprint away, half guilty, half pleased, his promises to kick my ass in the morning echoing after me as I go.

WARNER

I've joined Juliette on her morning walk today.

She seems deeply nervous now, more so than ever before, and I blame myself for not better preparing her for what she might face as supreme commander. She came back to our room last night in a panic, said something about wishing she spoke more languages, and then refused to talk about it.

I feel like she's hiding from me.

Or maybe I've been hiding from her.

I've been so absorbed in my own head, in my own issues, that I haven't had much of a chance to speak with her, at length, about how she's doing lately. Yesterday was the first time she'd ever brought up her worries about being a good leader, and it makes me wonder how long these fears have been wearing away at her. How long she's been bottling everything up. We have to find more time to talk this all through; but I worry we might both be drowning in revelations.

I'm certain I am.

My mind is still full of Castle's nonsense. I'm fairly certain he'll be proven misinformed, that he's misunderstood some crucial detail. Still, I'm desperate for real answers, and I haven't yet had a chance to go through my father's files.

So I remain here, in this uncertain state.

I'd been hoping to find some time today, but I don't trust Haider and Nazeera to be alone with Juliette. I gave her the space she needed when she first met Haider, but leaving her alone with them now would just be irresponsible. Our visitors are here for all the wrong reasons and likely looking for any reason to play cruel mental Olympics with her emotions. I'd be surprised if they didn't want to terrify and confuse her. To bully her into cowardice. And I'm beginning to worry.

There's so much Juliette doesn't know.

I think I've not made enough of an effort to imagine how she must be feeling. I take too much for granted in this military life, and things that seem obvious to me are still brand-new to her. I need to remember that. I need to tell her that she has her own armory. That she has a fleet of private cars; a personal chauffeur. Several private jets and pilots at her disposal. And then I wonder, suddenly, whether she's ever been on a plane.

I stop, suspended in thought.

Of course she hasn't. She has no recollection of a life lived anywhere but in Sector 45. I doubt she's ever gone for a *swim*, much less sailed on a ship in the middle of the ocean. She's never lived anywhere but in books and memories.

There's still so much she has to learn. So much to overcome. And while I sympathize deeply with her struggles, I really do not envy her in this, the enormity of the task ahead. After all, there's a simple reason I never wanted the job of supreme commander myself—

I never wanted the responsibility.

It's a tremendous amount of work with far less freedom than one might expect; worse, it's a position that requires a great deal of people skills. The kind of people skills that include both killing *and* charming a person at a moment's notice. Two things I detest.

I tried to convince Juliette that she was perfectly capable of stepping into my father's shoes, but she doesn't seem at all persuaded. And with Haider and Nazeera now here, I understand why she seems more uncertain than ever. The two of them—well, it was only Haider, really—asked to join Juliette on her morning walk to the water this morning. She and Kenji had been discussing the matter under their breaths, but Haider has sharper hearing than we suspected. So here we are, the five of us walking along the beach in an awkward silence. Haider and Juliette and I have unintentionally formed a group. Nazeera and Kenji follow some paces behind.

No one is speaking.

Still, the beach isn't a terrible place to spend a morning, despite the strange stench arising from the water. It's actually rather peaceful. The sounds of the breaking waves make for a soothing backdrop against the otherwise already-stressful day.

"So," Haider finally says to me, "will you be attending the Continental Symposium this year?"

"Of course," I answer quietly. "I will attend as I always

have." A pause. "Will you be returning home to attend your own event?"

"Unfortunately not. Nazeera and I were hoping to accompany you to the North American arm, but of course—I wasn't sure if Supreme Commander Ferrars"—he glances at Juliette—"would be making an appearance, so—"

She leans in, eyes wide. "I'm sorry, what are we talking about?"

Haider frowns only a little in response, but I can feel the depth of his surprise. "The Continental Symposium," he says. "Surely you've heard of it?"

Juliette looks at me, confused, and then—

"Oh, yes, of course," she says, remembering. "I've gotten a bunch of letters about that. I didn't realize it was such a big deal."

I have to fight the impulse to cringe.

This was another oversight on my part.

Juliette and I have talked about the symposium, of course, but only briefly. It's a biannual congress of all 555 regents from across the continent. Every sector leader gathered in one place.

It's a massive production.

Haider tilts his head, studying her. "Yes, it's a very big deal. Our father," he says, "is busy preparing for the Asia event, so it's been on my mind quite a bit lately. But as the late Supreme Anderson never attended public gatherings, I wondered whether you would be following in his footsteps."

"Oh, no, I'll be there," Juliette says quickly. "I'm not

hiding from the world the way he did. Of course I'll be there."

Haider's eyes widen slightly. He looks from me to her and back again.

"When is it, exactly?" she says, and I feel Haider's curiosity grow suddenly more intense.

"You've not looked at your invitation?" he asks, all innocence. "The event is in two days."

She suddenly turns away, but not before I see that her cheeks are flushed. I can feel her sudden embarrassment and it breaks my heart. I hate Haider for toying with her like this.

"I've been very busy," she says quietly.

"It's my fault," I cut in. "I was supposed to follow up on the matter and I forgot. But we'll be finalizing the program today. Delalieu is already hard at work arranging all the details."

"Wonderful," Haider says to me. "Nazeera and I look forward to joining you. We've never been to a symposium outside of Asia before."

"Of course," I say. "We'll be delighted to have you with us."

Haider looks Juliette up and down then, examining her outfit, her hair, her plain, worn tennis shoes; and though he says nothing, I can feel his disapproval, his skepticism and ultimately—his disappointment in her.

It makes me want to throw him in the ocean.

"What are your plans for the rest of your stay here?" I

ask, watching him closely now.

He shrugs, perfect nonchalance. "Our plans are fluid. We're only interested in spending time with all of you." He glances at me. "Do old friends really need a reason to see each other?" And for a moment, the briefest moment, I sense genuine pain behind his words. A feeling of neglect.

It surprises me.

And then it's gone.

"In any case," Haider is saying, "I believe Supreme Commander Ferrars has already received a number of letters from our other friends. Though it seems their requests to visit were met with silence. I'm afraid they felt a bit left out when I told them Nazeera and I were here."

"What?" Juliette says, glancing at me before looking back at Haider. "What other friends? Do you mean the other supreme commanders? Because I haven't—"

"Oh—no," Haider says. "No, no, not the other commanders. Not yet, anyway. Just us kids. We were hoping for a little reunion. We haven't gotten the whole group together in far too long."

"The whole group," Juliette says softly. Then she frowns. "How many more kids are there?"

Haider's fake exuberance turns suddenly strange. Cold. He looks at me with both anger and confusion when he says, "You've told her nothing about us?"

Now Juliette is staring at me. Her eyes widen perceptibly; I can feel her fear spike. And I'm still trying to figure out how to tell her not to worry when Haider clamps down on my arm, hard, and pulls me forward.

"What are you doing?" he whispers, the words urgent, violent. "You turned your back on all of us—for what? For *this*? For a *child*? *Inta kullish ghabi,*" he says. "So very, very stupid. And I promise you, *habibi*, this won't end well."

There's a warning in his eyes.

I feel it then, when he suddenly lets go—when he unlocks a secret deep within his heart—and something awful settles into the pit of my stomach. A feeling of nausea. Terrible dread.

And I finally understand:

The commanders are sending their children to do the groundwork here because they don't think it's worth their time to come themselves. They want their offspring to infiltrate and examine our base—to use their youth to appeal to the new, young supreme commander of North America, to fake camaraderie—and, ultimately, to send back information. They're not interested in forging alliances.

They're only here to figure out how much work it will take to destroy us.

I turn away, anger threatening to undo my composure, and Haider clamps down harder on my arm. I meet his eyes. It's only my determination to keep things civil for Juliette's sake that prevents me from breaking his fingers off my body.

Hurting Haider would be enough to start a world war.

And he knows this.

"What's happened to you?" he says, still hissing in my ear. "I didn't believe it when I first heard that you'd fallen in love with some idiot psychotic girl. I had more faith in you. I *defended* you. But this," he says, shaking his head, "this is truly heartbreaking. I can't believe how much you've changed."

My fingers tense, itching to form fists, and I'm just about to respond when Juliette, who's been watching us closely from a distance, says, "Let go of him."

And there's something about the steadiness of her voice, something about the barely restrained fury in her words that captures Haider's attention.

He drops my arm, surprised. Spins around.

"Touch him one more time," Juliette says quietly, "and I will rip your heart out of your body."

Haider stares at her. "Excuse me?"

She steps forward. She looks suddenly terrifying. There's a fire in her eyes. A murderous stillness in her movements. "If I ever catch you putting your hands on him again, I will tear open your chest," she says, "and rip out your heart."

Haider's eyebrows fly up his forehead. He blinks. Hesitates. And then: "I didn't realize that was something you could do."

"For you," she says, "I'd do it with pleasure."

Now, Haider smiles. Laughs, out loud. And for the first time since he's arrived, he actually looks sincere. His eyes crinkle with delight. "Would you mind," he says to her, "if I borrowed your Warner for a bit? I promise I won't put my hands on him. I'd just like to speak with him."

She looks at me then, a question in her eyes.

But I can only smile at her. I want to scoop her up and carry her away. Take her somewhere quiet and lose myself in her. I love that the girl who blushes so easily in my arms is the same one who would kill a man for hurting me.

"I won't be long," I say.

And she returns my smile, her face transformed once again. It lasts only a couple of seconds, but somehow time slows down long enough for me to gather the many details of this moment and place it among my favorite memories. I'm grateful, suddenly, for this unusual, supernatural gift I have for sensing emotions. It's still my secret, known only by a few—a secret I'd managed to keep from my father, and from the other commanders and their children. I like how it makes me feel separate—different—from the people I've always known. But best of all, it makes it possible for me to know how deeply Juliette loves me. I can always feel the rush of emotion in her words, in her eyes. The certainty that she would fight for me. Protect me. And knowing this makes my heart feel so full that, sometimes, when we're together, I can hardly breathe.

I wonder if she knows that I would do anything for her.

JULIETTE

"Oh, look! A fish!" I run toward the water and Kenji catches me around the waist, hauls me back.

"That water is *disgusting*, J. You shouldn't get near it."

"What? Why?" I say, still pointing. "Can't you see the fish? I haven't seen a fish in the water in a really long time."

"Yeah, well, it's probably dead."

"What?" I look again, squinting. "No—I don't think—"

"Oh, yeah, it's definitely dead."

We both look up.

It's the first thing Nazeera has said all morning. She's been very quiet, watching and listening to everything with an eerie stillness. Actually, I've noticed she spends most of her time watching her brother. She doesn't seem interested in me the way Haider seems to be, and I find it confusing. I don't understand yet exactly why they're here. I know they're curious about who I am—which, honestly, I get—but there's got to be more to it than just that. And it's this unknowable part—the tension between brother and sister, even—that I can't comprehend.

So I wait for her to say more.

She doesn't.

She's still watching her brother, who's off in the distance

with Warner now, the two of them discussing something we can no longer hear.

It's an interesting scene, the two of them.

Warner is wearing a dark, bloodred suit today. No tie, and no overcoat—even though it's freezing outside—just a black shirt underneath the blazer, and a pair of black boots. He's clutching the handle of a briefcase and a pair of gloves in the same hand, and his cheeks are pink from the cold. Beside him, Haider's hair is a wild, untamed shock of blackness in the gray morning light. He's wearing slim black slacks and yesterday's chain-link shirt underneath a long blue velvet coat, and doesn't seem at all bothered by the wind blowing the jacket open to reveal his heavily built, very bronzed upper body. In fact, I'm pretty sure it's intentional. The two of them walking tall and alone on the deserted beach—heavy boots leaving prints in the sand—makes for a striking image, but they're definitely overdressed for the occasion.

If I were being honest, I'd be forced to admit that Haider is just as beautiful as his sister, despite his aversion to wearing shirts. But Haider seems deeply aware of how handsome he is, which somehow works against him. In any case, none of that matters. I'm only interested in the boy walking beside him. So it's Warner I'm staring at when Kenji says something that pulls me suddenly back to the present.

"I think we better get back to base, J." He checks the time on the watch he's only recently started wearing.

"Castle said he needs to talk to you ASAP."

"Again?"

Kenji nods. "Yeah, and I have to talk to the girls about their progress with James, remember? Castle wants a report. By the way, I think Winston and Alia are finally done fixing your suit, and they actually have a new design for you to look at when you have a chance. I know you still have to get through the rest of your mail from today, but whenever you're done maybe we could—"

"Hey," Nazeera says, waving at us as she walks up. "If you guys are heading back to base, could you do me a favor and grant me clearance to walk around the sector on my own today?" She smiles at me. "I haven't been back here in over a year, and I'd like to look around a little. See what's changed."

"Sure," I say, and smile back. "The soldiers at the front desk can take care of that. Just give them your name, and I'll have Kenji send them my pre-authorizati—"

"Oh—yeah, actually, you know what? Why don't I just show you around myself?" Kenji beams at her. "This place changed a lot in the last year. I'd be happy to be your tour guide."

Nazeera hesitates. "I thought I just heard you say you had a bunch of things to do."

"What? No." He laughs. "Zero things to do. I'm all yours. For whatever. You know."

"Kenji—"

He flicks me in the back and I flinch, scowling at him.

"Um, okay," Nazeera says. "Well, maybe later, if you have time—"

"I've got time now," he says, and he's grinning at her like an idiot. Like, an actual idiot. I don't know how to save him from himself. "Should we get going?" he says. "We can start here—I can show you around the compounds first, if you like. Or, I mean, we can start in unregulated territory, too." He shrugs. "Whatever you prefer. Just let me know."

Nazeera looks suddenly fascinated. She's staring at Kenji like she might chop him up and put him in a stew. "Aren't you a member of the Supreme Guard?" she says. "Shouldn't you stay with your commander until she's safely back to base?"

"Oh, uh, yeah—no, she'll be fine," he says in a rush. "Plus we've got these dudes"—he waves at the six soldiers shadowing us—"watching her all the time, so, she'll be safe."

I pinch him, hard, in the side of his stomach.

Kenji gasps, spins around. "We're only like five minutes from base," he says. "You'll be okay getting back by yourself, won't you?"

I glare at him. "Of course I can get back by myself," I shout-whisper. "That's not why I'm mad. I'm mad because you have a million things to do and you're acting like an idiot in front of a girl who is obviously not interested in you."

Kenji steps back, looking injured. "Why are you trying to hurt me, J? Where's your vote of confidence? Where's the love and support I require at this difficult hour? I need you to be my wingwoman."

"You do know that I can hear you, right?" Nazeera tilts her head to one side, her arms crossed loosely against her chest. "I'm standing right here."

She looks somehow even more stunning today, her hair wrapped up in silks that look like liquid gold in the light. She's wearing an intricately braided red sweater, a pair of black, textured leather leggings, and black boots with steel platforms. And she's still got those heavy gold knuckles on both her fists.

I wish I could ask her where she gets her clothes.

I only realize Kenji and I have both been staring at her for too long when she finally clears her throat. She drops her arms and steps cautiously forward, smiling—not unkindly—at Kenji, who seems suddenly unable to breathe. "Listen," she says softly. "You're cute. Really cute. You've got a great face. But this," she says, gesturing between them, "is not happening."

Kenji doesn't appear to have heard her. "You think I've got a great face?"

She laughs and frowns at the same time. Waves two fingers and says, "Bye."

And that's it. She walks away.

Kenji says nothing. His eyes are fixed on Nazeera's disappearing form in the distance.

I pat his arm, try to sound sympathetic. "It'll be okay," I say. "Rejection is har—"

"That was amazing."

"Uh. What?"

He turns to look at me. "I mean, I've always known I had a great face. But now I know, like, for sure that I've got a great face. And it's just so validating."

"You know, I don't think I like this side of you."

"Don't be like that, J." Kenji taps me on the nose. "Don't be jealous."

"I'm not je—"

"I mean, I deserve to be happy, too, don't I?" And he goes suddenly quiet. His smile slips, his laugh dies away, and Kenji looks, if only for a moment—sad. "Maybe one day."

I feel my heart seize.

"Hey," I say gently. "You deserve to be the happiest."

Kenji runs a hand through his hair and sighs. "Yeah. Well."

"Her loss," I say.

He glances at me. "I guess that was pretty decent, as far as rejections go."

"She just doesn't know you," I say. "You're a total catch."

"I know, right? I keep trying to tell people."

"People are dumb." I shrug. "I think you're wonderful."

"Wonderful, huh?"

"Yep," I say, and link my arm in his. "You're smart and funny and kind and—"

"Handsome," he says. "Don't forget handsome."

"And very handsome," I say, nodding.

"Yeah, I'm flattered, J, but I don't like you like that."

My mouth drops open.

"How many times do I have to ask you to stop falling in love with me?"

"Hey!" I say, shoving away from him. "You're terrible."

"I thought I was wonderful."

"Depends on the hour."

And he laughs, out loud. "All right, kid. You ready to head back?"

I sigh, look off into the distance. "I don't know. I think I need a little more time alone. I've still got a lot on my mind. A lot I need to sort through."

"I get it," he says, shooting me a sympathetic look. "Do your thing."

"Thanks."

"Do you mind if I get going, though? All jokes aside, I really do have a lot to take care of today."

"I'll be fine. You go."

"You sure? You'll be okay out here on your own?"

"Yes, yes," I say, and shove him forward. "I'll be more than okay. I'm never really on my own, anyway." I gesture with my head toward the soldiers. "These guys are always following me."

Kenji nods, gives me a quick squeeze on the arm, and jogs off.

Within seconds, I'm alone. I sigh and turn toward the water, kicking at the sand as I do.

I'm so confused.

I'm caught between different worries, trapped by a fear of what seems my inevitable failure as a leader and my fears of Warner's inscrutable past. And today's conversation with Haider didn't help with the latter. His unmasked shock that Warner hadn't even bothered to mention the other families—and the children—he grew up with, really blew me away. It made me wonder how much more I don't know. How much more there is to unearth.

I know exactly how I feel when I look into his eyes, but sometimes being with Warner gives me whiplash. He's so unused to communicating basic things—to anyone—that every day with him comes with new discoveries. The discoveries aren't all bad—in fact, most of the things I learn about him only make me love him more—but even the harmless revelations are occasionally confusing.

Last week I found him sitting in his office listening to old vinyl records. I'd seen his record collection before—he has a huge stack that was apportioned to him by The Reestablishment along with a selection of old books and artwork—he was supposed to be sorting through it all, deciding what to keep and what to destroy. But I'd never seen him just sit and listen to music.

He didn't notice me when I'd walked in that day.

He was sitting very still, looking only at the wall, and listening to what I later discovered was a Bob Dylan record. I know this because I peeked in his office many hours later, after he'd left. I couldn't shake my curiosity; Warner had only listened to one of the songs on the record—he'd reset the needle every time the song finished—and I wanted to know what it was. It turned out to be a song called "Like a Rolling Stone."

I still haven't told him what I saw that day; I wanted to see if he would share the story with me himself. But he never mentioned it, not even when I asked him what he did that afternoon. It wasn't a lie, exactly, but the omission made me wonder why he'd keep it from me.

There's a part of me that wants to rip his history open. I want to know the good and the bad and just get all the secrets out and be done with it. Because right now I feel certain that my imagination is much more dangerous than any of his truths.

But I'm not sure how to make that happen.

Besides, everything is moving so quickly now. We're all so busy, all the time, and it's hard enough to keep my own thoughts straight. I'm not even sure where our resistance is headed at the moment. Everything is worrying me. Castle's worries are worrying me. Warner's mysteries are worrying me. The children of the supreme commanders are worrying me.

I take in a deep breath and exhale, long and loud.

I'm staring out across the water, trying to clear my mind by focusing on the fluid motions of the ocean. It was just three weeks ago that I'd felt stronger than I ever had in my whole life. I'd finally learned how to make use of my powers; I'd learned how to moderate my strength, how to project—and, most important, how to turn my abilities on and off. And then I'd crushed Anderson's legs in my bare hands. I stood still while soldiers emptied countless rounds of lead into my body. I was invincible.

But now?

This new job is more than I bargained for.

Politics, it turns out, is a science I don't yet understand. Killing things, breaking things—destroying things? That, I understand. Getting angry and going to war, I understand. But patiently playing a confusing game of chess with a bunch of strangers from around the world?

God, I'd so much rather shoot someone.

I'm making my way back to base slowly, my shoes filling with sand as I go. I'm actively dreading whatever it is Castle wants to talk to me about, but I've been gone for too long already. There's too much to do, and there's no way out of this but through. I have to face it. Deal with it, whatever it is. I sigh as I flex and unflex my fists, feeling the power come in and out of my body. It's still a strange thrill for me, to be able to disarm myself at will. It's nice to be able to walk around most days with my powers turned off; it's nice to be able to accidentally touch Kenji's skin without worrying I'll hurt him. I scoop up two handfuls of sand. Powers on: I close my fist and the sand is pulverized to dust. Powers off: the sand leaves a vague, pockmarked impression on my skin.

I drop the sand, dusting off the remaining grains from my palms, and squint into the morning sun. I'm searching for the soldiers who've been following me this whole time, because, suddenly, I can't spot them. Which is strange, because I just saw them a minute ago.

And then I feel it—

Pain

It explodes in my back.

It's a sharp, searing, violent pain and I'm blinded by it in an instant. I spin around in a fury that immediately dulls, my senses dimming even as I attempt to harness them. I pull up my Energy, thrumming suddenly with *electricum,* and wonder at my own stupidity for forgetting to turn my powers back on, especially out in the open like this. I was too distracted. Too frustrated. I can feel the bullet in my shoulder blade incapacitating me now, but I fight through the agony to try and spot my attacker.

Still, I'm too slow.

Another bullet hits my thigh, but this time I feel it leave only a flesh wound, bouncing off before it can make much of a mark. My Energy is weak—and weakening by the minute—I think because of the blood I'm losing—and I'm frustrated, so frustrated by how quickly I've been overtaken.

Stupid stupid stupid—

I trip as I try to hurry on the sand; I'm still an open target here. My assailant could be anyone—could be anywhere—and I'm not even sure where to look when suddenly three more bullets hit me: in my stomach, my wrist, my chest. The bullets break off my body and still manage to draw blood, but the bullet buried, buried in my back, is sending blinding flashes of pain through my veins and I gasp, my mouth frozen open and I can't catch my breath and the torment is so intense I can't help but wonder if this is a special gun, if these are special bullets—

oh

The small, breathless sound leaves my body as my knees hit the sand and I'm now pretty sure, fairly certain these bullets have been laced with poison, which would mean that even these, these flesh wounds would be dangero—

I fall, head spinning, backward onto the sand, too dizzy to see straight. My lips feel numb, my bones loose and my blood, my blood all sloshing together fast and weird and I start laughing, thinking I see a bird in the sky—not just one but many of them all at once flying flying *flying*

Suddenly I can't breathe.

Someone has their arm around my neck; they're dragging me backward and I'm choking, spitting up and losing lungs and I can't feel my tongue and I'm kicking at the sand so hard I've lost my shoes and I think here it is, death again, so soon so soon I was too tired anyway and then

The pressure is gone

So swiftly

I'm gasping and coughing and there's sand in my hair and in my teeth and I'm seeing colors and birds, so many birds, and I'm spinning and—

crack

Something breaks and it sounds like bone. My eyesight sharpens for an instant and I manage to see something in front of me. Someone. I squint, feeling like my mouth might swallow itself and I think it must be the poison but it's not; it's Nazeera, so pretty, so pretty standing in front of me, her hands around a man's limp neck and then she drops him to the ground

Scoops me up

You're so strong and so pretty I mumble, so strong and I want to be like you, I say to her

And she says shhh and tells me to be still, tells me I'll be fine

and carries me away.

WARNER

Panic, terror, guilt—unbounded fears—

I can hardly feel my feet as they hit the ground, my heart beating so hard it physically hurts. I'm bolting toward our half-built medical wing on the fifteenth floor and trying not to drown in the darkness of my own thoughts. I have to fight an instinct to squeeze my eyes shut as I run, taking the emergency stairs two at a time because, of course, the nearest elevator is temporarily closed for repairs.

I've never been such a fool.

What was I thinking? What was I *thinking*? I simply walked away. I keep making mistakes. I keep making assumptions. And I've never been so desperate for Kishimoto's inelegant vocabulary. God, the things I wish I could say. The things I'd like to shout. I've never been so angry with myself. I was so sure she'd be fine, I was so sure she knew to never move out in the open unprotected—

A sudden rush of dread overwhelms me.

I will it away.

I will it away, even as my chest heaves with exhaustion and outrage. It's irrational, to be mad at agony—it's futile, I know, to be angry with this pain—and yet, here I am. I feel powerless. I want to see her. I want to hold her. I want to ask her how she could've possibly let her guard down while walking *alone*, out in the *open*—

Something in my chest feels like it might rip apart as I reach the top floor, my lungs burning from the effort. My heart is pumping furiously. Even so, I tear down the hall. Desperation and terror fuel my need to find her.

I stop abruptly in place when the panic returns.

A wave of fear bends my back and I'm doubled over, hands on my knees, trying to breathe. It's unbidden, this pain. Overwhelming. I feel a startling prick behind my eyes. I blink, hard, fight the rush of emotion.

How did this happen? I want to ask her.

Didn't you realize that someone would try to kill *you?*

I'm nearly shaking when I reach the room they're keeping her in. I almost can't make sense of her limp, blood-smeared body laid out on the metal table. I rush forward half blind and ask Sonya and Sara to do again what they've done once before: help me heal her.

It's only then that I realize the room is full.

I'm ripping off my blazer when I notice the others. Figures are pressed up against the walls—forms of people I probably know and can't be bothered to name. Still, somehow, *she* stands out to me.

Nazeera.

I could close my hands around her throat.

"Get out of here," I choke out in a voice that doesn't sound like my own.

She looks genuinely shocked.

"I don't know how you managed this," I say, "but this is your fault—you, and your brother—you did this to her—"

"If you'd like to meet the man responsible," she says, flat and cold, "you're welcome to. He has no identification, but the tattoos on his arms indicate he might be from a neighboring sector. His dead body is in a holding cell underground."

My heart stops, then starts. "What?"

"Aaron?" It's Juliette, Juliette, my Juliette—

"Don't worry, love," I say quickly, "we're going to fix this, okay? The girls are here and we're going to do this again, just like last time—"

"Nazeera," she says, eyes closed, lips half mumbling.

"Yes?" I freeze. "What about Nazeera?"

"Saved"—her mouth halts midmotion, then swallows—"my life."

I look at Nazeera, then. Study her. She seems just about carved from stone, motionless in the middle of chaos. She's staring at Juliette with a curious look on her face, and I can't read her at all. But I don't need a supernatural ability to tell me that something is off about this girl. Basic human instinct tells me there's something she knows—something she's not telling me—and it makes me distrust her.

So when she finally turns in my direction, her eyes deep and steady and frighteningly serious, I feel a bolt of panic pierce me through the chest.

Juliette is sleeping now.

I'm never more grateful for my inhuman ability to steal

and manifest other people's Energies than I am in these unfortunate moments. We've often hoped that now, in the wake of Juliette learning to turn on and off her lethal touch, that Sonya and Sara would be able to heal her—that they'd be able to place their hands on her body in case of emergency without concern for their own safety. But Castle has since pointed out that there's still a chance that, once Juliette's body has begun to heal, her half-healed trauma could instinctively trigger old defenses, even without Juliette's permission. In that state of emergency, Juliette's skin might, accidentally, become lethal once more. It is a risk—an experiment—we were hoping to never again have to face. But now?

What if I weren't around? What if I didn't have this strange gift?

I can't bring myself to think on it.

So I sit here, head in my hands. I wait quietly outside her door as she sleeps off her injuries. The healing properties are still working their way through her body.

Until then, waves of emotion continue to assault me.

It's immeasurable, this frustration. Frustration with Kenji for having left Juliette all alone. Frustration with the six soldiers who were so easily relieved of their guns and their faculties by this single, unidentified assailant. But most of all, *God,* most of all, I've never been so frustrated with myself.

I've been remiss.

I let this happen. My oversights. My stupid infatuation with my own father—the fallout with my own feelings after his death—the pathetic dramas of my past. I let myself get distracted; I was self-absorbed, consumed by my own concerns and daily dealings.

It's my fault.

It's my fault for misunderstanding.

It's my fault for thinking she was fine, that she didn't require more from me—more encouragement, more motivation, more guidance—on a daily basis. She kept showing these tremendous moments of growth and change, and they disarmed me. I'm only now realizing that these moments are misleading. She needs more time, more opportunities to solidify her new strength. She needs to practice; and she needs to be pushed to practice. To be unyielding, to always and forever fight for herself.

And she's come so far.

She is, today, almost unrecognizable from the trembling young woman I first met. She's strong. She's no longer terrified of everything. But she's still only seventeen years old. And she's only been doing this for a short while.

And I keep forgetting.

I should have advised her when she said she wanted to take over the job of supreme commander. I should've said something then. I should've made sure she understood the breadth of what she'd be getting herself into. I should've warned her that her enemies would inevitably make an attempt on her *life*—

I have to pry my hands away from my face. I've unconsciously pressed my fingers so hard into my skin that I've given myself a brand-new headache.

I sigh and fall back against the chair, extending my legs as my head hits the cold, concrete wall behind me. I feel numb and somehow, still electric. With anger. With impotence. With this impossible need to yell at someone, anyone. My fists clench. I close my eyes. *She has to be okay.* She has to be okay for her sake and for my sake, because I need her, and because I need her to be safe—

A throat clears.

Castle sits down in the seat beside me. I do not look in his direction.

"Mr. Warner," he says.

I do not respond.

"How are you holding up, son?"

An idiotic question.

"This," he says quietly, waving a hand toward her room, "is a much bigger problem than anyone will admit. I think you know that, too."

I stiffen.

He stares at me.

I turn only an inch in his direction. I finally notice the faint lines around his eyes, his forehead. The threads of silver gleaming through the neat dreadlocks tied at his neck. I don't know how old Castle is, but I suspect he's old enough to be my father. "Do you have something to say?"

"She can't lead this resistance," he says, squinting at something in the distance. "She's too young. Too inexperienced. Too angry. You know that, don't you?"

"No."

"It should've been you," Castle says. "I always secretly hoped—from the day you showed up at Omega Point—that it would've been you. That you would join us. And lead us." He shakes his head. "You were born for this. You would've managed it all beautifully."

"I didn't want this job," I say to him, sharp and clipped. "Our nation needed change. It needed a leader with heart and passion and I am not that person. Juliette cares about these people. She cares about their hopes, their fears—and she will fight for them in a way I never would."

Castle sighs. "She can't fight for anyone if she's dead, son."

"Juliette is going to be fine," I say angrily. "She's resting now."

Castle is quiet for a time.

When he finally breaks the silence, he says, "It is my great hope that, very soon, you will stop pretending to misunderstand me. I certainly respect your intelligence too much to reciprocate the pretense." He's staring at the floor. His eyebrows pull together. "You know very well what I'm trying to get at."

"And what is your point?"

He turns to look at me. Brown eyes, brown skin, brown hair. The white flash of his teeth as he speaks. "You say you love her?"

I feel my heart pound suddenly, the sound drumming in my ears. It's so hard for me to admit this sort of thing out loud. To a veritable stranger.

"Do you really love her?" he asks again.

"Yes," I whisper. "I do."

"Then stop her. Stop her before they do. Before this experiment destroys her."

I turn away, my chest heaving.

"You still don't believe me," he says. "Even though you know I'm telling the truth."

"I only know that you *think* you're telling me the truth."

Castle shakes his head. "Her parents are coming for her," he says. "And when they do you'll know for certain that I've not led you astray. But by then," he says, "it'll be too late."

"Your theory doesn't make any sense," I say, frustrated. "I have documents stating that Juliette's biological parents died a long time ago."

He narrows his eyes. "Documents are easily falsified."

"Not in this case," I say. "It isn't possible."

"I assure you that it is."

I'm still shaking my head. "I don't think you understand," I say. "I have all of Juliette's files," I say to him, "and her biological parents' date of death has always been clearly noted. Maybe you confused these people with her *adoptive* parents—"

"The adoptive parents only ever had custody of one child—Juliette—correct?"

"Yes."

"Then how do you explain the second child?"

"What?" I stare at him. "What second child?"

"Emmaline, her older sister. You remember Emmaline, of course."

Now I'm convinced Castle is unhinged. "My God," I say. "You really have lost your mind."

"Nonsense," he says. "You've met Emmaline many times, Mr. Warner. You may not have known who she was at the time, but you've lived in her world. You've interacted with her at length. Haven't you?"

"I'm afraid you're deeply misinformed."

"Try to remember, son."

"Try to remember *what*?"

"You were sixteen. Your mother was dying. There were whispers that your father would soon be promoted from commander and regent of Sector 45 to supreme commander of North America. You knew that, in a couple of years, he was going to move you to the capital. You didn't want to go. You didn't want to leave your mother behind, so you offered to take his place. To take over Sector 45. And you were willing to do anything."

I feel the blood exit my body.

"Your father gave you a job."

"No," I whisper.

"Do you remember what he made you do?"

I look into my open, empty hands. My pulse picks up. My mind spirals.

"Do you remember, son?"

"How much do you know?" I say, but my face feels paralyzed. "About me—about *this*?"

"Not quite as much as you do. But more than most."

I sink into the chair. The room spins around me.

I can only imagine what my father would say if he were alive to see this now. *Pathetic. You're pathetic. You have no one to blame but yourself,* he'd say. *You're always ruining everything, putting your emotions before your duty—*

"How long have you known?" I look at him, anxiety sending waves of unwelcome heat up my back. "Why have you never said anything?"

Castle shifts in his chair. "I'm not sure how much I should say on this matter. I don't know how much I can trust you."

"You can't trust *me*?" I say, losing control. "You're the one who's been holding back—all this time"—I glance up suddenly, realizing—"does Kishimoto know about this?"

"No."

My features rearrange. Surprised.

Castle sighs. "He'll know soon enough. Just as everyone else will."

I shake my head in disbelief. "So you're telling me that—that girl—that was her sister?"

Castle nods.

"That's not possible."

"It is a fact."

"How can any of this be true?" I say, sitting up straighter. "I would *know* if it were true. I would have the classified data, I would have been briefed—"

"You're still only a child, Mr. Warner. You forget that

sometimes. You forget that your father didn't tell you everything."

"Then how do *you* know? How do you know any of this?"

Castle looks me over. "I know you think I'm foolish," he says, "but I'm not as simple as you might hope. I, too, once tried to lead this nation, and I did a great deal of my own research during my time underground. I spent decades building Omega Point. Do you think I did so without also understanding my enemies? I had files three feet deep on every supreme commander, their families, their personal habits, their favorite colors." He narrows his eyes. "Surely you didn't think I was that naive.

"The supreme commanders of the world have a great deal of secrets," Castle says. "And I'm privy to only a few of them. But the information I gathered on the beginnings of The Reestablishment have proven true."

I can only stare at him, uncomprehending.

"It was on the strength of what I'd uncovered that I knew a young woman with a lethal touch was being held in an asylum in Sector 45. Our team had already been planning a rescue mission when you first discovered her existence—as Juliette Ferrars, an alias—and realized how she might be useful to your own research. So we at Omega Point waited. Bided our time. In the interim, I had Kenji enlist. He was gathering information for several months before your father finally approved your request to move her out of the asylum. Kenji infiltrated the base in Sector 45 on my orders; his mission was always to retrieve Juliette.

I've been searching for Emmaline ever since."

"I still don't understand," I whisper.

"Mr. Warner," he says impatiently, "Juliette and her sister have been in the custody of The Reestablishment for twelve years. The two sisters are part of an ongoing experiment for genetic testing and manipulation, the details of which I'm still trying to unravel."

My mind might explode.

"Will you believe me now?" he says. "Have I done enough to prove I know more about your life than you think?"

I try to speak but my throat is dry; the words scrape the inside of my mouth. "My father was a sick, sadistic man," I say. "But he wouldn't have done this. He couldn't have done this to me."

"And yet," Castle says. "He did. He allowed you to bring Juliette on base knowing very well who she was. Your father had a disturbing obsession with torture and experimentation."

I feel disconnected from my mind, my body, even as I force myself to breathe. "Who are her real parents?"

Castle shakes his head. "I don't know yet. Whoever they were, their loyalties to The Reestablishment ran deep. These girls were not stolen from their parents," he says. "They were offered willingly."

My eyes widen. I feel suddenly sick.

Castle's voice changes. He sits forward, his eyes sharp. "Mr. Warner," he says. "I'm not sharing this information with you because I'm trying to hurt you. You must know that this isn't fun for me, either."

I look up.

"I need your help," he says, studying me. "I need to know what you did for those two years. I need to know the details of your assignment to Emmaline. What were you tasked to do? Why was she being held? How were they using her?"

I shake my head. "I don't know."

"You do know," he says. "You must know. *Think*, son. Try to remember—"

"I don't know!" I shout.

Castle sits back, surprised.

"He never told me," I say, breathing hard. "That was the job. To follow orders without questioning them. To do whatever was asked of me by The Reestablishment. To prove my loyalty."

Castle falls back into his seat, crestfallen. He looks shattered. "You were my one remaining hope," he says. "I thought I might finally be able to crack this."

I glance at him, heart pounding. "And I still have no idea what you're talking about."

"There's a reason why no one knows the truth about these sisters, Mr. Warner. There's a reason why Emmaline is kept under such high security. She is critical, somehow, to the structure of The Reestablishment, and I still don't know how or why. I don't know what she's doing for them." He looks me straight in the eye, then, his gaze piercing through me. "Please," he says. "Try to remember. What did he make you do to her? Anything you can remember—anything at all—"

"No," I whisper. I want to scream the word. "I don't want to remember."

"Mr. Warner," he says. "I understand that this is hard for you—"

"Hard for me?" I stand up suddenly. My body is shaking with rage. The walls, the chairs, the tables around us begin to rattle. The light fixtures swing dangerously overhead, the bulbs flickering. "You think this is *hard* for me?"

Castle says nothing.

"What you are telling me right now is that Juliette was planted here, in my life, as part of a larger experiment—an experiment my father had always been privy to. You're telling me that Juliette is not who I think she is. That Juliette Ferrars isn't even her real name. You're telling me that not only is she a girl with a set of living parents, but that I also spent two years unwittingly torturing her sister." My chest heaves as I stare at him. "Is that about right?"

"There's more."

I laugh, out loud. The sound is insane.

"Ms. Ferrars will find out about all this very soon," Castle says to me. "So I would advise you to get ahead of these revelations. Tell her everything as soon as possible. You must confess. Do it now."

"What?" I say, stunned. "Why me?"

"Because if you don't tell her soon," he says, "I assure you, Mr. Warner, that someone else will—"

"I don't care," I say. "You tell her."

"You're not hearing me. It is imperative that she hear this from *you*. She trusts you. She loves you. If she finds out on her own, from a less worthy source, we might lose her."

"I'll never let that happen. I'll never let anyone hurt her again, even if that means I'll have to guard her myself—"

"No, son." Castle cuts me off. "You misunderstand me. I did not mean we would lose her physically." He smiles, but the result is strange. Scared. "I meant we would *lose* her. Up here"—he taps his head—"and here"—he taps his heart.

"What do you mean?"

"Simply that you must not live in denial. Juliette Ferrars is not who you think she is, and she is not to be trifled with. She seems, at times, entirely defenseless. Naive. Even innocent. But you cannot allow yourself to forget the fist of anger that still lives in her heart."

My lips part, surprised.

"You've read about it, haven't you? In her journal," he says. "You've read where her mind has gone—how dark it's been—"

"How did you—"

"And I," he says, "I have seen it. I've seen her lose control of that quietly contained rage with my own eyes. She nearly destroyed all of us at Omega Point long before your father did. She broke the ground in a fit of madness inspired by a simple *misunderstanding*," he says. "Because she was upset about the tests we were running on Mr. Kent. Because she was confused and a little scared. She wouldn't listen to reason—and she nearly killed us all."

"That was different," I say, shaking my head. "That was a long time ago. She's different now." I look away, failing to control my frustration at his thinly veiled accusations. "She's *happy—*"

"How can she be truly happy when she's never dealt with her past? She's never addressed it—merely set it aside. She's never had the time, or the tools, to examine it. And that anger—that kind of rage," Castle says, shaking his head, "does not simply disappear. She is volatile and unpredictable. And heed my words, son: Her anger will make an appearance again."

"No."

He looks at me. Picks me apart with his eyes. "You don't really believe that."

I do not respond.

"Mr. Warner—"

"Not like that," I say. "If it comes back, it won't be like that. Anger, maybe—*yes*—but not rage. Not uncontrolled, uninhibited rage—"

Castle smiles. It's so sudden, so unexpected, I stop mid-sentence.

"Mr. Warner," he says. "What do you think is going to happen when the truth of her past is finally revealed to her? Do you think she will accept it quietly? Calmly? If my sources are correct—and they usually are—the whispers underground affirm that her time here is up. The experiment has come to an end. Juliette murdered a supreme commander. The system won't let her go on like this, her powers unleashed, unchecked. And I have heard that the plan is to obliterate Sector 45." He hesitates. "As for Juliette herself," he says, "it is likely they will either kill her, or place her in another facility."

My mind spins, explodes. "How do you know this?"

Castle laughs briefly. "You can't possibly believe that Omega Point was the only resistance group in North America, Mr. Warner. I'm very well connected underground. And my point still stands." A pause. "Juliette will soon have access to the information necessary to piece together her past. And she will find out, one way or another, your part in all of it."

I look away and back again, eyes wide, my voice fraying. "You don't understand," I whisper. "She would never forgive me."

Castle shakes his head. "If she learns from someone else that you've always known she was adopted? If she hears from someone else that you tortured her sister?" He nods. "Yes, it's true, she will likely never forgive you."

For a sudden, terrible moment, I lose feeling in my knees. I'm forced to sit down, my bones shaking inside me.

"But I didn't know," I say, hating how it sounds, hating that I feel like a child. "I didn't know who that girl was, I didn't know Juliette had a sister— I didn't know—"

"It doesn't matter. Without you, without context, without an explanation or an apology, all of this will be much harder to forgive. But if you tell her yourself and tell her *now*? Your relationship might still stand a chance." He shakes his head. "Either way, you must tell her, Mr. Warner. Because we have to warn her. She needs to know what's coming, and we have to start planning. Your silence on the subject will end only in devastation."

JULIETTE

I am a thief.

I stole this notebook and this pen from one of the doctors, from one of his lab coats when he wasn't looking, and I shoved them both down my pants. This was just before he ordered those men to come and get me. The ones in the strange suits with the thick gloves and the gas masks with the foggy plastic windows hiding their eyes. They were aliens, I remember thinking. I remember thinking they must've been aliens because they couldn't have been human, the ones who handcuffed my hands behind my back, the ones who strapped me to my seat. They stuck Tasers to my skin over and over for no reason other than to hear me scream but I wouldn't. I whimpered but I never said a word. I felt the tears streak down my cheeks but I wasn't crying.

I think it made them angry.

They slapped me awake even though my eyes were open when we arrived. Someone unstrapped me without removing my handcuffs and kicked me in both kneecaps before ordering me to rise. And I tried. I tried but I couldn't and finally six hands shoved me out the door and my face was bleeding on the concrete for a while. I can't really remember the part where they dragged me inside.

I feel cold all the time.

I feel empty, like there is nothing inside of me but this broken heart, the only organ left in this shell. I feel the bleats echo within me, I feel the thumping reverberate around my skeleton. I have a heart, says science, but I am a monster, says society. And I know it, of course I know it. I know what I've done. I'm not asking for sympathy. But sometimes I think—sometimes I wonder—if I were a monster—surely, I would feel it by now?

I would feel angry and vicious and vengeful. I'd know blind rage and bloodlust and a need for vindication.

Instead, I feel an abyss within me that's so deep, so dark I can't see within it; I can't see what it holds. I do not know what I am or what might happen to me.

I do not know what I might do again.

—AN EXCERPT FROM JULIETTE'S JOURNALS IN THE ASYLUM

I'm dreaming about birds again.

I wish they would go away already. I'm tired of thinking about them, hoping for them. Birds, birds, birds—why won't they go away? I shake my head as if to clear it, but feel my mistake at once. My mind is still dense and foggy, swimming in confusion. I blink open my eyes slowly, tentatively, but no matter how far I force them open, I can't seem to take in any light. It takes me too long to understand that I've awoken in the middle of the night.

A sharp gasp.

That's me, my voice, my breath, my quickly beating heart. Where is my head? Why is it so heavy? My eyes close fast, sand stuck in the lashes, sticking them together. I try to clear the haze—try to remember—but parts of me still feel numb, like my teeth and toes and the spaces between my ribs and I laugh, suddenly, and I don't know why—

I was shot.

My eyes fly open, my skin breaking into a sudden, cold sweat.

Oh my God I was shot, I was shot I was shot

I try to sit up and can't. I feel so heavy, so heavy with blood and bone and suddenly I'm freezing, my skin is cold rubber and clammy against the metal table I'm sticking to and all at once

I want to cry

all at once I'm back in the asylum, the cold and the metal and the pain and the delirium all confusing me and then I'm weeping, silently, hot tears warming my cheeks and I can't speak but I'm scared and I hear them, I hear them

the others

screaming

Flesh and bone breaking in the night, hushed, muffled voices—suppressed shouts—cellmates I'd never see—

Who were they? I wonder.

I haven't thought about them in so long. What happened to them. Where they came from. Who did I leave behind?

My eyes are sealed shut, my lips parted in quiet terror. I haven't been haunted like this in so long so long so long

It's the drugs, I think. *There was poison in those bullets.*

Is that why I can see the birds?

I smile. Giggle. Count them. Not just the white ones, white with streaks of gold like crowns atop their heads, but blue ones and black ones and yellow birds, too. I see them when I close my eyes but I saw them today, too, on the beach and they looked so real, so real

Why?

Why would someone try to kill me?

Another sudden jolt to my senses and I'm more alert,

more myself, panic clearing the poison for a single moment of clarity and I'm able to push myself up, onto my elbows, head spinning, eyes wild as they scan the darkness and I'm just about to lie back down, exhausted, when I see something—

"Are you awake?"

I inhale sharply, confused, trying to make sense of the sounds. The words are warped like I'm hearing them underwater and I swim toward them, trying, trying, my chin falling against my chest as I lose the battle.

"Did you see anything today?" the voice says to me. "Anything . . . strange?"

"Who—where, where are you—" I say, reaching blindly into the dark, eyes only half open now. I feel resistance and wrap my fingers around it. A hand? A strange hand. It's a mix of metal and flesh, a fist with a sharp edge of steel.

I don't like it.

I let go.

"Did you see anything today?" it says again.

I mumble.

"What did you see?" it says.

And I laugh, remembering. I could hear them—hear their *caw caws* as they flew far above the water, could hear their little feet walking along the sand. There were so many of them. Wings and feathers, sharp beaks and talons.

So much motion.

"What did you *see*—?" the voice demands again, and it makes me feel strange.

"I'm cold," I say, and lie down again. "Why is it so cold?"

A brief silence. A rustle of movement. I feel a heavy blanket drape over the simple sheet already covering my body.

"You should know," the voice says to me, "that I'm not here to hurt you."

"I know," I say, though I don't understand why I've said it.

"But the people you trust are lying to you," the voice is saying. "And the other supreme commanders only want to kill you."

I smile wide, remembering the birds. "Hello," I say.

Someone sighs.

"I'll see you in the morning. We'll talk another time," the voice says. "When you're feeling better."

I'm so warm now, warm and tired and drowning again in strange dreams and distorted memories. I feel like I'm swimming in quicksand and the harder I pull away, the more quickly I am devoured and all I can think is

here

in the dark, dusty corners of my mind

I feel a strange relief.

I am always welcome here

in my loneliness, in my sadness

in this abyss, there is a rhythm I remember. The steady drop of tears, the temptation to retreat, the shadow of my past

the life I choose to forget has not
will never
ever
forget *me*

WARNER

I've been awake all night.

Infinite boxes lie open before me, their innards splayed across the room. Papers are stacked on desks and tables, spread open on my floor. I'm surrounded by files. Many thousands of pages of paperwork. My father's old reports, his work, the documents that ruled his life—

I have read them all.

Obsessively. Desperately.

And what I've found within these pages does nothing to soothe me, no—

I am distraught.

I sit here, cross-legged on the floor of my office, suffocated on all sides by the sight of a familiar typeset and my father's too-legible scrawl. My right hand is caught behind my head, desperate for a length of hair to yank out of my skull and finding none. This is so much worse than I had feared, and I don't know why I'm so surprised.

This is not the first time my father has kept secrets from me.

It was after Juliette escaped Sector 45, after she ran away with Kent and Kishimoto and my father came here to clean up the mess—that was when I learned, for the first time, that my father had knowledge of their world. Of others with abilities.

He'd kept it from me for so long.

I'd heard rumors, of course—from the soldiers, from the civilians—of various unusual sightings and stories, but I brushed them off as nonsense. A human need to find a magical portal to escape our pain.

But there it was—all true.

After my father's revelation, my thirst for information became suddenly insatiable. I needed to know more—who these people were, where they'd come from, how much we'd known—

And I unearthed truths I wish every day I could unlearn.

There are asylums, just like Juliette's, all over the world. *Unnaturals,* as The Reestablishment calls them, were rounded up in the name of science and discovery. But now, finally, I'm understanding how it all began. Here, in these stacks of papers, are all the horrible answers I sought.

Juliette and her sister were the very first Unnatural finds of The Reestablishment. The discovery of these girls' unusual abilities led to the discoveries of other people like them, all over the world. The Reestablishment went on to collect as many Unnaturals as they could find; they told the civilians they were cleansing them of their old and their ill and imprisoning them in camps for closer medical examination.

But the truth was rather more complicated.

The Reestablishment quickly weeded out the useful Unnaturals from the nonuseful for their own benefit. The ones with the best abilities were absorbed by the system—divvied up around the world by the supreme commanders for their personal use in perpetuating the wrath of The Reestablishment—and the others were disposed of. This led to the eventual rise of The Reestablishment, and, with it, the many asylums that would house the other Unnaturals around the globe. For further studies, they'd said. For testing.

Juliette had not yet manifested abilities when she was donated to The Reestablishment by her parents. No. It was her *sister* who started it all.

Emmaline.

It was Emmaline whose preternatural gifts startled everyone around them; the sister, Emmaline, was the one who unwittingly drew attention to herself and her family. The unnamed parents were frightened by their daughter's frequent and incredible displays of psychokinesis.

They were also fanatics.

There's limited information in my father's files about the mother and father who willingly gave up their children for experimentation. I've scoured every document and was able to glean only a little about their motives, ultimately piecing together from various notes and extraneous details a startling depiction of these characters. It seems these people had an unhealthy obsession with The Reestablishment. Juliette's biological parents were devoted to the cause long before it had even gained momentum as an international movement, and they thought that studying their daughter might help shed light on the current world and its many ailments. If this was happening to Emmaline, they theorized, maybe it was happening to others—and maybe, somehow, this was information that could be used to help better the world. In no time at all The Reestablishment had Emmaline in custody.

Juliette was taken as a precaution.

If the older sibling had proven herself capable of incredible feats, The Reestablishment thought the younger sister might, too. Juliette was only five years old, and she was held under close surveillance.

After a month in a facility, Juliette showed no signs of a special ability. So she was injected with a drug that would destroy critical parts of her memory, and sent to live in Sector 45, under my father's supervision. Emmaline had kept her real name, but the younger sister, unleashed into the real world, would need an alias. They renamed her Juliette, planted false memories in her head, and assigned her adoptive parents who, only too happy to bring home a child into their childless family, followed instructions to never tell the child that she'd been adopted. They also had no idea that they were being watched. All other useless Unnaturals were, generally, killed off, but The Reestablishment chose to monitor Juliette in a more neutral setting. They hoped a home life would inspire a latent ability within her. She was too valuable as a blood relation to the very talented Emmaline to be so quickly disposed of.

It is the next part of Juliette's life that I was most familiar with.

I knew of Juliette's troubles at home, her many moves. I

knew of her family's visits to the hospital. Their calls to the police. Her stays in juvenile detention centers. She lived in the general area that used to be Southern California before she settled in a city that became firmly a part of what is now Sector 45, always within my father's reach. Her upbringing among the ordinary people of the world was heavily documented by police reports, teachers' complaints, and medical files attempting to understand what she was becoming. Eventually, upon finally discovering the extremes of Juliette's lethal touch, the vile people chosen to be her adoptive parents would go on to abuse her—for the rest of her adolescent life with them—and, ultimately, return her to The Reestablishment, which was only too happy to receive her.

It was The Reestablishment—my own father—who put Juliette back in isolation. For more tests. More surveillance.

And this was when our worlds collided.

Tonight, in these files, I was finally able to make sense of something both terrible and alarming:

The supreme commanders of the world have always known Juliette Ferrars.

They've been watching her grow up. She and her sister were handed over by their psychotic parents, whose allegiance to The Reestablishment overruled all else. Exploiting these girls—understanding their powers—was what helped The Reestablishment dominate the world. It was through the exploitation of other innocent Unnaturals that The Reestablishment was able to conquer and manipulate people and places so quickly.

This, I now realize, is why they've been so patient with a seventeen-year-old who's declared herself ruler of an entire continent. This is why they've so quietly abided the truth of her having slaughtered one of their fellow commanders.

And Juliette has no idea.

She has no idea she's being played and preyed upon. She has no idea that she has no real power here. No chance at change. No opportunity to make a difference in the world. She was, and will forever be nothing more than a toy to them—a science experiment to watch carefully, to make certain the concoction doesn't boil over too soon.

But it did.

Juliette failed their tests over a month ago, and my father tried to kill her for it. He tried to kill her because he'd decided that she'd become a distraction. Gone was the opportunity for this *Unnatural* to grow into an adversary.

The monster we've bred has tried to kill my own son. She's since attacked me like a feral animal, shooting me in both my legs. I've never seen such wildness—such blind, inhuman rage. Her mind shifts without warning. She showed no signs of psychosis upon first arrival in the house, but appeared to dissociate from any structure of rational thought while attacking me. Having seen her instability with my own eyes makes me only more certain of what needs to be done. I write this now as a decree from my hospital bed, and as a precaution to my fellow commanders. In the case that I don't recover from these wounds and am unable to follow through with what needs to be done: You, who are reading this now, you must react. Finish what I could not do. The younger sister is a failed experiment. She is, as we feared, disconnected from humanity. Worse, she's become a distraction for Aaron. He's become—in a toxic turn of events—impossibly drawn to her, with no apparent regard for his own safety. I have no idea what she's done to his mind. I only know now that I should never have entertained my own curiosity by allowing him to bring her on base. It's a shame, really, that she is nothing like her elder sister. Instead, Juliette Ferrars has become an incurable cancer we must cut out of our lives for good.

—AN EXCERPT FROM ANDERSON'S DAILY LOG

Juliette threatened the balance of The Reestablishment.

She was an experiment gone wrong. And she'd become a liability. She needed to be expunged from the earth.

My father tried so hard to destroy her.

And I see now that his failure has been of great interest to the other commanders. My father's daily logs were shared; all the supreme commanders shared their logs with one another. It was the only way for the six of them to remain apprised, at all times, of each other's daily goings-on.

So. They knew his story. They've known about my feelings for her.

And they have their orders to kill Juliette.

But they're waiting. And I have to assume there's something more—some other explanation for their hesitation.

Maybe they think they can rehabilitate her. Maybe they're wondering whether Juliette cannot still be of service to them and to their cause, much like her sister has been.

Her sister.

I'm haunted at once by a memory of her.

Brown-haired and bony. Jerking uncontrollably underwater. Long brown waves suspended, like jittery eels, around her face. Electric wires threaded under her skin. Several tubes permanently attached to her neck and torso. She'd been living underwater for so long when I first saw her that she hardly resembled a person. Her flesh was milky and shriveled, her mouth stretched out in a grotesque O, wrapped around a regulator that forced air into her lungs. She's only a year older than Juliette. And she's been held in captivity for twelve years.

Still alive, but only barely.

I had no idea she was Juliette's sister. I had no idea she was anyone at all. When I first met my assignment, she had no name. I was given only instructions, and ordered to follow them. I didn't know who or what I'd been assigned to oversee. I understood only that she was a prisoner—and I knew she was being tortured—but I didn't know then that there was anything supernatural about the girl. I was an idiot. A child.

I slam the back of my head against the wall, once. Hard. My eyes squeeze shut.

Juliette has no idea she ever had a real family—a horrible, insane family—but a family nonetheless. And if Castle is to be believed, The Reestablishment is coming for her. To kill her. To exploit her. So we have to act. I have to warn her, and I have to do it as soon as possible.

But how—how do I tell her any of this? How do I tell her without explaining my part in all of this?

I've always known Juliette was adopted, but I never told her this truth simply because I thought it would make things worse. My understanding was that Juliette's biological parents were long dead. I didn't see how telling her that she had real, dead parents would make her life any better.

But that doesn't change the fact that I knew.

And now I have to confess. Not just this, but the truth about her sister—that she is still alive and being actively tortured by The Reestablishment. That I contributed to that torture.

Or this:

That I am the true monster, completely and utterly unworthy of her love.

I close my eyes, press the back of my hand to my mouth and feel my body break apart within me. I don't know how to extricate myself from the mess made by my own father. A mess in which I was unintentionally complicit. A mess that, upon its unveiling, will destroy the little bit of happiness I've managed to piece together in my life.

Juliette will never, ever forgive me.

I will lose her.

And it will kill me.

JULIETTE

I wonder what they're thinking. My parents. I wonder where they are. I wonder if they're okay now, if they're happy now, ~~if they finally got what they wanted.~~ I wonder if my mother will have another child. I wonder if someone will ever be kind enough to kill me and I wonder if hell is better than here. I wonder what my face looks like now. I wonder if I'll ever breathe fresh air again.

I wonder about so many things.

Sometimes I'll stay awake for days just counting everything I can find. I count the walls, the cracks in the walls, my fingers and toes. I count the springs in the bed, the threads in the blanket, the steps it takes to cross the room and back. I count my teeth and the individual hairs on my head and the number of seconds I can hold my breath.

But sometimes I get so tired that I forget I'm not allowed to wish for things anymore and I find myself wishing for the one thing I've always wanted. The only thing I've always dreamt about.

I wish all the time for a friend.

I dream about it. I imagine what it would be like. To smile and be smiled upon. To have a person to confide in, someone who wouldn't throw things at me or stick my hands in the fire or beat me for being born. Someone who would hear that I'd been thrown away and would try to find me, who would never be afraid of me.

Someone who'd know I'd never try to hurt them.

I fold myself into a corner of this room and bury my head in my knees and rock back and forth and back and forth and back and forth and I wish and I wish and I wish and I dream of impossible things until I've cried myself to sleep.

I wonder what it would be like to have a friend.

And then I wonder who else is locked in this asylum. I wonder where the other screams are coming from.

I wonder if they're coming from me.

—AN EXCERPT FROM JULIETTE'S JOURNALS IN THE ASYLUM

I feel strange this morning.

I feel slow, like I'm wading through mud, like my bones have filled with lead and my head, *oh*—

I flinch.

My head has never been heavier.

I wonder if it's the last dregs of the poison still haunting my veins, but something feels wrong with me today. My memories of my time in the asylum are suddenly too present—perched too fully at the forefront of my mind. I thought I'd managed to shove those memories out of my head but no, here they are again, dredged out of the darkness. 264 days in perfect isolation. Nearly a year without access or outlet to the outside. To another human being.

So long, so long, so very, very long without the warmth of human contact.

I shiver involuntarily. Jerk upward.

What's wrong with me?

Sonya and Sara must've heard me moving because they're now standing before me, their voices clear but somehow, vibrating. Echoing off the walls. My ears won't stop ringing. I squint to make sense of their faces but I feel dizzy suddenly, disoriented, like my body is sideways or maybe flat on the ground or maybe *I* need to be flat on the ground, or *oh*

oh I think I might be sick—

"Thank you for the bucket," I say, still nauseous. I try to sit up and for some reason I can't remember how. My skin has broken out in a cold sweat. "What's wrong with me?" I say. "I thought you healed—healed—"

I'm gone again.

Head spinning.

Eyes closed against the light. The floor-to-ceiling windows we've installed can't seem to block the sun from invading the room and I can't help but wonder when I've ever seen the sun shine so brightly. Over the last decade our world collapsed inward, the atmosphere unpredictable, the weather changing in sharp and dramatic spikes. It snows where it shouldn't; rains where it once couldn't; the clouds are always gray; the birds gone forever from the sky. The once-bright green leaves of trees and lawns are now dull and brittle with decay. It's March now, and even as we approach spring the sky shows no sign of change. The earth is still cold, still iced over, still dark and muddy.

Or at least, it was yesterday.

Someone places a cool rag on my forehead and the cold is welcome; my skin feels inflamed even as I shiver. Slowly, my muscles unclench. But I wish someone would do something about the glaring sunlight. I'm squinting, even with my eyes closed, and it's making my headache worse.

"The wound is fully healed," I hear someone saying, "but it looks like the poison hasn't worked its way out of her system—"

"I don't understand," says another voice. "How is that possible? Why aren't you able to heal her completely?"

"Sonya," I manage to say. "Sara?"

"Yes?" The twin sisters answer at the same time, and I can feel the rush of their footsteps, hard like drumbeats against my head, as they hurry to my bedside.

I try to gesture toward the windows. "Can we do something about the sun?" I say. "It's too bright."

They help me up into a seated position and I feel my head-spin begin to steady. I blink my eyes open with a great deal of effort just in time to have someone hand me a cup of water.

"Drink this," Sonya says. "Your body is severely dehydrated."

I gulp the water down quickly, surprised by my own thirst. They hand me another glass. I drink that, too. I have to drink five glasses of water before I can hold my head up without immense difficulty.

When I finally feel more normal, I look around. Eyes wide-open. I have a massive headache, but the other symptoms are beginning to fade.

I see Warner first.

He's standing in a corner of the room, eyes bloodshot, yesterday's clothes rumpled on his body, and he's staring at me with a look of unmasked fear that surprises me. It's entirely unlike him. Warner rarely shows emotion in public.

I wish I could say something, but it doesn't feel like the right time. Sonya and Sara are still watching me carefully, their hazel eyes bright against their brown skin. But something about them looks different to me. Maybe it's that I've never looked at them this closely anywhere but underground, but the brilliant light of the sun has reduced their pupils to the size of pinpricks, and it makes their eyes look different. Bigger. *New.*

"The light is so strange today," I can't help saying. "Has it ever been this bright?"

Sonya and Sara glance out the window, glance back at me, and frown at each other. "How are you feeling?" they say. "Does your head still hurt? Do you feel dizzy?"

"My head is killing me," I say, and try to laugh. "What was in those bullets?" I pinch the bridge of my nose between my thumb and index finger. "Do you know if the headache will go away soon?"

"Honestly—we're not sure what's happening right now." This, from Sara.

"Your wound is mended," says Sonya, "but it seems the poison is still affecting your mind. We can't know for sure if it was able to cause permanent damage before we got to you."

At this, I look up. Feel my spine stiffen. "Permanent damage?" I say. "To my brain? Is that really possible?"

They nod. "We'll monitor you closely for the next couple of weeks just to be sure. The illusions you're experiencing might end up being nothing."

"What?" I look around. Look at Warner, who still won't speak. "What illusions? I just have a headache." I squint again, turning away from the window. "Yikes. Sorry," I say, eyes narrowed against the light, "it's been so long since we've had days like this"—I laugh—"I think I'm more accustomed to the dark." I place my hand over my eyes like a visor. "We really need to get some shades on these windows. Someone remind me to tell Kenji about that."

Warner has gone gray. He looks frozen in his skin.

Sonya and Sara share a look of concern.

"What is it?" I say, my stomach sinking as I look at the three of them. "What's wrong? What are you not telling me?"

"There's no sun today," Sonya says quietly. "It's snowing again."

"It's dark and cloudy, just like every other day," says Sara.

"What? What are you talking about?" I say, laughing and frowning at the same time. I can *feel* the heat of the sun on my face. I see it make a direct impact in their eyes, their pupils dilating as they move into the shadows. "You're joking, right? The sun is so bright I can barely look out the window."

Sonya and Sara shake their heads.

Warner is staring at the wall, both hands locked behind his neck.

I feel my heart begin to race. "So I'm seeing things?" I say to them. "I'm hallucinating?"

They nod.

"Why?" I say, trying not to panic. "What's happening to me?"

"We don't know," Sonya says, looking into her hands. "But we're hoping these effects are just temporary."

I try to slow my breathing. Try to remain calm. "Okay. Well. I need to go. Can I go? I have a thousand things to do—"

"Maybe you should stay here a little while longer," says Sara. "Let us watch you for a few more hours."

But I'm shaking my head. "I need to get some air—I need to go outside—"

"No—"

It's the first thing Warner's said since I woke up, and he nearly shouts the word at me. He's holding up his hands in a silent plea.

"No, love," he says, sounding strange. "You can't go outside again. Not—not just yet. Please."

The look on his face is enough to break my heart.

I slow down, feel my racing pulse steady as I stare at him. "I'm so sorry," I say. "I'm sorry I scared everyone. It was a moment of stupidity and it was totally my fault. I let my guard down for just a *second.*" I sigh. "I think someone had been watching me, waiting for the right moment. Either way, it won't happen again."

I try to smile, and he doesn't budge. Won't smile back.

"Really," I try again. "Don't worry. I should've realized there would be people out there waiting to kill me the moment I seemed vulnerable, but"—I laugh—"believe me, I'll be more careful next time. I'll even ask to have a larger guard follow me around."

He shakes his head.

I study him, his terror. I don't understand it.

I make an effort to get to my feet. I'm in socks and a hospital gown, and Sonya and Sara hurry me into a robe and slippers. I thank them for everything they've done and they squeeze my hands.

"We'll be right outside if you need anything," they say in unison.

"Thank you again," I say, and smile. "I'll let you know how it goes with the, um"—I point to my head—"weird visions."

They nod and disappear.

I take a tentative step toward Warner.

"Hey," I say gently. "I'm going to be okay. Really."

"You could've been killed."

"I know," I say. "I've been so off lately—I wasn't thinking. But this was a mistake I will never make again." A short laugh. "Really."

Finally, he sighs. He releases the tension in his shoulders. Runs a hand along the length of his face, the back of his neck.

I've never seen him like this before.

"I'm so sorry I scared you," I say.

"Please don't apologize to me, love. You don't have to worry about me," he says, shaking his head. "I've been worried about *you*. How are you feeling?"

"Other than the hallucinating, you mean?" I crack a half grin. "I feel okay. It took me a minute to come back to myself this morning, but I feel much better now. I'm sure the strange visions will be gone soon, too." I smile, wide, more for his benefit than mine. "Anyway, Delalieu wants me to meet with him ASAP to talk about my speech for the symposium, so I'm thinking maybe I should go do that. I can't believe it's happening *tomorrow*." I shake my head. "I can't afford to waste any more time. Although"—I look down at myself—"maybe I should take a shower first? Put on some real clothes?"

I try to smile at him again, to convince him that I'm feeling fine, but he seems unable to speak. He just looks at me, his eyes red-rimmed and raw. If I didn't know him any better I'd think he'd been crying.

I'm just about to ask him what's wrong, when he says

"Sweetheart."

and for some reason I hold my breath.

"I have to talk to you," he says.

He whispers it, actually.

"Okay," I say, and exhale. "Talk to me."

"Not here."

I feel my stomach flip. My instincts tell me to panic. "Is everything okay?"

It takes him a long time to say, "I don't know."

I stare at him, confused.

He stares back, his eyes such a pale green in the light

that, for a moment, he doesn't even seem human. He says nothing more.

I take a deep breath. Try to be calm. "Okay," I say. "Okay. But if we're going to go back to the room, can I at least shower first? I'd really like to get all this sand and dried blood off my body."

He nods. Still no emotion.

And now I'm really beginning to panic.

WARNER

I'm pacing the length of the hall just outside of our room, impatiently waiting for Juliette to finish her shower. My mind is ravaged. Hysteria has been clawing at my insides for hours. I have no idea what she'll say to me. How she'll react to what I need to tell her. And I'm so horrified by what I'm about to do that I don't even hear someone calling my name until they've touched me.

I spin around too fast, my reflexes faster than even my mind. I've got his hand pinched up at the wrist and wound behind his back and I've slammed him chest-first into the wall before I realize it's Kent. Kent, who's not fighting back, just laughing and telling me to let go of him.

I do.

I drop his arm. Stunned. Shake my head to clear it. I don't remember to apologize.

"Are you okay?" someone else says to me.

It's James. He's still the size of a child, and for some reason this surprises me. I take a careful breath. My hands are shaking. I've never felt further from *okay,* and I'm too confused by my anxiety to remember to lie.

"No," I say to him. I step backward, hitting the wall behind me and slumping to the floor. "No," I say again, and this time I don't know who I'm speaking to.

"Oh. Do you want to talk about it?" James is still blathering. I don't understand why Kent won't make him stop.

I shake my head.

But this only seems to encourage him. He sits down beside me. "Why not? I think you should talk about it," he says.

"C'mon, buddy," Kent finally says to him. "Maybe we should give Warner some privacy."

James will not be convinced. He peers into my face. "Were you *crying*?"

"Why do you ask so many questions?" I snap, dropping my head in one hand.

"What happened to your hair?"

I look up at Kent, astounded. "Will you please retrieve him?"

"You shouldn't answer questions with other questions," James says to me, and puts a hand on my shoulder. I nearly jump out of my skin.

"Why are you touching me?"

"You look like you could use a hug," he says. "Do you want a hug? Hugs always make me feel better when I'm sad."

"No," I say, fast and sharp. "I do not want a *hug*. And I'm not sad."

Kent appears to be laughing. He stands a few feet away from us with his arms crossed, doing nothing to help the situation. I glare at him.

"Well you *seem* sad," James says.

"Right now," I say stiffly, "all I'm feeling is irritation."

"Bet you feel better though, huh?" James smiles. Pats my arm. "See—I told you it helps to talk about it."

I blink, surprised. Stare at him.

He's not exactly correct in his theory, but oddly enough, I do feel better. Getting frustrated just now, with him—it helped clear my panic and focus my thoughts. My hands have steadied. I feel a little sharper.

"Well," I say. "Thank you for being annoying."

"*Hey.*" He frowns. He gets to his feet, dusts off his pants. "I'm not annoying."

"You most certainly are annoying," I tell him. "Especially for a child your size. Why haven't you have learned to be quieter by now? When I was your age I only spoke when I was spoken to."

James crosses his arms. "Wait a second—what do you mean, *for a child my size*? What's wrong with my size?"

I squint at him. "How old are you? Nine?"

"I'm about to turn eleven!"

"You're very small for eleven."

And then he punches me. Hard. In the thigh.

"*Owwwwwww,*" he cries, overzealous in his exaggeration of the simple sound. He shakes out his fingers. Scowls at me. "Why does your leg feel like *stone*?"

"Next time," I say, "you should try picking on someone your own size."

He narrows his eyes at me.

"Don't worry," I say to him. "I'm sure you'll get taller

soon. I didn't hit my growth spurt until I was about twelve or thirteen, and if you're anything like me—"

Kent clears his throat, hard, and I catch myself.

"That is—if you're anything like, ah, your brother, I'm sure you'll be just fine."

James looks back at Kent and smiles, the awkward punch apparently forgotten. "I really hope I'm like my brother," James says, beaming now. "Adam is the best, isn't he? I hope I'm just like him."

I feel the smile break off my face. This little boy. He's also mine, *my brother,* and he may never know it.

"Isn't he?" James says, still smiling.

I startle. "Excuse me?"

"Adam," he says. "Isn't Adam the best? He's the best big brother in the world."

"Oh—yes," I say to him, clearing the catch in my throat. "Yes, of course. Adam is, ah, the best. Or some approximation thereof. In any case, you're very lucky to have him."

Kent shoots me a look, but says nothing.

"I know," James says, undeterred. "I got really lucky."

I nod. Feel something twist in my gut. I get to my feet. "Yes, well, if you'll excuse me—"

"Yep. Got it." Kent nods. Waves good-bye. "We'll see you around, yeah?"

"Certainly."

"Bye!" James says as Kent tugs him down the hall. "Glad you're feeling better!"

Somehow I feel worse.

I walk back into the bedroom not quite as panicked as before, but more somber, somehow. And I'm so distracted I almost don't notice Juliette stepping out of the bathroom as I enter.

She's wearing nothing but a towel.

Her cheeks are pink from the shower. Her eyes are big and bright as she smiles as me. She's so beautiful. So unbelievably beautiful.

"I just have to grab some fresh clothes," she says, still smiling. "Do you mind?"

I shake my head. I can only stare at her.

Somehow, my reaction is insufficient. She hesitates. Frowns as she looks at me. And then, finally, moves toward me.

I feel my lungs malfunction.

"Hey," she says.

But all I can think about is what I have to say to her and how she might react. There's a small, desperate hope in my heart that's still trying to be optimistic about the outcome.

Maybe she'll understand.

"Aaron?" She steps closer, closing the gap between us. "You said you wanted to talk to me, right?"

"Yes," I say, whispering the word. "Yes." I feel dazed.

"Can it wait?" she says. "Just long enough for me to change?"

I don't know what comes over me.

Desperation. Desire. Fear.

Love.

It hits me with a painful force, the reminder. Of just how much I love her. God, I love all of her. Her impossibilities, her exasperations. I love how gentle she is with me when we're alone. How soft and kind she can be in our quiet moments. How she never hesitates to defend me.

I love her.

And she's standing in front of me now, a question in her eyes, and I can't think of anything but how much I want her in my life, forever.

Still, I say nothing. I do nothing.

And she won't walk away.

I realize, with a start, that she's still waiting for an answer.

"Yes, of course," I say quickly. "Of course it can wait."

But she's trying to read my face. "What's wrong?" she says.

I shake my head as I take her hand. Gently, so gently. She steps closer, and my hands close lightly over her bare shoulders. It's a small, simple movement, but I feel it when her emotions change. She trembles suddenly as I touch her, my hands traveling down her arms, and her reaction trips my senses. It kills me, every time, it leaves me breathless every time she reacts to me, to my touch. To know that she feels something for me. That she wants me.

Maybe she'll understand, I think. We've been through so much together. We've overcome so much. Maybe this, too, will be surmountable.

Maybe she'll understand.

"Aaron?"

Blood rushes through my veins, hot and fast. Her skin is soft and smells of lavender and I pull back, just an inch. Just to look at her. I graze her bottom lip with my thumb before my hand slips behind her neck.

"Hi," I say.

And she meets me here, in this moment, in an instant.

She kisses me without restraint, without hesitation, and wraps her arms around my neck and I'm overwhelmed, lost in a rush of emotion—

And the towel falls off her body.

Onto to the floor.

I step back, surprised, taking in the sight of her. My heart is pounding furiously in my chest. I can hardly remember what I was trying to do.

Then she steps forward, stands on tiptoe and reels me in, all warmth and heat and sweetness and I pull her against me, drugged by the feel of her, lost in the smooth expanse of her bare skin. I'm still fully clothed. She's naked in my arms. And somehow that difference between us only makes this moment more surreal. She's pushing me back gently, even as she continues to kiss me, even as she searches my body through this fabric and I fall backward onto the bed, gasping.

She climbs on top of me.

And I think I've lost my goddamned mind.

JULIETTE

This, I think, is the way to die.

I could drown in this moment and I'd never regret it. I could catch fire from this kiss and happily turn to ash. I could live here, die here, right *here,* against his hips, his lips. In the emotion in his eyes as he sinks into me, his heartbeats indistinguishable from mine.

This. Forever. This.

He kisses me again, his occasional gasps for air hot against my skin, and I taste him, his mouth, his neck, the hard line of his jaw and he fights back a groan, pulls away, pain and pleasure twining together as he moves deeper, harder, his muscles taught, his body rock solid against mine. He has one hand around the back of my neck, the other around the back of my thigh and he wraps us together, impossibly closer, overwhelming me with an extraordinary pleasure that feels like nothing I've ever known. It's nameless. Unknowable, impossible to plan for. It's different every time.

And there's something wild and beautiful in him today, something I can't explain in the way he touches me—the way his fingers linger along my shoulder blades, down the curve of my back—like I might evaporate at any moment, like this might be the first and last time we'll ever touch.

I close my eyes.

Let go.

The lines of our bodies have merged. It's wave after wave of ice and heat, melting and catching fire and it's his mouth on my skin, his strong arms wrapping me up in love and warmth. I'm suspended in midair, underwater, in outer space, all at the same time and clocks are frozen, inhibitions are out the window and I've never felt so safe, so loved or so protected than I have here, in the private fusion of our bodies.

I lose track of time.

I lose track of my mind.

I only know I want this to last forever.

He's saying something to me, running his hands down my body, and his words are soft and desperate, silky against my ear, but I can hardly hear him over the sound of my own heart beating against my chest. But I see it, when the muscles in his arms strain against his skin, as he fights to stay here, with me—

He gasps, out loud, squeezing his eyes shut as he reaches out, grabs a fistful of the bedsheets and I turn my face into his chest, trail my nose up the line of his neck and breathe him in and I'm pressed against him, every inch of my skin hot and raw with want and need and

"I love you," I whisper

even as I feel my mind detach from my body

even as stars explode behind my eyes and heat floods my

veins and I'm overcome, I'm stunned and overcome every time, every time

It's a torrent of feeling, a simultaneous, ephemeral taste of death and bliss and my eyes close, white-hot heat flashes behind my eyelids and I have to fight the need to call out his name even as I feel us shatter together, destroyed and restored all at once and he gasps

He says, *"Juliette—"*

I love the sight of his naked body.

Especially in these quiet, vulnerable moments. These brackets of time stapled between dreams and reality are my favorite. There's a sweetness in this hesitant consciousness—a careful, gentle return of form to function. I've found I love these minutes most for the delicate way in which they unfold. It's tender.

Slow motion.

Time tying its shoes.

And Warner is so still, so soft. So unguarded. His face is smooth, his brow unfurrowed, his lips wondering whether to part. And the first seconds after he opens his eyes are the sweetest. Some days I'm lucky enough to look up before he does. Today I watch him stir. I watch him blink open his eyes and orient himself. But then, in the time it takes him to find me—the way his face lights up when he sees me staring—that part makes something inside of me sing. I know everything, everything that ever matters, just by the way he looks at me in that moment.

And today, something is different.

Today, when he opens his eyes he looks suddenly disoriented. He blinks and looks around, sitting up too fast like he might want to run and doesn't remember how. Today, something is wrong.

And when I climb into his lap he stills.

And when I take his chin in my hands he turns away.

When I kiss him, softly, he closes his eyes and something inside him thaws, something unclenches in his bones, and when he opens his eyes again he looks terrified and I feel suddenly sick to my stomach.

Something is terribly, terribly wrong.

"What is it?" I say, my words scarcely making a sound. "What happened? What's wrong?"

He shakes his head.

"Is it me?" My heart is pounding. "Did I do something?"

His eyes go wide. "No, no, Juliette—you're perfect. You're—God, you're perfect," he says. He grips the back of his head, looks at the ceiling.

"Then why won't you look at me?"

So he meets my eyes. And I can't help but marvel at how much I love his face, even now, even in his fear. He's so classically handsome. So remarkably beautiful, even like this: his hair shorn, short and soft; his face unshaven, a silver-blond shadow contouring the already hard lines of his face. His eyes are an impossible shade of green. Bright. Blinking. And then—

Closed.

"I have to tell you something," he says quietly. He's looking down. He lifts a hand to touch me and his fingers trail down the side of my torso. Delicate. Terrified. "Something I should've told you earlier."

"What do you mean?" I fall back. I ball up a section of the bedsheet and hold it tightly against my body, feeling suddenly vulnerable.

He hesitates for too long. Exhales. He drags his hand across his mouth, his chin, down the back of his neck—

"I have no idea where to start."

Every instinct in my body is telling me to run. To shove cotton in my ears. To tell him to stop talking. But I can't. I'm frozen.

And I'm scared.

"Start at the beginning," I say, surprised I can even bring myself to speak. I've never seen him like this before. I can't imagine what he has to say. He's now clasping his hands together so tightly I worry he might break his own fingers by accident.

And then, finally. Slowly.

He speaks.

"The Reestablishment," he says, "went public with their campaigns when you were seven years old. I was nine. But they'd been meeting and planning for many years before that."

"Okay."

"The founders of the The Reestablishment," he says, "were once military men and women turned defense contractors. And they were responsible, in part, for the rise of the military industrial complex that built the foundation of the *de facto* military states composing what is now The Reestablishment. They'd had their plans in place for a long time before this regime went live," he says. "Their jobs had made it possible for them to have had access to weapons and technology no one had even heard of. They had extensive surveillance, fully equipped facilities, acres of private property, unlimited access to information—all for years before you were even born."

My heart is pounding in my chest.

"They'd discovered *Unnaturals*—a term The Reestablishment uses to describe those with supernatural abilities—a few years later. You were about five years old," he says, "when they made their first discovery." He looks at the wall. "That's when they started collecting, testing, and using people with abilities to expedite their goals in dominating the world."

"This is all really interesting," I say, "but I'm kind of freaking out right now and I need you to skip ahead to the part where you tell me what any of this has to do with me."

"Sweetheart," he says, finally meeting my eyes. "All of this has to do with you."

"How?"

"There was one thing I knew about your life that I never told you," he says. He swallows. He's looking into his hands when he says, "You were adopted."

The revelation is like a thunderclap.

I stumble off the bed, clutch the sheet to my body and

stand there, staring at him, stunned. I try to stay calm even as my mind catches fire.

"I was adopted."

He nods.

"So you're saying that the people who raised me—*tortured me*—are not my real parents?"

He shakes his head.

"Are my biological parents still alive?"

"Yes," he whispers.

"And you never told me this?"

No, he says quickly

No, no I didn't know they were still alive, he says

I didn't know anything except that you were adopted, he says, *I just found out, just yesterday, that your parents are still alive, because Castle,* he says, *Castle told me—*

And every subsequent revelation is like a shock wave, a sudden, unforeseen detonation that implodes within me—

BOOM

Your life has been an experiment, he says

BOOM

You have a sister, he says, *she's still alive*

BOOM

Your biological parents gave you and your sister to The Reestablishment for scientific research

and it's like the world has been knocked off its axis, like I've been flung from the earth and I'm headed directly for the sun,

like I'm being burned alive and somehow, I can still

hear him, even as my skin melts inward, as my mind turns inside-out and everything I've ever known, everything I ever thought to be true about who I am and where I come from

v a n i s h e s

I inch away from him, confused and horrified and unable to form words, unable to speak

And he says he *didn't know,* and his voice breaks when he says it, when he says he didn't know until recently that my biological parents were still alive, didn't know until Castle told him, never knew how to tell me that I'd been adopted, didn't know how I would take it, didn't know if I needed that pain, but Castle told him that The Reestablishment is coming for me, that they're coming to take me back

and your sister, he says

but I'm crying now, unable to see him through the tears and still I cannot speak and

your sister, he says, her name is Emmaline, she's one year older than you, she's very, very powerful, she's been the property of The Reestablishment *for twelve years*

I can't stop shaking my head

"Stop," I say

"No," I say

Please don't do this to me—

But he won't stop. He says I have to know. He says I have to know this now—that I have to know the truth—

STOP TELLING ME THIS, I scream

I didn't know she was your sister, he's saying,

I didn't know you had a sister

I swear I didn't know

"There were nearly twenty men and women who put together the beginnings of The Reestablishment," he says, "but there were only six supreme commanders. When the man originally chosen for North America became terminally ill, my father was being considered to replace him. I was sixteen. We lived here, in Sector 45. My father was then CCR. And becoming supreme commander meant he would be moving away, and he wanted to take me with him. My mother," he says, "was to be left behind."

Please don't say any more

Please don't say anything else, I beg him

"It was the only way I could convince him to give me his job," he says, desperate now. "To allow me to stay behind, to watch her closely. He was sworn in as supreme commander when I was eighteen. And he made me spend the two years in between—

"Aaron, please," I say, feeling hysterical, "I don't want to know—I didn't ask you to tell me— I don't want to know—"

"I perpetuated your sister's torture," he says, his voice raw, broken, "her confinement. I was ordered to oversee her continued imprisonment. I gave the orders that kept her there. Every day. I was never told why she was there or what was wrong with her. I was told to maintain her. That was it. She was allowed only four twenty-minute breaks from the water tank every twenty-four hours and she used to scream—she'd beg me to release her," he says, his voice catching. "She begged for mercy and I never gave it to her."

And I stop

Head spinning

I drop the sheet from my body as I run, run away

I'm shoving clothes on as fast as I can and when I return to the room, half wild, caught in a nightmare, I catch him half dressed, too, no shirt, just pants, and he doesn't even speak as I stare at him, stunned, one hand covering my mouth as I shake my head, tears spilling fast down my face and I don't know what to say, I don't know that I can ever say anything to him, ever again—

"It's too much," I say, choking on the words. "It's too much—it's too much—"

"Juliette—"

And I shake my head, hands trembling as I reach for the door and

"Please," he says, and tears are falling silently down his face, and he's visibly shaking as he says, "You have to believe me. I was young. And stupid. I was desperate. I thought I had nothing to live for then—nothing mattered to me but saving my mother and I was willing to do anything that would keep me here, close to her—"

"You lied to me!" I explode, anger squeezing my eyes shut as I back away from him. "You lied to me all this time, you've *lied* to me—about everything—"

"No," he says, all terror and desperation. "The only thing I've kept from you was the truth about your parents, I swear to you—"

"How could you keep that from me? All this time, all

this—*everything*—all you did was *lie to me*—"

He's shaking his head when he says *No, no, I love you, my love for you has never been a lie*—

"Then why didn't you tell me this sooner? Why would you keep this from me?"

"I thought your parents had died a long time ago—I didn't think it would help you to know about them. I thought it would only hurt you more to know you'd lost them. And I didn't know," he says, shaking his head, "I didn't know anything about your real parents or your sister, please believe me—I swear I didn't know, not until yesterday—"

His chest is heaving so hard that his body bows, his hands planted on his knees as he tries to breathe and he's not looking at me when he says, whispers, "I'm so sorry. I'm so, so sorry."

"Stop it—stop talking—"

"Please—"

"How—h-how can I ever—ever trust you again?" My eyes are wide and terrified and searching him for an answer that will save us both but he doesn't answer. He can't. He leaves me with nothing to hold on to. "How can we ever go back?" I say. "How can you expect me to forget all of this? That you lied to me about my parents? That you tortured my sister? There's so much about you I don't know," I say, my voice small and broken, "so much—and I can't—I can't do this—"

And he looks up, frozen in place, staring at me like he's finally understanding that I won't pretend this never happened, that I can't continue to be with someone I can't trust and I can see it, can see the hope go out of his eyes, his hand caught behind his head. His jaw is slack; his face is stunned, suddenly pale and he takes a step toward me, lost, desperate, pleading with his eyes

but I have to go.

I'm running down the hall and I don't know where I'm going until I get there.

WARNER

So this—

This is agony.

This is what they talk about when they talk about heartbreak. I thought I knew what it was like before. I thought I knew, with perfect clarity, what it felt like to have my heart broken, but now—now I finally understand.

Before? When Juliette couldn't decide between myself and Kent? That pain? That was child's play.

But this.

This is suffering. This is full, unadulterated torture. And I have no one to blame for this pain but myself, which makes it impossible to direct my anger anywhere but inward. If I weren't better informed, I'd think I were having an actual heart attack. It feels as though a truck has run over me, broken every bone in my chest, and now it's stuck here, the weight of it crushing my lungs. I can't breathe. I can't even see straight.

My heart is pounding in my ears. Blood is rushing to my head too quickly and it's making me hot and dizzy. I'm strangled into speechlessness, numb in my bones. I feel nothing but an immense, impossible pressure breaking apart my body. I fall backward, hard. My head is against the wall. I try to calm myself, calm my breathing. I try to be rational.

This is not a heart attack, I tell myself. *Not a heart attack.*

I know better.

I'm having a panic attack.

This has happened to me just once before, and then the pain had materialized as if out of a nightmare, out of nowhere, with no warning. I'd woken up in the middle of the night seized by a violent terror I could not articulate, convinced beyond a shadow of a doubt that I was dying. Eventually, the episode passed, but the experience never left me.

And now, this—

I thought I was prepared. I thought I had steeled myself against the possible outcome of today's conversation. I was wrong.

I can feel it devouring me.

This pain.

I've struggled with occasional anxiety over the course of my life, but I've generally been able to manage it. In the past, my experiences had always been associated with this work. With my father. But the older I got, the less powerless I became, and I found ways to manage my triggers; I found the safe spaces in my mind; I educated myself in cognitive behavioral therapies; and with time, I learned to cope. The anxiety came on with far less weight and frequency. But very rarely, it morphs into something else. Sometimes it spirals entirely out of my control.

And I don't know how to save myself this time.

I don't know if I'm strong enough to fight it now, not when I no longer know what I'm fighting for. And I've just collapsed, supine on the floor, my hand pressed against the pain in my chest, when the door suddenly opens.

I feel my heart restart.

I lift my head half an inch and wait. Hoping against hope.

"Hey, man, where the hell are you?"

I drop my head with a groan. Of all the people.

"Hello?" Footsteps. "I know you're in here. And why is this room such a mess? Why are there boxes and bedsheets everywhere?"

Silence.

"Bro, where are you? I just saw Juliette and she was freaking out, but she wouldn't tell me why, and I know your punkass is probably hiding in here like a little—"

And then there he is.

His boots right next to my head.

Staring at me.

"Hi," I say. It's all I can manage at the moment.

Kenji is looking down at me, stunned.

"What in the fresh hell are you doing on the ground? Why aren't you wearing any clothes?" And then, "Wait—were you *crying*?"

I close my eyes, pray to die.

"What's going on?" His voice is suddenly closer than it was before, and I realize he must be crouching next to me. "What's wrong with you, man?"

"I can't breathe," I whisper.

"What do you mean, *you can't breathe*? Did she shoot you again?"

That reminder spears straight through me. Fresh, searing pain.

God, I hate him so much.

I swallow, hard. "Please. Leave."

"Uh, no." I hear the rustle of movement as he sits down beside me. "What is this?" he says, gesturing to my body. "What's happening to you right now?"

Finally, I give up. Open my eyes. "I'm having a panic attack, you inconsiderate ass." I try to take a breath. "And I'd really like some privacy."

His eyebrows fly up. "You're having a what-now?"

"Panic." I breathe. "Attack."

"What the hell is that?"

"I have medicine. In the bathroom. *Please*."

He shoots me a strange look, but does as I ask. He returns in a moment with the right bottle, and I'm relieved.

"This it?"

I nod. I've never actually taken this medication before, but I've kept the prescription current at my medic's request. In case of emergencies.

"You want some water with that?"

I shake my head. Snatch the bottle from him with shaking hands. I can't remember the right dosage, but as I so rarely have an attack this severe, I take a guess. I pop three of the pills in my mouth and bite down, hard, welcoming the vile, bitter taste on my tongue.

It's only several minutes later, after the medicine begins to work its magic, that the metaphorical truck is finally extricated from its position on my chest. My ribs magically restitch themselves. My lungs remember to do their job.

And I feel suddenly limp. Exhausted.

Slow.

I drag myself up, stumble to my feet.

"*Now* do you want to tell me what's going on here?" Kenji is still staring at me, arms crossed against his chest. "Or should I go ahead and assume you did something horrible and just beat the shit out of you?"

I feel so tired suddenly.

A laugh builds in my chest and I don't know where it's coming from. I manage to fight back the laugh, but fail to hide a stupid, inexplicable smile as I say, "You should probably just beat the shit out of me."

It was the wrong thing to say.

Kenji's expression changes. His eyes are suddenly, genuinely concerned and I worry I've said too much. These drugs are slowing me down, softening my senses. I touch a hand to my lips, beg them to stay closed. I hope I haven't taken too much of the medicine.

"Hey," Kenji says gently. "What happened?"

I shake my head. Close my eyes. "What happened?" Now I actually laugh. "What happened, what happened." I open my eyes long enough to say, "Juliette broke up with me."

"What?"

"That is, I think she did?" I stop. Frown. Tap a finger against my chin. "I imagine that's why she ran out of here screaming."

"But—why would she break up with you? Why was she crying?"

At this, I laugh again. "Because I," I say, pointing at myself, "am a monster."

Kenji looks confused. "And how is that news to anyone?"

I smile. He's funny, I think. Funny guy.

"Where did I leave my shirt?" I mumble, feeling suddenly numb in a whole new way. I cross my arms. Squint. "Hmm? Have you seen it anywhere?"

"Bro, are you drunk?"

"What?" I slap at the air. Laugh. "I don't drink. My father is an alcoholic, didn't you know? I don't touch the stuff. No, wait"—I hold up a finger—"*was* an alcoholic. My father *was* an alcoholic. He's dead now. Quite dead."

And then I hear Kenji gasp. It's loud and strange and he whispers, "*Holy shit*," and it's enough to sharpen my senses for a second.

I turn around to face him.

He looks terrified.

"What is it?" I say, annoyed.

"What happened to your back?"

"Oh." I look away, newly irritated. "That." The many, many scars that make up the disfiguration of my entire back. I take a deep breath. Exhale. "Those are just, you know, birthday gifts from dear old dad."

"Birthday gifts from your *dad*?" Kenji blinks, fast. Looks around, speaks to the air. "What the hell kind of soap opera did I just walk into here?" He runs a hand through his hair and says, "Why am I always getting involved in other people's personal shit? Why can't I just mind my own business? Why can't I just keep my mouth shut?"

"You know," I say to him, tilting my head slightly, "I've always wondered the same thing."

"Shut up."

I smile, big. Lightbulb bright.

Kenji's eyes widen, surprised, and he laughs. He nods at my face and says, "Aw, you've got dimples. I didn't know that. That's cute."

"Shut up." I frown. "Go away."

He laughs harder. "I think you took way too many of those medicine thingies," he says to me, picking up the bottle I left on the floor. He scans the label. "It says you're only supposed to take one every three hours." He laughs again. Louder this time. "Shit, man, if I didn't know you were in a world of pain right now, I'd be filming this."

"I'm very tired," I say to him. "Please go directly to hell."

"No way, freak show. I'm not missing this." He leans against the wall. "Plus, I'm not going anywhere until your drunkass tells me why you and J broke up."

I shake my head. Finally manage to find a shirt and put it on.

"Yeah, you put that on backward," Kenji says to me.

I glare at him and fall into bed. Close my eyes.

"So?" he says, sitting down next to me. "Should I get the popcorn? What's going on?"

"It's classified."

Kenji makes a sound of disbelief. "What's classified? Why you broke up is classified? Or did you break up over classified information?"

"Yes."

"Throw me a freaking bone here."

"We broke up," I say, pulling a pillow over my eyes, "because of information I shared with her that is, as I said, *classified*."

"What? Why? That doesn't make any sense." A pause. "Unless—"

"Oh good, I can practically hear the tiny gears in your tiny brain turning."

"You lied to her about something?" he says. "Something you should've told her? Something classified—about *her*?"

I wave a hand at nothing in particular. "The man's a genius."

"Oh, *shit*."

"Yes," I say. "Very much shit."

He exhales a long, hard breath. "That sounds pretty serious."

"I am an idiot."

He clears his throat. "So, uh, you really screwed up this time, huh?"

"Quite thoroughly, I'm afraid."

Silence.

"Wait—tell me again why all these sheets are on the floor?"

At that, I pull the pillow away from my face. "Why do you think they're on the floor?"

A second's hesitation and then,

"Oh, what—*c'mon,* man, what the hell." Kenji jumps off the bed looking disgusted. "Why would you let me sit here?" He stalks off to the other side of the room. "You guys are just—*Jesus*—that is just *not okay*—"

"Grow up."

"I *am* grown." He scowls at me. "But Juliette's like my sister, man, I don't want to think about that shit—"

"Well, don't worry," I say to him, "I'm sure it'll never happen again."

"All right, all right, drama queen, calm down. And tell me about this classified business."

JULIETTE

Run, I said to myself.

Run until your lungs collapse, until the wind whips and snaps at your tattered clothes, until you're a blur that blends into the background.

Run, Juliette, run faster, run until your bones break and your shins split and your muscles atrophy and your heart dies because it was always too big for your chest and it beat too fast for too long and run.

Run run run until you can't hear their feet behind you. Run until they drop their fists and their shouts dissolve in the air. Run with your eyes open and your mouth shut and dam the river rushing up behind your eyes. Run, Juliette.

Run until you drop dead.

Make sure your heart stops before they ever reach you. Before they ever touch you.

Run, I said.

—AN EXCERPT FROM JULIETTE'S JOURNALS IN THE ASYLUM

My feet pound against the hard, packed earth, each steady footfall sending shocks of electric pain up my legs. My lungs burn, my breaths coming in fast and sharp, but I push through the exhaustion, my muscles working harder than they have in a long time, and keep moving. I never used to be any good at this. I've always had trouble breathing. But I've been doing a lot of cardio and weight training since moving on base, and I've gotten much stronger.

Today, that training is paying off.

I've covered at least a couple of miles already, panic and rage propelling me most of the way through, but now I have to break through my own resistance in order to maintain momentum. I cannot stop. I will not stop.

I'm not ready to start thinking yet.

It's a disturbingly beautiful day today; the sun is shining high and bright, impossible birds chirping merrily in half-blooming trees and flapping their wings in vast, blue skies. I'm wearing a thin cotton shirt. Dark blue jeans. Another pair of tennis shoes. My hair, loose and long, waves behind me, locked in a battle with the wind. I can feel the sun warm my face; I feel beads of sweat roll down my back.

Could this possibly be real? I wonder.

Did someone shoot me with those poison bullets on purpose? To try and tell me something?

Or are my hallucinations an altogether different issue?

I close my eyes and push my legs harder, will myself to move faster. I don't want to think yet. I don't want to stop moving.

If I stop moving, my mind might kill me.

A sudden gust of wind hits me in the face. I open my eyes again, remember to breathe. I'm back in unregulated territory now, my powers turned fully on, the energy humming through me even now, in perpetual motion. The streets of the old world are paved, but pockmarked by potholes and puddles. The buildings are abandoned, tall and cold, electric lines strapped across the skyline like the staffs of unfinished songs, swaying gently in the afternoon light. I run under a crumbling overpass and down several cascading, concrete stairs manned on either side by unkempt palm trees and burned-out lampposts, their wrought-iron handrails rough and peeling paint. I turn up and down a few side streets and then I'm surrounded, on all sides, by the skeleton of an old freeway, twelve lanes wide, an enormous metal structure half collapsed in the middle of the road. I squint more closely and count three equally massive green signs, only two of which are still standing. I read the words—

405 SOUTH LONG BEACH

—and I stop.

I fall forward, elbows on my knees, hands clasped behind my head, and fight the urge to tumble to the ground.

Inhale.

Exhale.

Over and over and over

I look up, look around.

An old bus sits not far from me, its many wheels mired in a pool of still water, rotting, half rusted, like an abandoned child steeping in its own filth. Freeway signs, shattered glass, shredded rubber, and forgotten bumpers litter what's left of the broken pavement.

The sun finds me and shines in my direction, a spotlight for the fraying girl stopped in the middle of nowhere and I'm caught in its focused rays of heat, melting slowly from within, quietly collapsing as my mind catches up to my body like an asteroid barreling to earth.

And then it hits me—

The reminders like reverberations

The memories like hands around my throat

There it is

There she is

shattered again.

I'm curled into myself against the back of the filthy bus and I've got a hand clamped over my mouth to try and trap the screams but their desperate attempts to escape my lips are fighting a tide of unshed tears I cannot allow and—

breathe

My body shakes with unspent emotion.

Vomit inches up my esophagus.

Go away, I whisper, but only in my head

go away, I say

Please *die*

I'd chained the terrified little girl of my past in some unknowable dungeon inside of me where she and her fears had been carefully stored, sealed away.

Her memories, suffocated.

Her anger, ignored.

I do not speak to her. I don't dare look in her direction. I *hate* her.

But right now I can hear her crying.

Right now I can see her, this other version of myself, I can see her dragging her dirty fingernails against the chambers of my heart, drawing blood. And if I could reach inside myself and rip her out of me with my own two hands, I would.

I would snap her little body in half.

I would toss her mangled limbs out to sea.

I would be rid of her then, fully and truly, bleached forevermore of her stains on my soul. But she refuses to die. She remains within me, an echo. She haunts the halls of my heart and mind and though I'd gladly murder her for a chance at freedom, I cannot. It's like trying to choke a ghost.

So I close my eyes and beg myself to be brave. I take deep breaths. I cannot let the broken girl inside of me inhale all that I've become. I cannot revert back to another version of myself. I will not shatter, not again, in the wake of an emotional earthquake.

But where do I even begin?

How do I deal with any of this? These past weeks had already been too much for me; too much to handle; too much to juggle. It's been hard to admit that I'm unqualified, that I'm in way over my head, but I got there. I was willing to recognize that all this—this new life, this new world—would take time and experience. I was willing to put in the hours, to trust my team, to try to be diplomatic. But now, in light of everything—

My entire life has been an experiment.

I have a sibling. A sister. And an altogether different set of parents, biological parents, who treated me no differently than my adoptive ones did, donating my body to research as if I were nothing more than a science experiment.

Anderson and the other supreme commanders have always known me. Castle has always known the truth about me. Warner knew I'd been adopted.

And now, to know that those I've trusted most have been lying to me—manipulating me—

Everyone has been *using me*—

It rips itself from my lungs, the sudden scream. It wrenches free from my chest without warning, without permission, and it's a scream so loud, so harsh and violent it brings me to my knees. My hands are pressed against the pavement, my head half bent between my legs. The sound of my agony is lost in the wind, carried off by the clouds.

But here, between my feet, the ground has fissured open.

I jump up, surprised, and look down, spin around. I suddenly can't remember if that crack was there before.

The force of my frustration and confusion sends me back to the bus, where I exhale and lean against the back doors, hoping for a place to rest my head—except that my hands and head rip through the exterior wall as though it were made of tissue, and I fall hard on the filthy floor, my hands and knees going straight through the metal underfoot.

Somehow this only makes me angrier.

My power is out of control, stoked by my reckless mind, my wild thoughts. I can't focus my energy the way Kenji taught me to, and it's everywhere, all around me, within and without me and the problem is, I don't care anymore.

I don't care, not right now.

I reach without thinking and rip one of the bus seats from its bolts, and throw it, hard, through the windshield. Glass splinters everywhere; a large shard hits me in the eye and several more fly into my open, angry mouth; I lift a hand to find slivers stuck in my sleeve, glittering like miniature icicles. I spit the spare bits from my mouth. Remove the glass shards from my shirt. And then I pull an inch-long piece of glass out of the inside of my eyelid and toss it, with a small clatter, to the ground.

My chest is heaving.

What, I think, as I rip another seat from its bolts, *do I do now?* I throw this seat straight through a window, shattering more glass and ripping open more metal innards. Instinct alone moves my arm up to protect my face from the flying debris, but I don't flinch. I'm too angry to care. I'm too powerful at the moment to feel pain. Glass ricochets off my body. Razor-thin ribbons of steel bounce off my skin. I almost wish I felt something. Anything.

What do I do?

I punch the wall and there's no relief in it; my hand goes straight through. I kick a chair and there's no comfort in it; my foot rips through the cheap upholstery. I scream again, half outrage, half heartbreak, and watch this time as a long, dangerous crack forms along the ceiling.

That's new.

And I've hardly had time to think the thought when the bus gives a sudden, lurching heave, yawns itself into a deep shudder, and splits clean in half.

The two halves collapse on either side of me, tripping me backward. I fall into a pile of shredded metal and wet, dirty glass and, stunned, I stumble up to my feet.

I don't know what just happened.

I knew I was able to project my abilities—my strength, for certain—but I didn't know that there was any projectional power in my voice. Old impulses make me wish I had someone to discuss this with. But I have no one to talk to anymore.

Warner is out of the question.

Castle is complicit.

And Kenji—*what about Kenji?* Did he know about my parents—my sister—too? Surely, Castle would've told him?

The problem is, I can't be sure of anything anymore.

There's no one left to trust.

But those words—that simple thought—suddenly inspires

in me a memory. It's something hazy I have to reach for. I wrap my hands around it and pull. A voice? A female voice, I remember now. Telling me—

I gasp.

It was Nazeera. Last night. In the medical wing. It was her. I remember her voice now—I remember reaching out and touching her hand, I remember the feel of the metal knuckles she's always wearing and she said—

". . . the people you trust are lying to you—and the other supreme commanders only want to kill you . . ."

I spin around too fast, searching for something I cannot name.

Nazeera was trying to warn me. Last night—she's barely known me and she was trying to tell me the truth long before any of the others ever did—

But why?

Just then, something hard and loud lands heavily on the half-bent steel structure blocking the road. The old freeway signs shudder and sway.

I'm looking straight at it as it happens. I'm watching this in real time, frame by frame, and yet, I'm still so shocked by what I see that I forget to speak.

It's Nazeera, fifty feet in the air, sitting calmly atop a sign that says—

10 EAST LOS ANGELES

—and she's waving at me. She's wearing a loose, brown leather hood attached to a holster that fits snugly around her shoulders. The leather hood covers her hair and shades her eyes so that only the bottom half of her face is visible from where I stand. The diamond piercing under her bottom lip catches fire in the sunlight.

She looks like a vision from an unknowable time.

I still have no idea what to say.

Naturally, she does not share my problem.

"You ready to talk yet?" she says to me.

"How—how did you—"

"Yeah?"

"How did you get here?" I spin around, scanning the distance. *How did she know I was here? Was I being followed?*

"I flew."

I turn back to face her. "Where's your plane?"

She laughs and jumps off the freeway sign. It's a long, hard fall that would've injured any normal person. "I really hope you're joking," she says to me, and then grabs me around the waist and leaps up, into the sky.

WARNER

I've seen a lot of strange things in my life, but I never thought I'd have the pleasure of seeing Kishimoto shut his mouth for longer than five minutes. And yet, here we are. In any other situation, I might be relishing this moment. Sadly, I'm unable to enjoy even this small pleasure.

His silence is unnerving.

It's been fifteen minutes since I finished sharing with him the same details I shared with Juliette earlier today, and he hasn't said a word. He's sitting quietly in the corner, his head pressed against the wall, face in a frown, and he will not speak. He only stares, his eyes narrowed at some invisible point across the room.

Occasionally he sighs.

We've been here for almost two hours, just he and I. Talking. And of all the things I thought would happen today, I certainly did not think it would involve Juliette running away from me, and my befriending this idiot.

Oh, the best-laid plans.

Finally, after what feels like a tremendous amount of time, he speaks.

"I can't believe Castle didn't tell me," is the first thing he says.

"We all have our secrets."

He looks up, looks me in the eye. It's not pleasant. "You have any more secrets I should know about?"

"None you should know about, no."

He laughs, but it sounds sad. "You don't even realize what you're doing, do you?"

"Realize what?"

"You're setting yourself up for a lifetime of pain, bro. You can't keep living like this. This," he says, pointing at my face, "this old you? This messed-up dude who never talks and never smiles and never says anything nice and never allows anyone to really know him—you can't be this guy if you want to be in any kind of relationship."

I raise an eyebrow.

He shakes his head. "You just can't, man. You can't be with someone and keep that many secrets from them."

"It's never stopped me before."

Here, Kenji hesitates. His eyes widen, just a little. "What do you mean, *before?*"

"Before," I say. "In other relationships."

"So, uh, you've been in other relationships? Before Juliette?"

I tilt my head at him. "You find that hard to believe."

"I'm still trying to wrap my head around the fact that you have *feelings,* so yeah, I find that hard to believe."

I clear my throat very quietly. Look away.

"So—umm—you, uh"—he laughs, nervously—"I'm sorry but, like, does Juliette know you've been in other relationships? Because she's never mentioned anything about that, and I think that would've been, like, I don't know? Relevant?"

I turn to face him. "No."

"No, what?"

"No, she doesn't know."

"Why not?"

"She's never asked."

Kenji gapes at me. "I'm sorry—but are you—I mean, are you actually as stupid as you sound? Or are you just messing with me right now?"

"I'm nearly twenty years old," I say to him, irritated. "Do you really think it so strange that I've been with other women?"

"No," he says, "I, personally, don't give a shit how many women you've been with. What I think is strange is that you never told your *girlfriend* that you've been with other women. And to be perfectly honest it's making me wonder whether your relationship wasn't already headed to hell."

"You have no idea what you're talking about." My eyes flash. "I *love* her. I never would've done anything to hurt her."

"They why would you lie to her?"

"Why do you keep pressing this? Who cares if I've been with other women? They meant nothing to me—"

"You're messed up in the head, man."

I close my eyes, feeling suddenly exhausted. "Of all the things I've shared with you today, *this* is the issue you're most interested in discussing?"

"I just think it's important, you know, if you and J ever try to repair this damage. You have to get your shit together."

"What do you mean, *repair this damage*?" I say, my eyes flying open. "I've already lost her. The damage is done."

At this, he looks surprised. "So that's it? You're just going to walk away? All this talk of *I love her* blah blah and that's it?"

"She doesn't want to be with me. I won't try to convince her she's wrong."

Kenji laughs. "Damn," he says. "I think you might need to get your bolts tightened."

"I beg your pardon?"

He gets to his feet. "Whatever, bro. Your life. Your business. I liked you better when you were drunk on your meds."

"Tell me something, Kishimoto—"

"What?"

"Why would I take relationship advice from *you*? What do you know about relationships aside from the fact that you've never been in one?"

A muscle twitches in his jaw. "Wow." He nods, looks away. "You know what?" He flips me off. "Don't pretend to know shit about me, man. You don't know me."

"You don't know me, either."

"I know that you're an *idiot*."

I suddenly, inexplicably, shut down.

My face pales. I feel unsteady. I don't have any fight left in me today and I don't have any interest in defending myself. I *am* an idiot. I know who I am. The terrible things I've done. It's indefensible.

"You're right," I say, but I say it quietly. "And I'm sure

you're right that there's a great deal I don't know about you, too."

Something in Kenji seems to relax.

His eyes are sympathetic when he says, "I really don't think you have to lose her. Not like this. Not over this. What you did was, like—yeah, that shit was beyond horrible. Torturing her freaking sister? I mean. Yeah. Absolutely. Like, ten out of ten you'll probably go to hell for that."

I flinch.

"But that happened before you knew her, right? Before all this"—he waves a hand—"you know, whatever it is that happened between you guys happened. And I know her—I know how she feels about you. There might be something to save. I wouldn't lose hope just yet."

I almost crack a smile. I almost laugh.

I don't do either.

Instead, I say, "I remember Juliette telling me you gave a similar speech to Kent shortly after they broke up. That you spoke expressly against her wishes. You told Kent she still loved him—that she wanted to get back together with him. You told him the exact opposite of what she felt. And she was furious."

"That was different." Kenji frowns. "That was just . . . like . . . you know—I was just trying to help? Because, like, logistically the situation was really complicated—"

"I appreciate your trying to help me," I say to him. "But I will not beg her to return to me. Not if it's not what she wants." I look away. "In any case, she's always deserved to be with someone better. Maybe this is her chance."

"Uh-huh." Kenji lifts an eyebrow. "So if, like, tomorrow she hooks up with some other dude you're just gonna shrug and be like—I don't know? Shake the guy's hand? Take the happy couple out to dinner? Seriously?"

It's just an idea.

A hypothetical scenario.

But the possibility blooms in my mind: Juliette smiling, laughing with another man—

And then worse: his hands on her body, her eyes half closed with desire—

I feel suddenly like I've been punched in the stomach.

I close my eyes. Try to be steady.

But now I can't stop picturing it: someone else knowing her the way I've known her, in the dark, in the quiet hours before dawn—her gentle kisses, her private moans of pleasure—

I can't do it. I can't do it.

I can't breathe.

"Hey—I'm sorry—it was just a question—"

"I think you should go," I say. I whisper the words. "You should leave."

"Yeah—you know what? Yeah. Excellent idea." He nods several times. "No problem." Still, he doesn't move.

"What?" I snap at him.

"I just, uh"—he rocks back and forth on his heels—"I was wondering if you, uh, wanted any more of those medicine thingies though? Before I get out of here?"

"Get. Out."

"All right, man, no problem, yeah, I'm just gonna—"

Suddenly, someone is banging on my door.

I look up. Look around.

"Should I, um"—Kenji is looking at me, a question in his eyes—"you want me to get that?"

I glare at him.

"Yeah, I'll get it," he says, and runs to answer the door.

It's Delalieu, looking panicked.

It takes more than a concerted effort, but I manage to pull myself together.

"You couldn't have called, Lieutenant? Isn't that what our phones are for?"

"I've been trying, sir, for over an hour, but no one would answer your phone, sir—"

I roll my neck and sigh, stretching the muscles even as they tense up again.

My fault.

I disconnected my phone last night. I didn't want any distractions while I was looking through my father's files, and in the insanity of the morning I forgot to reconnect the line. I was beginning to wonder why I've had so much uninterrupted time to myself today.

"That's fine," I say, cutting him off. "What's the problem?"

"Sir," he says, swallowing hard, "I've tried to contact both you and Madam Supreme, but the two of you have been unavailable all day and, and—"

"What is it, Lieutenant?"

"The supreme commander of Europe has sent her

daughter, sir. She showed up unannounced a couple of hours ago, and I'm afraid she's making quite a fuss about being ignored and I wasn't sure what to d-do—"

"Well, tell her to sit her ass down and wait," Kenji says, irritated. "What do you mean she's making a *fuss*? We've got shit to do around here."

But I've gone unexpectedly solid. Like the blood in my veins has congealed.

"I mean—right?" Kenji is saying, nudging me with his arm. "What's the deal, man? Delalieu," he says, ignoring me. "Just tell her to chill. We'll be down in a bit. This guy needs to shower and put his shirt on straight. Give her some lunch or something, okay? We'll be right there."

"Yes, sir," Delalieu says quietly. He's talking to Kenji, but flashes me another look of concern. I do not respond. I'm not sure what to say.

Things are happening too quickly. Fission and fusion in all the wrong places, all at once.

It's only once Delalieu has gone and the door is closed that Kenji finally says, "What was that about? Why do you look so freaked?"

And I unfreeze. Feeling returns slowly to my limbs.

I turn around to face him.

"You really think," I say carefully, "that I need to tell Juliette about the other women I've been with?"

"Uh, yeah," he says, "but what does that have to do with—"

I stare at him.

He stares back. His mouth drops open. "You mean—with

this girl—the one downstairs—?"

"The children of the supreme commanders," I try to explain, squeezing my eyes shut as I do, "we—we all basically grew up together. I've known most of these girls all my life." I look at him, attempting nonchalance. "It was inevitable, really. It shouldn't be surprising."

But Kenji's eyebrows are high. He's trying to fight a smile as he slaps me on the back, too hard. "Oh, you are in for a world of pain, bro. A world. Of. Pain."

I shake my head. "There's no need to make this dramatic. Juliette doesn't have to know. She's not even speaking to me at the moment."

Kenji laughs. Looks at me with something that resembles pity. "You don't know anything about women, do you?" When I don't respond, he says, "Trust me, man, I bet you anything that wherever J is right now—out there somewhere—she already knows. And if she doesn't, she will soon. Girls talk about everything."

"How is that possible?"

He shrugs.

I sigh. Run a hand over my hair. "Well," I say. "Does it really matter? Don't we have more important things to contend with than the staid details of my previous relationships?"

"Normally? Yes. But when the supreme commander of North America is your ex-girlfriend, and she's already feeling really stressed about the fact that you've been lying to her? And then all of a sudden your other ex-girlfriend shows up and Juliette doesn't even *know* about her? And she realizes there are, like, a thousand other things you've lied to her about—"

"I never lied to her about any of this," I interject. "She never *asked*—"

"—and then our very powerful supreme commander gets, like, super, super pissed?" Kenji shrugs. "I don't know, man, I don't see that ending well."

I drop my head in my hands. Close my eyes. "I need to shower."

"And . . . yeah, that's my cue to go."

I look up, suddenly. "Is there anything I can do?" I say. "To stop this from getting worse?"

"Oh, so *now* you're taking relationship advice from me?"

I fight the impulse to roll my eyes.

"I don't really know man," Kenji says, and sighs. "I think, this time, you just have to deal with the consequences of your own stupidity."

I look away, bite back a laugh, and nod several times as I say, "Go to hell, Kishimoto."

"I'm right behind you, bro." He winks at me. Just once.

And disappears.

JULIETTE

There's something simmering inside of me.

Something I've never dared to tap into, something I'm afraid to acknowledge. There's a part of me clawing to break free from the cage I've trapped it in, banging on the doors of my heart begging to be free.

Begging to let go.

Every day I feel like I'm reliving the same nightmare. I open my mouth to shout, to fight, to swing my fists but my vocal cords are cut, my arms are heavy and weighted down as if trapped in wet cement and I'm screaming but no one can hear me, no one can reach me and I'm caught. And it's killing me.

I've always had to make myself submissive, subservient, twisted into a pleading, passive mop just to make everyone else feel safe and comfortable. My existence has become a fight to prove I'm harmless, that I'm not a threat, that I'm capable of living among other human beings without hurting them.

And I'm so tired I'm so tired I'm so tired I'm so tired and sometimes I get so angry.

I don't know what's happening to me.

—AN EXCERPT FROM JULIETTE'S JOURNALS IN THE ASYLUM

We land in a tree.

I have no idea where we are—I don't even know if I've ever been this high, or this close to nature—but Nazeera doesn't seem bothered at all.

I'm breathing hard as I turn to face her, adrenaline and disbelief colliding, but she's not looking at me. She looks calm—happy, even—as she looks out across the sky, one foot propped up on a tree branch while the other hangs, swinging gently back and forth in the cool breeze. Her left arm rests on her left knee and her hand is relaxed, almost too casual, as it clenches and unclenches around something I can't see. I tilt my head, part my lips to ask the question when she interrupts me.

"You know," she says suddenly, "I've never, ever shown anyone what I can do."

I'm caught off guard.

"No one? Ever?" I say, stunned.

She shakes her head.

"Why not?"

She's quiet for a minute before she says, "The answer to that question is one of the reasons why I wanted to talk to you." She touches an absent hand to the diamond piercing at her lip, tapping the tip of one finger against the glittering stone. "So," she says. "Do you know anything real about your past?"

And the pain is swift, like cold steel, like knives in my chest. Painful reminders of today's revelations. "I know some things," I finally say. "I learned most of it this morning, actually."

She nods. "And that's why you ran off like you did."

I turn to face her. "You were watching me?"

"I've been shadowing you, yeah."

"Why?"

She smiles, but it looks tired. "You really don't remember me, do you?"

I stare at her, confused.

She sighs. Swings both her legs under her and looks out into the distance. "Never mind."

"No, wait—what do you mean? Am I supposed to remember you?"

She shakes her head.

"I don't understand," I say.

"Forget it," she says. "It's nothing. You just look really familiar, and for a split second I thought we'd met before."

"Oh," I say. "Okay." But now she won't look at me, and I have a strange feeling she's holding something back.

Still, she says nothing.

She looks lost in thought, chewing on her lip as she looks off in the distance, and doesn't say anything for what feels like a long time.

"Um. Excuse me? You put me in a *tree*," I finally say. "What the hell am I doing here? What do you want?"

She turns to face me. That's when I realize that the object in her hand is actually a bag of little hard candies. She holds it out to me, indicating with her head that I should take one.

But I don't trust her. "No thanks," I say.

She shrugs. Unwraps one of the colorful candies and pops it in her mouth. "So," she says. "What'd Warner tell you today?"

"Why do you want to know?"

"Did he tell you that you have a sister?"

I feel a knot of anger beginning to form in my chest. I say nothing.

"I'll take that as a yes," she says. She bites down hard on the candy in her mouth. Crunches quietly beside me. "Did he tell you anything else?"

"What do you want from me?" I say. "Who are you?"

"What did he tell you about your parents?" she asks, ignoring me even as she glances at me out of the corner of her eye. "Did he tell you that you were adopted? That your biological parents are still alive?"

I only stare at her.

She tilts her head. Studies me. "Did he tell you their names?"

My eyes widen automatically.

Nazeera smiles, and the action brightens her face. "There it is," she says, with a triumphant nod. She peels another candy from its wrapper and pops it in her mouth. "Hmm."

"There *what* is?"

"The moment," she says, "where the anger ends, and the curiosity begins."

I sigh, irritated. "You know my parents' names?"

"I never said that."

I feel suddenly exhausted. Powerless. "Does everyone know more about my life than I do?"

She glances at me. Looks away. "Not everyone," she says. "Those of us with ranks high enough in The Reestablishment know a lot, yeah," she says. "It's our business to know. Especially *us*," she says, meeting my eyes for a second. "The kids, I mean. Our parents expect us to take over one day. But, no, not everyone knows everything." She smiles at something, a private joke shared only with herself, when she says, "Most people don't know shit, actually." And then, a frown. "Though I guess Warner knows more than I thought he did."

"So," I say. "You've known Warner for a long time."

Nazeera pushes her hood back a bit so I can better see her face, leans against a branch, and sighs. "Listen," she says quietly. "I only know what my dad told us about you guys, and I'm wise enough to the game now to know that most of the things I've heard are probably nonsense. But—"

She hesitates. Bites her lip and hesitates.

"Just say it," I tell her, shaking my head as I do. "I've already heard so many people tell me I'm crazy for falling for him. You wouldn't be the first."

"What? No," she says, and laughs. "I don't think you're crazy. I mean, I get why people might think he's trouble, but he's my people, you know? I knew his parents. Anderson made my own dad seem like a nice guy. We're all kind of messed up, that's true, but Warner's not a bad person. He's just trying to find a way to survive this insanity, just like the rest of us."

"Oh," I say. Surprised.

"Anyway," she says with a shrug, "no, I understand why you like him. And even if I didn't, I mean—I'm not blind." She raises a knowing eyebrow at me. "I get you, girl."

I'm still stunned. This might be the very first time I've heard anyone but myself make an argument for Warner.

"No, what I'm trying to say is that I think it might be a good time for you to focus on yourself for a little while. Take a beat. And anyway, Lena's going to be here any minute, so it's probably best for you to stay away from that situation for as long as you can." She shoots me another knowing look. "I really don't think you need any more drama in your life, and that whole"—she gestures to the air—"*thing* is bound to just—you know—get really ugly."

"What?" I frown. "What thing? What situation? Who's Lena?"

Nazeera's surprise is so swift, so genuine, I can't help but feel instantly concerned. My pulse picks up as Nazeera turns fully in my direction and says, very, very slowly, "Lena. Lena Mishkin. She's the daughter of the supreme commander of Europe."

I stare at her. Shake my head.

Nazeera's eyes widen. "Girl, what the hell?"

"What?" I say, scared now. "Who is she?"

"Who is she? Are you serious? She's Warner's *ex-girlfriend*."

I nearly fall out of the tree.

It's funny, I thought I'd feel more than this.

Old Juliette would've cried. Broken Juliette would've split open from the sudden impact of today's many heartbreaking revelations, from the depth of Warner's lies, from the pain of feeling so deeply betrayed. But this new version of me is refusing to react; instead, my body is shutting down.

I feel my arms go numb as Nazeera offers me details about Warner's old relationship—details I do and don't want to hear. She says Lena and Warner were a big deal for the world of The Reestablishment and suddenly three fingers on my right hand begin to twitch without my permission. She says that Lena's mom and Warner's dad were excited about an alliance between their families, about a bond that would only make their regime stronger, and electric currents bolt down my legs, shocking and paralyzing me all at once.

She says that Lena was in love with him—really in love with him—but that Warner broke her heart, that he never treated her with any real affection and she's hated him for it, that "Lena's been in a rage ever since she heard the stories of how he fell for you, especially because you were supposed to be, like, fresh out of a mental asylum, you know? Apparently it was a huge blow to her ego" and hearing this does nothing to soothe me. It makes me feel strange and foreign, like a specimen in a tank, like my life was never my own, like I'm an actor in a play directed by strangers and I feel an exhalation of arctic wind blow steadily into my chest, a bitter breeze circling my heart and I close my eyes as frostbite eases my pain, its icy hands closing around the wounds festering in my flesh.

Only then

Only then do I finally breathe, luxuriating in the disconnection from this pain.

I look up, feeling broken and brand-new, eyes cold and unfeeling as I blink slowly and say, "How do you know all this?"

Nazeera breaks a leaf off a nearby branch and folds it between her fingers. She shrugs. "It's a small, incestuous circle we move in. I've known Lena forever. She and I were never close, exactly, but we move in the same world." Another shrug. "She was really messed up over him. It's all she ever wanted to talk about. And she'd talk to anyone about it."

"How long were they together?"

"Two years."

Two years.

The answer is so unexpectedly painful it spears through my new defenses.

Two years? Two years with another girl and he never said a word about it. Two years with someone else. *And how many others?* A shock of pain tries to reach me, to circumvent my new, cold heart, and I manage to fight the worst of it. Even so, a brick of something hot and horrible buries itself in my chest.

Not jealousy, no.

Inferiority. Inexperience. Naïveté.

How much more will I learn about him? How much more has he kept from me? How will I ever be able to trust him again?

I close my eyes and feel the weight of loss and resignation settle deep, deep within me. My bones shift, rearranging to make room for these new hurts.

This wave of fresh anger.

"When did they break up?" I ask.

"Like . . . eight months ago?"

Now I stop asking questions.

I want to become a tree. A blade of grass. I want to become dirt or air or nothing. *Nothing*. Yes. I want to become nothing.

I feel like such a fool.

"I don't understand why he never told you," Nazeera is saying to me now, but I can hardly hear her. "That's crazy. It was pretty big news in our world."

"Why have you been following me?" I change the subject with zero finesse. My eyes are half lidded. My fists are clenched. I don't want to talk about Warner anymore. Ever again. I want to rip my heart out of my chest and throw it in our piss-filled ocean for all the good its ever done me.

I don't want to feel anything anymore.

Nazeera sits back, surprised. "There's a lot going on right now," she says. "There's so much you don't know, so much crap you're just beginning to wade into. I mean—hell, someone tried to kill you yesterday." She shakes her head. "I'm just worried about you."

"You don't even know me. Why bother worrying about me?"

This time, she doesn't respond. She just looks at me. Slowly, she unwraps another candy. Pops it in her mouth and looks away.

"My dad forced me to come here," she says quietly. "I didn't want to have any part in any of this. I never have. I hate everything The Reestablishment stands for. But I told myself that if I had to be here, I would look out for you. So that's what I'm doing now. I'm looking out for you."

"Well, don't waste your time," I say to her, feeling callous. "I don't need your pity or your protection."

Nazeera goes quiet. Finally, she sighs. "Listen—I'm really sorry," she says. "I honestly thought you knew about Lena."

"I don't care about Lena," I lie. "I have more important things to worry about."

"Right," she says. She clears her throat. "I know. Still, I'm sorry."

I say nothing.

"Hey," Nazeera says. "Really. I didn't mean to upset you.

I just want you to know that I'm not here to hurt you. I'm trying to look out for you."

"I don't need you to look out for me. I'm doing fine."

Now she rolls her eyes. "Didn't I just save your life?"

I mumble something dumb under my breath.

Nazeera shakes her head. "You have to get it together, girl, or you're not going to get through this alive," she says to me. "You have no idea what's going on behind the scenes or what the other commanders have in store for you." When I don't respond she says, "Lena won't be the last of us to arrive here, you know. And no one is coming here to play nice."

I look up at her. My eyes are dead of emotion. "Good," I say. "Let them come."

She laughs, but there's no life in it. "So you and Warner have some drama and now you just don't care about anything? That's real mature."

Fire flashes through me. My eyes sharpen. "If I'm upset right now, it's because I've just discovered that everyone closest to me has been *lying* to me. Using me. Manipulating me for their own needs. My parents," I say angrily, "are still *alive,* and apparently they're no better than the abusive monsters who adopted me. I have a sister being actively tortured by The Reestablishment—and I never even knew she existed. I'm trying to come to terms with the fact that *nothing* is going to be the same for me, not ever again, and I have no idea who to trust or how to move forward. So yeah," I say, nearly shouting the words, "right now I don't care about *anything*. Because I don't know what I'm fighting for anymore. And I don't know who my friends are. Right now," I say, "everyone is my enemy, including *you*."

Nazeera is unmoved. "You could fight for your sister," she says.

"I don't even know who she is."

Nazeera shoots me a sidelong look, heavy with disbelief. "Isn't it enough that she's an innocent girl being tortured? I thought there was some greater good you were fighting for."

I shrug. Look away.

"You know what? You don't have to care," she says. "But I do. I care about what The Reestablishment has done to innocent people. I care that our parents are all a bunch of psychopaths. I care a great deal about what The Reestablishment has done, in particular, to those of us with abilities.

"And to answer your earlier question: I never told anyone about my powers because I saw what they did to people like me. How they locked them up. Tortured and abused them." She looks me in the eye. "And I don't want to be the next experiment."

Something inside me hollows. Mellows out. I feel suddenly empty and sad. "I do care," I finally say to her. "I care too much, probably."

And Nazeera's anger subsides. She sighs.

"Warner said The Reestablishment wants to take me back," I say.

She nods. "Seems about right."

"Where do they want to take me?"

"I'm not sure," she says. Shrugs. "They might just kill you."

"Thanks for the pep talk."

"Or," she says, smiling a little, "they'll send you to another continent, maybe. New alias. New facility."

"Another continent?" I say, curious despite myself. "I've never even been on a plane before."

Somehow, I've said the wrong thing.

Nazeera looks almost stricken for a second. Pain flashes in and out of her eyes and she looks away. Clears her throat. But when she looks back her face is neutral once more. "Yeah. Well. You're not missing much."

"Do you travel a lot?" I ask.

"Yep."

"Where are you from?"

"Sector 2. Asian continent." And then, at the look at my face: "But I was born in Baghdad."

"Baghdad," I say, almost to myself. It sounds so familiar, and I'm trying to remember, trying to place it on the map, when she says

"Iraq."

"Oh," I say. "Wow."

"A lot to take in, huh?"

"Yeah," I say quietly. And then—hating myself even as I say the words—I can't help but ask, "Where's Lena from?"

Nazeera laughs. "I thought you said you didn't care about Lena."

I close my eyes. Shake my head, mortified.

"She was born in Peterhof, a suburb of Saint Petersburg."

"Russia," I say, relieved to finally recognize one of these cities. "*War and Peace*."

"Great book," Nazeera says with a nod. "Too bad it's still on the burn list."

"Burn list?"

"To be destroyed," she says. "The Reestablishment has big plans to reset language, literature, and culture. They want to create a new kind of, I don't know," she says, making a random gesture with one hand, "universal humanity."

I nod, quietly horrified. I already know this. I'd first heard about this from Adam right after he was assigned to become my cellmate in the asylum. And the idea of destroying art—culture—everything that makes human beings diverse and beautiful—

It makes me feel sick to my stomach.

"Anyway," she says, "it's obviously a garbage, grotesque experiment, but we have to go through the motions. We were given lists of books to sort through, and we have to read them, write reports, decide what to keep and what to get rid of." She exhales. "I finally finished reading most of the classics a couple of months ago—but early last year they forced all of us to read *War and Peace* in five languages, because they wanted us to analyze how culture plays a role in manipulating the translation of the same text." She hesitates, remembering. "It was definitely the most fun to read in French. But I think, ultimately, it's best in Russian. All other translations—especially the English ones—are missing that necessary . . . *toska*. You know what I mean?"

My mouth drops open a little.

It's the *way* she says it—like it's no big deal, like she's just said something perfectly normal, like anyone could read Tolstoy in five different languages and polish off the books in an afternoon. It's her easy, effortless self-assuredness that makes my heart deflate. It took me a month to read *War and Peace*. In *English*.

"Right," I say, and look away. "Yeah. That's, um, interesting."

It's becoming too familiar, this feeling of inferiority. Too powerful. Every time I think I've made progress in my life I seem to be reminded of how much further I still have to go. Though I guess it's not Nazeera's fault that she and the rest of these kids were bred to be violent geniuses.

"So," she says, clapping her hands together. "Is there anything else you want to know?"

"Yeah," I say. "What's the deal with your brother?"

She looks surprised. "Haider?" She hesitates. "What do you mean?"

"I mean, like"—I frown—"is he loyal to your dad? To The Reestablishment? Is he trustworthy?"

"I don't know if I'd call him trustworthy," she says, looking thoughtful. "But I think all of us have complicated relationships with The Reestablishment. Haider doesn't want to be here any more than I do."

"Really?"

She nods. "Warner probably doesn't consider any of us his friends, but Haider does. And Haider went through a really dark time last year." She pauses. Breaks another leaf off a nearby branch. Folds and refolds it between her fingers as she says, "My dad was putting a lot of pressure on him, forcing him through some really intense training—the details of which Haider still won't share with me—and a few weeks later he just started spiraling. He was exhibiting suicidal tendencies. Self-harming. And I got really scared. I called Warner because I knew Haider would listen to him." She shakes her head. "Warner didn't say a word. He just got on a plane. And he stayed with us for a couple of weeks. I don't know what he said to Haider," she says. "I don't know what he did or how he got him through it, but"—she looks off into the distance, shrugs—"it's hard to forget something like that. Even though our parents keep trying to pit us against each other. They're trying to keep us from getting too soft." She laughs. "But it's so much bullshit."

And I'm reeling, stunned.

There's so much to unpack here I don't even know where to begin. I'm not sure if I want to. All of Nazeera's comments about Warner just seem to spear me in the heart. They make me miss him.

They make me want to forgive him.

But I can't let my emotions control me. Not now. Not ever. So I force the feelings down, out of my head, and instead, I say, "Wow. And I just thought Haider was kind of a jerk."

Nazeera smiles. Waves an absent hand. "He's working on it."

"Does he have any . . . supernatural abilities?"

"None that I know of."

"Huh."

"Yeah."

"But you can fly," I say.

She nods.

"That's interesting."

She smiles, wide, and turns to face me. Her eyes are big and beautifully lit from the dappled light breaking through the branches, and her excitement is so pure that it makes something inside of me shrivel up and die.

"It's so much more than *interesting*," she says, and it's then that I feel a pang of something new:

Jealousy.

Envy.

Resentment.

My abilities have always been a curse—a source of endless pain and conflict. Everything about me is designed to kill and destroy and it's a reality I've never been able to fully accept. "Must be nice," I say.

She turns away again, smiling into the wind. "The best part?" she says. "Is that I can also do *this*—"

Nazeera goes suddenly invisible.

I jerk back sharply.

And then she's back, beaming. "Isn't it great?" she says, eyes glittering with excitement. "I've never been able to share this with anyone before."

"Uh . . . yeah." I laugh but it sounds fake, too high. "Very cool." And then, more quietly, "Kenji is going to be pissed."

Nazeera stops smiling. "What does he have to do with anything?"

"Well—" I nod in her general direction. "I mean, what you just did? That's Kenji's thing. And he's not good at sharing the spotlight, generally."

"I didn't know there could be someone else with the same power," she says, visibly heartbroken. "How is that possible?"

"I don't know," I say, and I feel a sudden urge to laugh. She's so determined to dislike Kenji that I'm starting to wonder why. And then I'm reminded, all at once, of today's horrible revelations, and the smile is wiped off my face. "So," I say quickly, "should we get back to base? I still have a ton of things to figure out, including how I'm going to deal with this stupid symposium tomorrow. I don't know if I should bail or just—"

"Don't bail." Nazeera cuts me off. "If you bail they might think you know something. Don't show your hand," she says. "Not yet. Just go through the motions until you get your own plan together."

I stare at her. Study her. Finally, I say, "Okay."

"And once you decide what you want to do, let me know. I can always help evacuate people. Hold down the fort. Fight. Whatever. Just say the word."

"What—?" I frown. "Evacuate people? What are you

talking about?"

She smiles as she shakes her head. "Girl, you still don't get it, do you? Why do you think we're here? The Reestablishment is planning on destroying Sector 45." She stares at me. "And that includes everyone in it."

WARNER

I never make it downstairs.

I've hardly had a second to put my shirt on straight when I hear someone banging on my door.

"I'm really sorry, bro," I hear Kenji shout, "she wouldn't listen to me—"

And then,

"Open the door, Warner. I promise this will only hurt a little."

Her voice is the same as it's always been. Smooth. Deceptively soft. Always a little rough around the edges.

"Lena," I say. "How nice to hear from you again."

"Open the door, asshole."

"You never did hold back with the flattery."

"I said *open the door—*"

Very carefully, I do.

And then I close my eyes.

Lena slaps me across the face so hard I feel it ring in my ears. Kenji screams, but only briefly, and I take a steadying breath. I look up at her without lifting my head. "Are you done?"

Her eyes go wide, enraged and offended, and I realize I've already pushed her too far. She swings without thinking, and even so, it's a punch perfectly executed. On impact she'd break, at the very least, my nose, but I can no longer entertain her daydreams of causing me physical harm. My reflexes are faster than hers—they always have been—and I catch her wrist just moments before impact. Her arm vibrates from the intensity of the unspent energy and she jerks back, shrieking as she breaks free.

"You son of a bitch," she says, breathing hard.

"I can't let you punch me in the face, Lena."

"I would do worse to you."

"And yet you wonder why things didn't work out between us."

"Always so cold," she says, and something in her voice breaks as she says it. "Always so cruel."

I rub the back of my head and smile, unhappily, at the wall. "Why have you come up to my room? Why engage me privately? You know I have little left to say to you."

"You never said *anything* to me," she suddenly screams. "Two years," she says, her chest heaving, "two years and you left a message with my *mother* telling her to let me know our relationship was over—"

"You weren't home," I say, squeezing my eyes shut. "I thought it more efficient—"

"You are a *monster*—"

"Yes," I say. "Yes, I am. I wish you'd forget about me."

Her eyes go glassy in an instant, heavy with unspent tears. I feel guilty for feeling nothing. I can only stare back at her, too tired to fight. Too busy nursing my own wounds.

Her voice is both angry and sad when she says, "Where's your new girlfriend? I'm dying to meet her."

At this, I look away again, my own heart breaking in my chest. "You should go get settled," I say. "Nazeera and Haider are here, too, somewhere. I'm sure you'll all have plenty to talk about."

"Warner—"

"Please, Lena," I say, feeling truly exhausted now. "You're upset, I understand. But it's not my fault you feel this way. I don't love you. I never have. And I never led you to believe I did."

She's quiet for so long I finally face her, realizing too late that somehow, again, I've managed to make things worse. She looks paralyzed, her eyes round, her lips parted, her hands trembling slightly at her sides.

I sigh.

"I have to go," I say quietly. "Kenji will show you to your quarters." I glance at Kenji and he nods, just once. His face is unexpectedly grim.

Still, Lena says nothing.

I take a step back, ready to close the door between us, when she lunges at me with a sudden cry, her hands closing around my throat so unexpectedly she almost knocks me over. She's screaming in my face, pushing me backward as she does, and it's all I can do to keep myself calm. My instincts are too sharp sometimes—it's hard for me to keep from reacting to physical threats—and I force myself to move in an almost liquid slow motion as I remove her hands from around my neck. She's still thrashing against me, landing several kicks at my shins when I finally manage to gentle her arms and pull her close.

Suddenly, she stills.

My lips are at her ear when I say her name once, very gently.

She swallows hard as she meets my eyes, all fire and rage. Even so, I sense her hope. Her desperation. I can feel her wonder whether I've changed my mind.

"Lena," I say again, even more softly. "Really, you must know that your actions do nothing to endear you to me."

She stiffens.

"Please go away," I say, and quickly close the door between us.

I fall backward onto my bed, cringing as she kicks violently at my door, and cradle my head in my hands. I have to stifle a sudden, inexplicable impulse to break something. My brain feels like it might split free of my skull.

How did I get here?

Unmoored. Disheveled and distracted.

When did this happen to me?

I have no focus, no control. I am every disappointment, every failure, every useless thing my father ever said I was. I am weak. I am a coward. I let my emotions win too often and now, now I've lost everything. Everything is falling apart. Juliette is in danger. Now, more than ever, she and I need to stand together. I need to talk to her. I need to warn her. I need to *protect* her—but she's gone. She despises me again.

And I'm here once more.

In the abyss.

Dissolving slowly in the acid of emotion.

JULIETTE

Loneliness is a strange sort of thing.

It creeps up on you, quiet and still, sits by your side in the dark, strokes your hair as you sleep. It wraps itself around your bones, squeezing so tight you almost can't breathe, almost can't hear the pulse racing in your blood as it rushes up your skin and touches its lips to the soft hairs at the back of your neck. It leaves lies in your heart, lies next to you at night, leaches the light out from every corner. It's a constant companion, clasping your hand only to yank you down when you're struggling to stand up, catching your tears only to force them down your throat. It scares you simply by standing by your side.

You wake up in the morning and wonder who you are. You fail to fall asleep at night and tremble in your skin. You doubt you doubt you doubt

do I

don't I

should I

why won't I

And even when you're ready to let go. When you're ready to break free. When you're ready to be brand-new. Loneliness is an old friend standing beside you in the mirror, looking you in the eye, challenging you to live your life without it. You can't find the words to fight yourself, to fight the words screaming that you're not enough never enough never ever enough.

Loneliness is a bitter, wretched companion.

Sometimes it just won't let go.

—AN EXCERPT FROM JULIETTE'S JOURNALS IN THE ASYLUM

The first thing I do upon my return back to base is order Delalieu to move all my things into Anderson's old rooms. I haven't really thought about how I'll deal with seeing Warner all the time. I haven't considered yet how to act around his ex-girlfriend. I have no idea what any of that will be like and right now I almost can't be bothered to care.

I'm too angry.

If Nazeera is to be believed, then everything we tried to do here—all of our efforts to play nice, to be diplomatic, to host an international conference of leaders—was for nothing. Everything we'd been working toward is garbage. She says they're planning on wiping out all of Sector 45. Every person. Not just the ones living at our headquarters. Not just the soldiers who stood alongside us. But all the civilians, too. Women, children—everyone.

They're going to make Sector 45 disappear.

And I'm feeling suddenly out of control.

Anderson's old quarters are enormous—they make Warner's rooms seem ridiculous in comparison—and after Delalieu has left me alone I'm free to drown in the many privileges that my fake role as supreme commander of The

Reestablishment has to offer. Two offices. Two meeting rooms. A full kitchen. A large master suite. Three bathrooms. Two guest rooms. Four closets, fully stocked—like father, like son, I realize—and countless other details. I've never spent much time in any of these rooms before; the dimensions are too vast. I need only one office and, generally, that's where I spend my time.

But today I take the time to look around, and the one space that piques my interest most is one I'd never noticed before. It's the one positioned closest to the bedroom: an entire room devoted to Anderson's enormous collection of alcohol.

I don't know very much about alcohol.

I've never had a traditional teenage experience of any kind; I've never had parties to attend; I've never been subjected to the kind of peer pressure I've read about in novels. No one has ever offered me drugs or a strong drink, and probably for good reason. Still, I'm mesmerized by the myriad bottles arranged perfectly on the glass shelves lining the dark, paneled walls of this room. There's no furniture but two big, brown leather chairs and the heavily lacquered coffee table stationed between them. Atop the coffee table sits a clear—jug?—filled with some kind of amber liquid; there's a lone drinking glass set beside it. Everything in here is dark, vaguely depressing, and reeks of wood and something ancient, musty—*old*.

I reach out, run my fingers along the wooden panels, and count. Three of the four walls of the room are dedicated to housing various, ancient bottles—637 in total—most of which are full of the same amber liquid; only a couple of bottles are full of clear liquid. I move closer to inspect the labels and learn that the clear bottles are full of vodka—this is a drink I've heard of—but the amber liquid is named different things in different containers. A great deal of it is called Scotch. There are seven bottles of tequila. But most of what Anderson keeps in this room is called bourbon—523 bottles in total—a substance I have no knowledge of. I've only really heard about people who drink wine and beer and margaritas—and there's none of that here. The only wall stocked with anything but alcohol is stacked with several boxes of cigars and more of the same short, intricately cut drinking glasses. I pick up one of the glasses and nearly drop it; it's so much heavier than it looks. I wonder if these things are made of real crystal.

And then I can't help but wonder about Anderson's motivations in designing this space. It's such a strange idea, to dedicate an entire room to displaying bottles of alcohol. Why not put them in a cabinet? Or in a refrigerator?

I sit down in one of the chairs and look up, distracted by the massive, glittering chandelier hanging from the ceiling.

Why I've gravitated toward this room, I can't say. But in here I feel truly alone. Walled off from all the noise and confusion of the day. I feel properly isolated here, among these bottles, in a way that soothes me. And for the first time all day, I feel myself relax. I feel myself withdraw. Retreat. Run away to some dark corner of my mind.

There's a strange kind of freedom in giving up.

There's a freedom in being angry. In living alone. And strangest of all: in here, within the walls of Anderson's old refuge I feel I finally understand him. I finally understand how he was able to live the way he did. He never allowed himself to feel, never allowed himself to hurt, never invited emotion into his life. He was under no obligation to anyone but himself—and it liberated him.

His selfishness set him free.

I reach for the jug of amber liquid, tug off the stopper, and fill the crystal glass sitting beside it. I stare at the glass for a while, and it stares back.

Finally, I pick it up.

One sip and I nearly spit it out, coughing violently as some of the liquid catches in my throat. Anderson's drink of choice is disgusting. Like death and fire and oil and smoke. I force myself to take one quick gulp of the vile drink before setting it down again, my eyes watering as the alcohol works its way through me. I'm not even sure why I've done it—why I wanted to try it or what I'm hoping it'll do for me. I have no expectations of anything.

I'm just curious.

I'm feeling careless.

And the seconds skip by, my eyes fluttering open and shut in the welcome silence and I drag a finger across the seam of my lips, I count the many bottles again, and I'm just beginning to think the terrible taste of the drink wasn't really that bad when slowly, happily, a bloom of warmth reaches up from deep within me and unfurls individual rays of heat inside my veins.

Oh, I think

oh

My mouth smiles but it feels a little crooked and I don't mind, not really, not even that my throat feels a little numb. I pick up the still-full glass and take another large gulp of fire and this time I don't dread it. It's pleasant to be lost like this, to fill my head with clouds and wind and nothing. I feel loose and a little clumsy as I stand but it feels nice, it feels nice and warm and pleasant and I find myself wandering toward the bathroom, smiling as I search its drawers for something

something

where is it

And then I find it, a set of electric hair clippers, and I decide it's time to give myself a haircut. My hair has been bothering me forever. It's too long, too long, a memento, a keepsake from all my time in the asylum, too long from all those years I was forgotten and left to rot in hell, too thick, too suffocating, too much, too this, too that, too annoying

My fingers fumble for the plug but eventually I manage to turn the thing on, the little machine buzzing in my hand and I think I should probably take off my clothes first, don't want to get hair everywhere do I, so I should probably take my clothes off first, definitely

And then I'm standing in my underwear, thinking about how much I've always secretly wanted to do this, how I always thought it would feel so nice, so liberating—

And I drag the clippers across my head in a slightly jagged motion.

Once.

Twice.

Over and over and over and I'm laughing as my hair falls to the floor, a sea of too-long brown waves lapping at my feet and I've never felt so light, so silly silly happy

I drop the still-buzzing clippers in the sink and step back, admiring my work in the mirror as I touch my newly shorn head. I have the same haircut as Warner now. The same sharp half inch of hair, except my hair is dark where his is light and I look so much older suddenly. Harsher. Serious. I have cheekbones. A jawline. I look angry and a little scary. My eyes are bright, huge in my face, the center of attention, wide and sharp and piercing and I love it.

I love it.

I'm still giggling as I teeter down the hall, wandering Anderson's rooms in my underwear, feeling freer than I have in years. I flop down onto the big leather chair and finish the rest of the glass in two swift gulps.

Years, centuries, lifetimes pass and dimly, I hear the sound of banging.

I ignore it.

I'm sideways on the chair now, my legs flung over the arm, leaning back to watch the chandelier spin—

Was it spinning before?

—and too soon my reverie is interrupted, too soon I hear

a rush of voices I vaguely recognize and I don't move, merely squint, turning only my head toward the sounds.

"Oh shit, J—"

Kenji charges into the room and freezes in place at the sight of me. I suddenly, faintly remember that I'm in my underwear, and that another version of myself would prefer not to have Kenji see me like this—but it's not enough to motivate me to move. Kenji, however, seems very concerned.

"Oh *shit shit shit*—"

It's only then that I notice he's not alone.

Kenji and Warner are standing in front of me, the two of them staring at me like they're horrified, like I've done something wrong, and it makes me angry.

"What?" I say, annoyed. "Go away."

"Juliette—love—what did you do—"

And then Warner is kneeling beside me. I try to look at him but it's suddenly hard to focus, hard to see straight at all. My vision blurs and I have to blink several times to get his face to stop moving but then I'm looking at him, really looking at him, and something inside of me is trying to remember that we are angry with Warner, that we don't like him anymore and we do not want to see him or speak to him but then he touches my face—

and I sigh

I rest my cheek against his palm and remember something beautiful, something kind, and a rush of feeling floods through me

"Hi," I say.

And he looks so sad so sad and he's about to respond but Kenji says, "Bro, I think she drank, like, I don't know, a whole glass of this stuff. Maybe half a pint? And at her weight?" He swears under his breath. "That much whisky would destroy *me*."

Warner closes his eyes. I'm fascinated by the way his Adam's apple moves up and down his throat and I reach out, trail my fingers down his neck.

"Sweetheart," he whispers, his eyes still closed. "Why—"

"Do you know how much I love you?" I say. "I love—loved you so much. So much."

When he opens his eyes again, they're bright. Shining. He says nothing.

"Kishimoto," he says quietly. "Please turn on the shower."

"On it."

And Kenji's gone.

Warner still says nothing to me.

I touch his lips. Lean forward. "You have such a nice mouth," I whisper.

He tries to smile. It looks sad.

"Do you like my hair?" I say.

He nods.

"Really?"

"You're beautiful," he says, but he can hardly get the words out. And his voice breaks when he says, "Why did you do this, love? Were you trying to hurt yourself?"

I try to answer but feel suddenly nauseous. My head spins. I close my eyes to steady the feeling but it won't abate.

"Shower's ready," I hear Kenji shout. And then, suddenly, his voice is closer. "You got this, bro? Or do you want me to take it from here?"

"No." A pause. "No, you can go. I'll make sure she's safe. Please tell the others I'm not feeling well tonight. Send my apologies."

"You got it. Anything else?"

"Coffee. Several bottles of water. Two aspirin."

"Consider it done."

"Thank you."

"Anytime, man."

And then I'm moving, everything is moving, everything is sideways and I open my eyes and quickly close them as the world blurs before me. Warner is carrying me in his arms and I bury my face in the crook of his neck. He smells so familiar.

Safe.

I want to speak but I feel slow. Like it takes forever to tell my lips to move, like it's slow motion when they do, like the words rush together as I say them, over and over again

"I miss you already," I mumble against his skin. "I miss this, miss you, miss you" and then he puts me down, steadies me on my feet, and helps me walk into the standing shower.

I nearly scream when the water hits my body.

My eyes fly open, my mind half sobered in an instant, as the cold water rushes over me. I blink fast, breathing hard as I lean against the shower wall, staring wildly at Warner through the warped glass. Water snakes down my skin, collects in my eyelashes, my open mouth. My shoulders slow their tremble as my body acclimates to the temperature and minutes pass, the two of us staring at each other and saying nothing. My mind steadies but doesn't clear, a fog still hanging over me even as I reach forward to turn the dial, heating the water by many degrees.

I can still see his face, beautiful even blurred by the glass between us, when he says, "Are you okay? Do you feel any better?"

I step forward, studying him silently, and say nothing as I unhook my bra and let it drop to the floor. There's no response from him save the slight widening of his eyes, the slight movement in his chest and I slip out of my underwear, kicking it off behind me and he blinks several times and steps backward, looks away, looks back again.

I push open the shower door.

"Come inside," I say.

But now he won't look at me.

"Aaron—"

"You're not feeling well," he says.

"I feel fine."

"Sweetheart, please, you just drank your weight in whisky—"

"I just want to touch you," I say. "Come here."

He finally turns to face me, his eyes moving slowly up my body and I see it, I see it happen when something inside of him seems to break. He looks pained and vulnerable and he swallows hard as he steps toward me, steam filling the room now, hot drops of water breaking on my bare hips and his lips part as he looks at me, as he reaches forward, and I think he might actually come inside when

instead

he closes the door between us and says

"I'll be waiting for you in the living room, love."

WARNER

Juliette is asleep.

She emerged from the shower, climbed into my lap and promptly fell asleep against my neck, all the while mumbling things I know for certain she'll regret having said in the morning. It took every bit of my self-control to unhook her soft, warm figure from around me, but somehow I managed it. I tucked her into bed and left, the pain of peeling myself away from her not unlike what I imagine it'd be like to peel the skin off my own body. She begged me to stay and I pretended not to hear her. She told me she loved me and I couldn't bring myself to respond.

She cried, even with her eyes closed.

But I can't trust that she knows what she's doing or saying in this compromised state; no, I know better. She has no experience with alcohol, but I can only imagine that when her good sense is returned to her in the daylight, she will not want to see my face. She won't want to know that she made herself so vulnerable in front of me. I wonder whether she'll even remember what happened.

As for me, I am beyond despair.

It's past three in the morning and I feel as though I've not slept in days. I can hardly bear to close my eyes; I can't be left alone with my mind or the many frailties of my person. I feel shattered, held together by nothing but necessity.

I have tried in vain to articulate the mess of emotion cluttering my mind—to Kenji, who wanted to know what happened after he left; to Castle, who cornered me not three hours ago, demanding to know what I'd said to her; even to Kent, who managed to look only a little pleased upon discovering that my brand-new relationship had already imploded.

I want to sink into the earth.

I can't go back to our bedroom—my bedroom—where the proof of her is still fresh, too alive; and I can no longer escape to the simulation chambers, as the soldiers are still stationed there, relocated in all the aftermath of the new construction.

I've no reprieve from the consequences of my actions.

Nowhere to rest my head for longer than a moment before I'm discovered and duly chastened.

Lena, laughing loudly in my face as I walked past her in the hall.

Nazeera shaking her head as I bid good night to her brother.

Sonya and Sara shooting me mournful looks upon discovering me crouched in a corner of the unfinished medical wing. Brendan, Winston, Lily, Alia, and Ian popping their heads out of their brand-new bedrooms, stopping me as I tried to get away, asking so many questions—so loudly and forcefully—that even a groggy James came to find me, tugging at my sleeve and asking me over and over again whether or not Juliette was okay.

Where did this life come from?

Who are all these people to whom I'm suddenly beholden?

Everyone is so justifiably concerned about Juliette—about the well-being of our new supreme commander—that I, because I am complicit in her suffering, am safe nowhere from prying eyes, questioning looks, and pitying faces. It's alarming, having so many people privy to my private life. When things were good between us I had to answer fewer questions; I was a subject of lesser interest. Juliette was the one who maintained these relationships; they were not for me. I never wanted any of this. I didn't want this accountability. I don't care for the responsibility of friendships. I only wanted Juliette. I wanted her love, her heart, her arms around me. And this was part of the price I paid for her affection: these people. Their questions. Their unvarnished scorn for my existence.

So. I've become a wraith.

I stalk these quiet halls. I stand in the shadows and hold myself still in the darkness and wait for something. For what, I don't know.

Danger.

Oblivion.

Anything at all to inform my next steps.

I want renewed purpose, a focus, a job to do. And then all at once I'm reminded that I am the chief commander and regent of Sector 45, that I have an infinite number of things to oversee and negotiate—and somehow that's no longer enough for me. My daily tasks are not enough to distract my mind; my deeply regimented routines have been dismantled; Delalieu is struggling under the weight of my emotional erosion and I cannot help but think of my father again and again—

How right he was about me.

He's always been right.

I've been undone by emotion, over and over. It was emotion that prompted me to take any job—at any cost—to be nearer to my mother. It was emotion that led me to find Juliette, to seek her out in search of a cure for my mother. It was emotion that prompted me to fall in love, to get shot and lose my mind, to become a broken boy all over again—one who'd fall to his knees and beg his worthless, monstrous father to spare the girl he loved. It was emotion, my flimsy emotions that cost me everything.

I have no peace. No purpose.

How I wish I'd ripped this heart from my chest long ago.

Still, there is work to be done.

The symposium is now less than twelve hours away and I never had a chance to go over the details with Juliette. I didn't think things would turn out like this. I never thought that business would go on as usual after the death of my father. I thought a greater war was imminent; I thought for certain the other supreme commanders would come for us before we'd had even a chance to pretend we had true control of Sector 45. It hadn't occurred to me that they'd have more sinister plans in mind. It hadn't occurred to me to spend more time prepping her for the tedious formalities—these monotonous routines—embedded in the structure of The Reestablishment. But I should have known better. I should have expected this. *I could have prevented this.*

I thought The Reestablishment would fall.

I was wrong.

Our supreme commander has hours to prepare before having to address a room of the 554 other chief commanders and regents in North America. She will be expected to lead. To negotiate the many intricacies of domestic and international diplomacy. Haider, Nazeera, and Lena will all be waiting to send word back to their murderous parents. And I should be by her side, helping and guiding and protecting her. Instead, I have no idea what kind of Juliette will emerge from my father's rooms in the morning. I have no idea what to expect from her, how she will treat me, or where her mind will go.

I have no idea what's going to happen.

And I have no one to blame but myself.

JULIETTE

I am not insane. I am not insane. I am not insane. I am not insane.
I am not insane. I am not insane. I am not insane. I am not insane.
I am not insane. I am not insane. I am not insane. I am not insane.
I am not insane. I am not insane. I am not insane. I am not insane.
I am not insane. I am not insane. I am not insane. I am not insane.
I am not insane. I am not insane. I am not insane. I am not insane.
I am not insane. I am not insane. I am not insane. I am not insane.
I am not insane. I am not insane. I am not insane. I am not insane.
I am not insane. I am not insane. I am not insane. I am not insane.
I am not insane. I am not insane. I am not insane. I am not insane.
I am not insane. I am not insane. I am not insane. I am not insane.
I am not insane. I am not insane. I am not insane. I am not insane.
I am not insane. I am not insane. I am not insane. I am not insane.
I am not insane. I am not insane. I am not insane. I am not insane.
I am not insane. I am not insane. I am not insane. I am not insane.
I am not insane. I am not insane. I am not insane. I am not insane.
I am not insane. I am not insane. I am not insane. I am not insane.
I am not insane. I am not insane. I am not insane. I am not insane.
I am not insane. I am not insane. I am not insane. I am not insane.
I am not insane. I am not insane. I am not insane. I am not insane.
I am not insane. I am not insane. I am not insane. I am not insane.
I am not insane. I am not insane. I am not insane. I am not insane.

~~I am not insane. I am not insane. I am not insane. I am not insane.~~
~~I am not insane. I am not insane. I am not insane. I am not insane.~~
~~I am not insane. I am not insane. I am not insane. I am not insane.~~
~~I am not insane. I am not insane. I am not insane. I am not insane.~~
~~I am not insane~~. I am not insane.

—AN EXCERPT FROM JULIETTE'S JOURNALS IN THE ASYLUM

When I open my eyes, everything comes rushing back to me.

The evidence is here, in this drumming, pounding headache, in this sour taste in my mouth and stomach—in this unbearable thirst, like every cell in my body is dehydrated. It's the strangest feeling. It's horrible.

But worse, worse than all that are the memories. Gauzy but intact, I remember everything. Drinking Anderson's bourbon. Lying in my underwear in front of Kenji. And then, with a sudden, painful gasp—

Stripping in the shower. Asking Warner to join me.

I close my eyes as a wave of nausea overtakes me, threatens to upend the meager contents of my stomach. Mortification floods through me with an almost breathtaking efficiency, manufacturing within me a feeling of absolute self-loathing I'm unable to shake. Finally, reluctantly, I squint open my eyes again and notice someone has left me three bottles of water and two small white pills.

Gratefully, I inhale everything.

It's still dark in this room, but somehow I know the day has broken. I sit up too fast and my brain swings, rocking in my skull like a weighted pendulum and I feel myself sway even as I remain motionless, planting my hands against the mattress.

Never, I think. *Never again. Anderson was an idiot. This is a terrible feeling.* And it's not until I make my way to the bathroom that I remember, with a sudden, piercing clarity, that I shaved my head.

I stand frozen in front of the mirror, remnants of my long, brown waves still littering the floor underfoot, and stare at my reflection in awe. Horror. Fascination.

I hit the light switch and flinch, the fluorescent bulbs triggering something painful in my newly stupid brain, and it takes me a minute to adjust to the light. I turn on the shower, letting the water warm while I study my new self.

Gingerly, I touch the soft buzz of what little hair I have left. Seconds pass and I get braver, stepping so close to the mirror my nose bumps the glass. So strange, so strange but soon my apprehension dulls. No matter how long I look at myself I'm unable to drum up appropriate feelings of regret. Shock, yes, but—

I don't know.

I really, really like it.

My eyes have always been big and blue-green, miniatures of the globe we inhabit, but I've never before found them particularly interesting. But now—for the first time—I find my own face interesting. Like I've stepped out of the shadows of my own self; like the curtain I used to hide behind has been, finally, pushed back.

I'm here. Right here.

Look at me, I seem to scream without speaking.

Steam fills the room in slow, careful exhalations that

cloud my reflection and eventually, I'm forced to look away. But when I do, I'm smiling.

Because for the first time in my life, I actually like the way I look.

I asked Delalieu to arrange to have my armoire moved into Anderson's quarters before I arrived yesterday—and I find myself standing before it now, examining its depths with new eyes. These are the same clothes I've seen every time I've opened these doors; but suddenly I'm seeing them differently.

But then, I *feel* differently.

Clothes used to perplex me. I could never understand how to piece together an outfit the way Warner did. I thought it was a science I'd never crack; a skill beyond my grasp. But I'm realizing now that my problem was that I never knew who I was; I didn't understand how to dress the imposter living in my skin.

What did I like?

How did I want to be perceived?

For years my goal was to minimize myself—to fold and refold myself into a polygon of nothingness, to be too insignificant to be remembered. I wanted to appear innocent; I wanted to be thought of as quiet and harmless; I was worried always about how my very existence was terrifying to others and I did everything in my power to diminish myself, my light, my soul.

I wanted so desperately to placate the ignorant. I wanted

so badly to appease the assholes who judged me without knowing me that I lost myself in the process.

But now?

Now, I laugh. Out loud.

Now, I don't give a shit.

WARNER

When Juliette joins us in the morning, she is almost unrecognizable.

I was forced, despite every inclination to bury myself in other duties, to rejoin our group today on account of what seems now to have been the inevitable arrival of our three final guests. The twin children of the South American supreme and the son of the supreme commander of Africa all arrived early this morning. The supreme commander of Oceania has no children, so I have to assume this is the last of our visitors. And all of them have arrived in time to accompany us to the symposium. Very convenient.

I should have realized.

I had just been in the middle of introducing the three of them to Castle and Kenji, who came down to greet our new visitors, when Juliette made her first appearance of the day. It's been less than thirty seconds since she walked in, and I'm still trying and failing to take her in.

She's *stunning*.

She's wearing a simple, fitted black sweater; slim, dark gray jeans; and a pair of flat, black, ankle-length boots. Her hair is both gone and not; it's like a soft, dark crown that suits her in a way I never could've expected. Without the distraction of her long hair my eyes have nowhere to focus but directly on her face. And she has the most incredible face—large, captivating eyes—and a bone structure that's never been more pronounced.

She looks shockingly different.

Raw.

Still beautiful, but sharper. Harder. She's not a girl with a ponytail in a pink sweater anymore, no. She looks a great deal more like the young woman who murdered my father and then drank four fingers of his most expensive Scotch.

She's looking from me to the stunned expressions of Kenji and Castle to the quietly confused faces of our three new guests, and all of us appear unable to speak.

"Good morning," she finally says, but she doesn't smile when she says it. There's no warmth, no kindness in her eyes as she looks around, and I falter.

"Damn, princess, is that really you?"

Juliette appraises Kenji once, swiftly, but doesn't respond.

"Who are you three?" she says, nodding at the newcomers. They stand slowly. Uncertainly.

"These are our new guests," I say, but now I can't bring myself to look at her. To face her. "I was just about to introduce them to Castle and Kishimo—"

"And you weren't going to include me?" says a new voice. "I'd like to meet the new supreme commander, too."

I turn around to find Lena standing in the doorway, not three feet from Juliette, looking around the room like she's never been so delighted in all her life. I feel my heart pick up, my mind racing. I still have no idea if Juliette knows who Lena is—or what we were together.

And Lena's eyes are bright, too bright, her smile wide and happy.

A chill runs through me.

With them standing so close together, I can't help but notice that the differences between her and Juliette are almost too obvious. Where Juliette is petite, Lena is tall. Juliette has dark hair and deep eyes, while Lena is pale in every possible way. Her hair is almost white, her eyes are the lightest blue, her skin is almost translucent, save the many freckles spanning her nose and cheeks. But what she lacks in pigment she makes up for in presence; she's always been loud, aggressive, passionate to a fault. Juliette, by comparison, is muted almost to an extreme this morning. She betrays no emotion, not a hint of anger or jealousy. She stands still and quiet, silently studying the situation. Her energy is tightly coiled. Ready to spring.

And when Lena turns to face her, I feel everyone in the room stiffen.

"Hi," Lena says loudly. False happiness disfigures her smile, morphing it into something cruel. She holds out her hand as she says, "It's nice to finally meet Warner's girlfriend." And then: "Oh, wait—I'm sorry. I meant *ex*-girlfriend."

I'm holding my breath as Juliette looks her up and down.

She takes her time, tilting her head as she devours Lena with her eyes and I can see Lena's offered hand beginning to tire, her open fingers starting to shake.

Juliette seems unimpressed.

"You can call me the supreme commander of North America," she says.

And then walks away.

I feel an almost hysterical laughter build in my chest; I have to look down, force myself to keep a straight face. And then I'm sobered, all at once, by the realization that Juliette is no longer mine. She's no longer mine to love, mine to adore. I've never been more attracted to her in all the time I've known her and there's nothing, nothing to be done about it. My heart pounds faster as she steps more completely into the room—a gaping Lena left in her wake—and I'm struck still with regret.

I can't believe I've managed to lose her. Twice.

That she loved me. Once.

"Please identify yourselves," she says to our three guests.

Stephan speaks first.

"I'm Stephan Feruzi Omondi," he says, reaching forward to shake her hand. "I'm here to represent the supreme commander of Africa."

Stephan is tall and dignified and deeply formal, and though he was born and raised in what used to be Nairobi, he studied English abroad, and speaks now with a British accent. And I can tell from the way Juliette's eyes linger on his face that she likes the look of him.

Something tightens in my chest.

"Your parents sent you to spy on me, too, Stephan?" she says, still staring.

Stephan smiles—the movement animating his whole face—and suddenly I hate him. "We're only here to say hello," he says. "Just a little friendly union."

"Uh-huh. And you two?" She turns to the twins. "Same thing?"

Nicolás, the elder twin, only smiles at her. He seems delighted. "I am Nicolás Castillo," he says, "son of Santiago and Martina Castillo, and this is my sister, Valentina—"

"*Sister?*" Lena cuts in. She's found another opportunity to be cruel and I've never hated her so much. "Are you still doing that?"

"Lena," I say, a warning in my voice.

"What?" She looks at me. "Why does everyone keep acting like this is normal? One day Santiago's son decides he wants to be a girl and we all just, what? Look the other way?"

"Eat shit, Lena," is the first thing Valentina has said all morning. "I should've cut off your ears when I had the chance."

Juliette's eyes go wide.

"Uh, I'm sorry"—Kenji pokes his head forward, waves a hand—"am I missing something?"

"Valentina likes to play pretend," Lena says.

"*Cállate la boca, cabrona,*" Nicolás snaps at her.

"No, you know what?" Valentina says, placing a hand on her brother's shoulder. "It's okay. Let her talk. Lena thinks I like to pretend, *pero* I won't be pretending *cuando cuelge su cuerpo muerto en mi cuarto.*"

Lena only rolls her eyes.

"Valentina," I say. "Please ignore her. *Ella no tiene ninguna idea de lo que está hablando. Tenemos mucho que hacer y no debemo—*"

"Damn, bro," Kenji cuts me off. "You speak Spanish, too, huh?" He runs a hand through his hair. "I'm going to have to get used to this."

"We all speak many languages," says Nicolás, a note of irritation still clinging to his voice. "We have to be able to communi—"

"Listen, guys, I don't care about your personal dramas," Juliette says suddenly, pinching the bridge of her nose. "I have a massive headache and a million things to do today, and I'd like to get started."

"Por su puesto, señorita." Nicolás bows his head a little.

"What?" she says, blinking at him. "I don't know what that means."

Nicolás only smiles. *"Entonces deberías aprender como hablar español."*

I almost laugh, even as I shake my head. Nicolás is being difficult on purpose. *"Basta ya,"* I say to him. *"Dejala sola. Sabes que ella no habla español."*

"What are you guys saying?" Juliette demands.

Nicolás only smiles wider, his blue eyes crinkling in delight. "Nothing of consequence, Madam Supreme. Only that we are pleased to meet you."

"And I take it you'll all be attending the symposium today?" she says.

Another slight bow. *"Claro que sí."*

"That's a yes," I say to her.

"What other languages do you speak?" Juliette says, spinning to face me, and I'm so surprised she's addressing me in public that I forget to respond.

It's Stephan who says, "We were taught many languages from a very young age. It was critical that the commanders and their families all knew how to communicate with one another."

"But I thought The Reestablishment wanted to get rid of all the languages," she says. "I thought you were working toward a single, universal language—"

"*Sí*, Madam Supreme," says Valentina with a slight nod. "That's true. But first we had to be able to speak with each other, no?"

Juliette looks fascinated. She's forgotten her anger for just long enough to be awed by the vastness of the world again; I can see it in her eyes. Her desire to escape. "Where are you from?" she asks, the question full of innocence; wonder. Something about it breaks my heart. "Before the world was remapped—what were the names of your countries?"

"We were born in Argentina," Nicolás and Valentina say at the same time.

"My family is from Kenya," says Stephan.

"And you've visited each other?" she says, turning to scan our faces. "You travel to each other's continents?"

We nod.

"Wow," she says quietly, but mostly to herself. "That must be incredible."

"You must come visit us, too, Madam Supreme," says a smiling Stephan. "We'd love to have you stay with us. After all, you are one of us now."

Juliette's smile vanishes. Gone too soon is the wistful, faraway look on her face. She says nothing, but I can sense the anger and sadness boiling over inside her.

Too suddenly, she says,

"Warner, Castle, Kenji?"

"Yeah?"

"Yes, Ms. Ferrars?"

I merely stare.

"If we're done here, I'd like to speak with the three of you alone, please."

JULIETTE

I keep thinking I need to stay calm, that it's all in my head, that everything is going to be fine and someone is going to open the door now, someone is going to let me out of here. I keep thinking it's going to happen. I keep thinking it has to happen, because things like this don't just happen. This doesn't happen. People aren't forgotten like this. Not abandoned like this.

This doesn't just happen.

My face is caked with blood from when they threw me on the ground and my hands are still shaking even as I write this. This pen is my only outlet, my only voice, because I have no one else to speak to, no mind but my own to drown in and all the lifeboats are taken and all the life preservers are broken and I don't know how to swim I can't swim I can't swim and it's getting so hard. It's getting so hard. It's like there are a million screams caught inside of my chest but I have to keep them all in because what's the point of screaming if you'll never be heard and no one will ever hear me in here. No one will ever hear me ever again.

I've learned to stare at things.

The walls. My hands. The cracks in the walls. The lines on my fingers. The shades of gray in the concrete. The shape of my fingernails. I pick one thing and stare at it for what must be hours. I keep time in my head by counting the seconds as they pass. I keep days in my head by writing them down. Today is day two. Today is the second day. Today is a day.

Today.

It's so cold. It's so cold it's so cold.

Please please please

—AN EXCERPT FROM JULIETTE'S JOURNALS IN THE ASYLUM

I'm still staring at the three of them, waiting for confirmation when, suddenly, Kenji speaks with a start.

"Uh, yeah—no, uh, no problem," he says.

"Certainly," says Castle.

And Warner says nothing at all, looking at me like he can see through me, and for a moment all I can remember is me, naked, begging him to join me in the shower; me, curled up in his arms crying, telling him how much I miss him; me, touching his lips—

I cringe, mortified. An old impulse to blush overtakes my entire body.

I close my eyes and look away, pivoting sharply as I leave the room without a word.

"Juliette, love—"

I'm already halfway down the hall when I feel his hand on my back and I stiffen, my pulse racing in an instant. The minute I spin around I see his face change, his features shifting from scared to surprised in less than a second and it makes me so angry that he has this ability, this gift of being able to sense other people's emotions, because I am always so transparent to him, so completely vulnerable and it's infuriating, *infuriating*

"What?" I say. I try to say it harshly but it comes out all wrong. Breathless. Embarrassing.

"I just—" But his hand falls. His eyes capture mine and suddenly I'm frozen in time. "I wanted to tell you—"

"What?" And now the word is quiet and nervous and terrified all at once. I take a step back to save my own life and I see Castle and Kenji walking too slowly down the hall; they're keeping their distance on purpose—giving us space to speak. "What do you want to say?"

But now Warner's eyes are moving, studying me. He looks at me with such intensity I wonder if he's even aware he's doing it. I wonder if he knows that when he looks at me like that I can feel it as acutely as if his bare skin were pressed against my own, that it does things to me when he looks at me like that and it makes me crazy, because I hate that I can't control this, that this thread between us remains unbroken and he says finally, softly,

something

something I don't hear

because I'm looking at his lips and feeling my skin ignite with memories of him and it was just yesterday, just yesterday that he was mine, that I felt his mouth on my body, that I could *feel him inside me—*

"What?" I manage to say, blinking upward.

"I said I really like what you've done with your hair."

And I hate him, hate him for doing this to my heart, hate my body for being so weak, for wanting him, missing him, despite everything and I don't know whether to cry or kiss him or kick him in the teeth, so instead I say, without meeting his eyes,

"When were you going to tell me about Lena?"

He stops then; motionless in a moment. "Oh"—he clears his throat—"I hadn't realized you'd heard about Lena."

I narrow my eyes at him, not trusting myself to speak, and I'm still deciding the best course of action when he says

"Kenji was right," but he whispers the words, and mostly to himself.

"Excuse me?"

He looks up. "Forgive me," he says softly. "I should've said something sooner. I see that now."

"Then why didn't you?"

"She and I," he says, "it was—we were nothing. It was a relationship of convenience and basic companionship. It meant nothing to me. Truly," he says, "you have to know—if I never said anything about her it was only because I never thought about her long enough to even consider mentioning it."

"But you were together for *two years—*"

He shakes his head before he says, "It wasn't like that. It wasn't two years of anything serious. It wasn't even two years of continuous communication." He sighs. "She lives in Europe, love. We saw each other briefly and infrequently. It was purely physical. It wasn't a real relationship—"

"Purely physical," I say, stunned. I rock backward, nearly tripping over my own feet and I feel his words tear through

my flesh with a searing physical pain I wasn't expecting. "Wow. Wow."

And now I can think of nothing but his body and hers, the two of them entwined, the *two years* he spent naked in her arms—

"No—please," he says, the urgency in his words jolting me back to the present. "That's not what I meant. I'm just—I'm—I don't know how to explain this," he says, frustrated like I've never seen him before. He shakes his head, hard. "Everything in my life was different before I met you," he says. "I was lost and all alone. I never cared for anyone. I never wanted to get close to anyone. I've never—you were the first person to ever—"

"Stop," I say, shaking my head. "Just stop, okay? I'm so tired. My head is *killing* me and I don't have the energy to hear any more of this."

"Juliette—"

"How many more secrets do you have?" I ask. "How much more am I going to learn about you? About me? My family? My history? The Reestablishment and the details of my *real life*?"

"I swear I never meant to hurt you like this," he says. "And I don't want to keep things from you. But this is all so new for me, love. This kind of relationship is so new for me and I don't—I don't know how to—"

"You've already kept so much from me," I say to him, feeling my strength falter, feeling the weight of this throbbing headache unclench my armor, feeling too much, too much all at once when I say "There's so much I don't know about you. There's so much I don't know about your past. Our present. And I have no idea what to believe anymore."

"Ask me anything," he says. "I'll tell you anything you want to know—"

"Except the truth about me? My parents?"

Warner looks suddenly pale.

"You were going to keep that from me forever," I say to him. "You had no plan to tell me the truth. That I was adopted. Did you?"

His eyes are wild, bright with feeling.

"Answer the question," I say. "Just tell me this much." I step forward, so close I can feel his breath on my face; so close I can almost hear his heart racing in his chest. "Were you ever going to tell me?"

"I don't know."

"Tell me the *truth*."

"Honestly, love," he says, shaking his head. "In all likelihood, I would have." And suddenly he sighs. The action seems to exhaust him. "I don't know how to convince you that I believed I was sparing you the pain of that particular truth. I really thought your biological parents were dead. I see now that keeping this from you wasn't the right thing to do, but then, I don't always do the right thing," he says quietly. "But you have to believe that my intention was never to hurt you. I never intended to lie to you or to purposely withhold information from you. And I do think that I would have, in time, told you what I knew to be the truth. I was just searching for the right moment."

Suddenly, I'm not sure what to feel.

I stare at him, his downcast eyes, the movement in his throat as he swallows against a swell of emotion. And something breaks apart inside of me. Some measure of resistance begins to crumble.

He looks so vulnerable. So young.

I take a deep breath and let it go, slowly, and then I look up, look into his face once more and I see it, I see the moment he senses the change in my feelings. Something comes alive in his eyes. He takes a step forward and now we're standing so close I'm afraid to speak. My heart is beating too hard in my chest and I don't have to do anything at all to be reminded of everything, every moment, every touch we've ever shared. His scent is all around me. His heat. His exhalations. Gold eyelashes and green eyes. I touch his face, almost without meaning to, gently, like he might be a ghost, like this might be a dream and the tips of my fingers graze his cheek, trail the line of his jaw and I stop when his breath catches, when his body shakes almost imperceptibly

and we lean in as if by memory

eyes closing

lips just touching

"Give me another chance," he whispers, resting his forehead against mine.

My heart aches, throbs in my chest.

"Please," he says softly, and he's somehow closer now, his lips touching mine as he speaks and I feel pinned in place by emotion, unable to move as he presses the words against my mouth, his hands soft and hesitant around my face and he says, "I swear on my life," he says, "I won't disappoint you"

and he kisses me

Kisses me

right here, in the middle of everything, in front of everyone and I'm flooded, overrun with feeling, my head spinning as he presses me against the hard line of his body and I can't save myself from myself, can't stop the sound I make when he parts my lips and I'm lost, lost in the taste of him, lost in his heat, wrapped up in his arms and

I have to tear myself away

pulling back so quickly I nearly stumble. I'm breathing too hard, my face flushed, my feelings panicked

And he can only look at me, his chest rising and falling with an intensity I feel from here, from two feet away, and I can't think of anything right or reasonable to say about what just happened or what I'm feeling except

"This isn't fair," I whisper. Tears threaten, sting my eyes. "This isn't *fair.*"

And I don't wait to hear his response before I tear down the hall, bolting the rest of the way back to my rooms.

WARNER

"Trouble in paradise, Mr. Warner?"

I've got him by the throat in seconds, shock disfiguring his expression as I slam his body against the wall. "You," I say angrily. "You forced me into this impossible position. *Why?*"

Castle tries to swallow but can't, his eyes wide but unafraid. When he speaks his words are raspy, suffocated. "You had to do it," he chokes out. "It had to happen. She needed to be warned, and it had to come from you."

"I don't believe you," I shout, shoving him harder against the wall. "And I don't know why I ever trusted you."

"Please, son. Put me down."

I ease up, only a little, and he takes in several lungfuls of air before saying, "I haven't lied to you, Mr. Warner. She had to hear the truth. And if she'd heard this from anyone else she'd never forgive you. But at least now"—he coughs—"with time, she might. It's your only chance at happiness."

"What?" I drop my hand. Drop him. "Since when have you cared about my happiness?"

He's quiet for too long, massaging his throat as he stares at me. Finally, he says, "You think I don't know what your father did to you? What he put you through?"

And now I take a step back.

"You think I don't know your story, son? You think I'd let you into my world—offer you sanctuary among my people—if I really thought you were going to hurt us?"

I'm breathing hard. Suddenly confused. Feeling exposed.

"You don't know anything about me," I say, feeling the lie even as I say it.

Castle smiles, but there's something wounded in it. "You're just a boy," he says quietly. "You're only nineteen years old, Mr. Warner. And I think you forget that all the time. You have no perspective, no idea that you've only barely lived. There's still so much life ahead of you." He sighs. "I try to tell Kenji the same thing, but he's like you. Stubborn," he says. "So stubborn."

"I'm *nothing* like him."

"Did you know that you're a year younger than him?"

"Age is irrelevant. Nearly all my soldiers are older than me."

Castle laughs.

"All of you kids," he says, shaking his head. "You suffer too much. You have these horrible, tragic histories. Volatile personalities. I've always wanted to help," he says. "I've always wanted to fix that. Make this world a better place for you kids."

"Well, you can go save the world somewhere else," I say. "And feel free to babysit Kishimoto all you like. But I'm not your responsibility. I don't need your pity."

Castle only tilts his head at me. "You will never escape my pity, Mr. Warner."

My jaw clenches.

"You boys," he says, his eyes distracted for a moment, "you remind me so much of my own sons."

I pause. "You have children?"

"Yes," he says. And I feel his sudden, breathtaking wave of pain wash over me as he says, "I did."

I take several unconscious steps backward, reeling from the rush of his shared emotions. I can only stare at him. Surprised. Curious.

Sorry.

"Hey."

At the sound of Nazeera's voice I spin around, startled. She's with Haider, the two of them looking grave.

"What is it?" I say.

"We need to talk." She looks at Castle. "Your name is Castle, right?"

He nods.

"Yeah, I know you're wise to this business, Castle, so I'm going to need you to get in on this, too." Nazeera whips her finger through the air to draw a circle around the four of us. "We all need to talk. *Now.*"

JULIETTE

It's a strange thing, to never know peace. To know that no matter where you go, there is no sanctuary. That the threat of pain is always a whisper away. I'm not safe locked into these 4 walls, I was never safe leaving my house, and I couldn't even feel safe in the 14 years I lived at home. The asylum kills people every day, the world has already been taught to fear me, and my home is the same place where my father locked me in my room every night and my mother screamed at me for being the abomination she was forced to raise.

She always said it was my face.

There was something about my face, she said, that she couldn't stand. Something about my eyes, the way I looked at her, the fact that I even existed. She'd always tell me to stop looking at her. She'd always scream it. Like I might attack her. Stop looking at me, she'd scream. You just stop looking at me, she'd scream.

She put my hand in the fire once.

Just to see if it would burn, she said. Just to check if it was a regular hand, she said.

I was 6 years old then.

I remember because it was my birthday.

—AN EXCERPT FROM JULIETTE'S JOURNALS IN THE ASYLUM

"Never mind," is all I say when Kenji shows up at my door.

"Never mind, what?" Kenji sticks his foot out to catch the closing door. Now he's squeezing his way in. "What's going on?"

"Never mind, I don't want to talk to any of you. Please go away. Or maybe you can all go to hell. I don't actually care."

Kenji looks stunned, like I just slapped him in the face. "Are you—wait, are you serious right now?"

"Nazeera and I are leaving for the symposium in an hour. I have to get ready."

"What? What's happening, J? What's wrong with you?"

Now, I turn to face him. "*What's wrong with me?* Oh, like you don't know?"

Kenji runs a hand through his hair. "I mean, I heard about what happened with Warner, yeah, but I'm pretty sure I just saw you guys making out in the hallway so I'm, uh, really confused—"

"He *lied* to me, Kenji. He lied to me this whole time. About so many things. And so did Castle. So did *you*—"

"Wait, what?" He grabs my arm as I turn away. "Wait—I didn't lie to you about shit. Don't mix me up in this mess. I had nothing to do with any of it. Hell, I still haven't figured out what to say to Castle. I can't believe he kept all of this from me."

I go suddenly still, my fists closing as my anger builds and breaks, holding fast to a sudden hope. "You weren't in on all of this?" I say. "With Castle?"

"Uh-uh. No way. I had no clue about any of this insanity until Warner told me about it yesterday."

I hesitate.

Kenji rolls his eyes.

"Well, how am I supposed to trust you?" I say, my voice rising in pitch like a child. "Everyone's been lying to me—"

"J," he says, shaking his head. "C'mon. You know me. You know I don't bullshit. That's not my style."

I swallow, hard, feeling suddenly small. Feeling suddenly broken inside. My eyes sting and I fight back the impulse to cry. "You promise?"

"Hey," he says softly. "Come here, kid."

I take a tentative step forward and he wraps me up in his arms, warm and strong and safe and I've never been so grateful for his friendship, for his steady existence in my life.

"It's going to be okay," he whispers. "I swear."

"Liar," I sniff.

"Well, there's a fifty percent chance I'm right."

"Kenji?"

"Mm?"

"If I find out you're lying to me about any of this I swear to God I will break all the bones in your body."

A short laugh. "Yeah, okay."

"I'm serious."

"Uh-huh." He pats my head.

"I will."

"I know, princess. I know."

Several more seconds of silence.

And then

"Kenji," I say quietly.

"Mm?"

"They're going to destroy Sector 45."

"Who is?"

"Everyone."

Kenji leans back. Raises an eyebrow. "Everyone who?"

"All the other supreme commanders," I say. "Nazeera told me everything."

Unexpectedly, Kenji's face breaks into a tremendous smile. "Oh, so Nazeera is one of the good guys, huh? She's on our team? Trying to help you out?"

"Oh my God, Kenji, please focus—"

"I'm just saying," he says, holding up his hands. "The girl is fine as hell is all I'm saying."

I roll my eyes. Try not to laugh as I wipe away errant tears.

"So." He nods his head at me. "What's the deal? The details? Who's coming? When? How? Et cetera?"

"I don't know," I say. "Nazeera is still trying to figure it out. She thinks maybe in the next week or so? The kids are here to monitor me and send back information, but they're coming to the symposium, specifically, because apparently the commanders want to know how the other sector leaders will react to seeing me. Nazeera says she thinks the information will help inform their next moves. I'm guessing we have maybe a matter of *days*."

Kenji's eyes go wide, panicked. "Oh, shit."

"Yeah, but when they decide to obliterate Sector 45 their plan is to also take me prisoner. The Reestablishment wants to bring me back in, apparently. Whatever that means."

"Bring you back in?" Kenji frowns. "For what? More testing? Torture? What do they want to do with you?"

I shake my head. "I have no idea. I have no clue who these people are. My sister," I say, the words feeling strange as I say them, "is apparently still being tested and tortured somewhere. So I'm pretty sure they're not bringing me back for a big family reunion, you know?"

"Wow." Kenji rubs his forehead. "That is some next-level drama."

"Yeah."

"So—what are we going to do?"

I hesitate. "I don't know, Kenji. They're coming to kill everyone in Sector 45. I don't think I have a choice."

"What do you mean?"

I look up. "I mean I'm pretty sure I'll have to kill them first."

WARNER

My heart is pounding frantically in my chest. My hands are clammy, unsteady. But I cannot make time to deal with my mind. Nazeera's confessions might cost me my sanity. I can only pray she is mistaken. I can only hope that she will be proven desperately and woefully wrong and there's no time, no time at all to deal with any of this. I can no longer make room in my day for these flimsy, unreliable human emotions.

I must live here now.

In my own solitude.

Today I will be a soldier only, a perfect robot if need be, and stand tall, eyes betraying no emotion as our supreme commander Juliette Ferrars takes the stage.

We're all here today, a small battalion posted up behind her like her own personal guard—myself, Delalieu, Castle, Kenji, Ian, Alia, Lily, Brendan, and Winston—even Nazeera and Haider, Lena, Stephan, Valentina, and Nicolás stand beside us, pretending to be supportive as she begins her speech. The only ones missing are Sonya, Sara, Kent, and James, who stayed behind on base. Kent cares little about anything these days but keeping James out of danger, and I can't say I blame him. Sometimes I wish I could opt out of this life, too.

I squeeze my eyes shut. Steady myself.

I just want this to be over.

The location of the biannual symposium is fairly fluid, and generally rotational. But in recognition of our new supreme commander, the event was relocated to Sector 45, an effort made possible entirely by Delalieu.

I can feel our collective group pulse with different kinds and levels of energy, but it's all so meshed together I can't tell fear and apathy apart. I'm focused instead on the audience and our leader, as their reactions are the most important. And of all the many events and symposiums I've attended over the years, I've never felt such an electric charge in the crowd as I do now.

554 of my fellow chief commanders and regents are in the audience, but so are their spouses, and even several members of their closest staff. It's unprecedented: every invitation was accepted. No one wanted to miss the opportunity to meet the new seventeen-year-old leader of North America, no. They're fascinated. They're hungry. Wolves sitting in human skin, eager to tear into the flesh of the young girl they've already underestimated.

If Juliette's powers didn't offer her body a level of functional invincibility I'd be deeply concerned about her standing alone and unguarded in front of all her enemies. The civilians of this sector may be rooting for her, but the rest of the continent has no interest in the disruption she's brought to the land—or to the threat she poses to their ranks in The Reestablishment. These men and women standing before her today are paid to be loyal to another party. They have no sympathy for her cause, for her fight for the common people.

I have no idea how long they'll let her speak before they rip into her.

But I don't have to wait long.

Juliette has only just started speaking—she's only just begun talking about the many failures of The Reestablishment and the need for a new beginning when the crowd becomes suddenly restless. They stand up, raise their fists and my mind disconnects as they shout at her, the events unfolding before my eyes as if in slow motion. She doesn't react.

One, two, sixteen people are on their feet now, and she keeps talking.

Half the room roars upward, angry words hurled in her direction and now I can feel her growing angrier, her frustration peaking, but somehow, she holds her ground. The more they protest, the more she projects her voice; she's speaking so loudly now she's practically shouting. I look quickly between her and the crowd, my mind working desperately to decide what to do. Kenji catches my eye and the two of us understand each other without speaking.

We have to intervene.

Juliette is now denouncing The Reestablishment's plans to obliterate languages and literature; she's outlining her hopes to transition the civilians out of the compounds; and she's just begun addressing our issues with the climate when a shot is fired into the room.

There's a moment of perfect silence, and then—

Juliette peels the dented bullet off her forehead. Tosses it to the ground. The gentle, tinkling sound of metal on marble reverberates around the room.

Mass chaos.

Hundreds and hundreds of people are suddenly on their feet, all of them shouting at her, threatening her, pointing guns at her, and I can feel it, I can feel it spiraling out of control.

More shots ring out, and in the seconds it takes us to form a plan, we're already too late. Brendan falls to the ground with a sudden, horrifying gasp. Winston screams; catches his body.

And that's it.

Juliette goes suddenly still, and my mind slows down.

I can feel it before it happens: I can feel the change, the static in the air. Heat ripples around her, tongues of power unfurling from her body like lightning preparing for a strike and there's no time to do anything but hold my breath when, suddenly—

She *screams.*

Long. Loud. Violent.

The world seems to blur for just a second—for just a moment everything seizes, freezes in place: contorted bodies; angry, distorted faces; all frozen in time—

Floorboards peel upward and fissure apart. Cracks like thunderclaps as they shatter up the walls. Light fixtures swing precariously before smashing to the floor.

And then, everyone.

Every single person in her line of sight. 554 people and all their guests. Their faces, their bodies, the seats they sit in: sliced open like fresh fish. Their flesh feathers outward, swelling slowly as a steady gush of blood gathers in pools around their feet.

They all drop dead.

JULIETTE

I started screaming today.

—AN EXCERPT FROM JULIETTE'S JOURNALS IN THE ASYLUM

Were you happy

Were you sad

Were you scared

Were you mad

the first time you screamed?

Were you fighting for your life your decency your dignity your humanity

When someone touches you now, do you scream?

When someone smiles at you now, do you smile back?

Did he tell you not to scream did he hit you when you cried?

Did he have one nose two eyes two lips two cheeks two ears two eyebrows.

Was he one human who looked just like you.

Color your personality.

Shapes and sizes are variety.

Your heart is an anomaly.

Your actions

are

the

only

traces

you leave

behind.

—AN EXCERPT FROM JULIETTE'S JOURNALS IN THE ASYLUM

Sometimes I think the shadows are moving.

Sometimes I think someone might be watching.

Sometimes this idea scares me and sometimes the idea makes me so absurdly happy I can't stop crying. And then sometimes I think I have no idea when I started losing my mind in here. Nothing seems real anymore and I can't tell if I'm screaming out loud or only in my head.

There's no one here to hear me.

To tell me I'm not dead.

—AN EXCERPT FROM JULIETTE'S JOURNALS IN THE ASYLUM

I don't know when it started.

I don't know why it started.

I don't know anything about anything except for the screaming.

My mother screaming when she realized she could no longer touch me. My father screaming when he realized what I'd done to my mother. My parents screaming when they'd lock me in my room and tell me I should be grateful. For their food. For their humane treatment of this thing that could not possibly be their child. For the yardstick they used to measure the distance I needed to keep away.

I ruined their lives, is what they said to me.

I stole their happiness. Destroyed my mother's hope for ever having children again.

Couldn't I see what I'd done? is what they'd ask me. Couldn't I see that I'd ruined everything?

I tried so hard to fix what I'd ruined. I tried every single day to be what they wanted. I tried all the time to be better but I never really knew how.

I only know now that the scientists are wrong.

The world is flat.

I know because I was tossed right off the edge and I've been trying to hold on for seventeen years. I've been trying to climb back up for seventeen years but it's nearly impossible to beat gravity when no one is willing to give you a hand.

When no one wants to risk touching you.

—AN EXCERPT FROM JULIETTE'S JOURNALS IN THE ASYLUM

Am I insane yet?

Has it happened yet?

How will I ever know?

—AN EXCERPT FROM JULIETTE'S JOURNALS IN THE ASYLUM

There's a moment of pure, perfect silence before everything, everything explodes. At first, I don't even realize what I've done. I don't understand what just happened. I didn't mean to kill *these* people—

And then, suddenly

It hits me

The crushing realization that I've just slaughtered a room of six hundred people.

It seems impossible. It seems fake. There were no bullets. No excess force, no violence. Just one, long, angry cry.

"*Stop it,*" I screamed. I squeezed my eyes shut and screamed it, anger and heartbreak and exhaustion and crushing devastation filling my lungs. It was the weight of recent weeks, the pain of all these years, the embarrassment of false hopes manufactured in my heart, the betrayal, the loss—

Adam. Warner. Castle.

My parents, real and imagined.

A sister I might never know.

The lies that make up my life. The threats against the innocent people of Sector 45. The certain death that awaits me. The frustration of having so much power, so much power and feeling so utterly, completely powerless

"Please," I screamed. *"Please stop—"*

And now—

Now this.

My limbs have gone numb from disbelief. My ears feel full of wind, my mind disconnected from my body. I couldn't have killed this many people, I think, I couldn't have just killed all these people that isn't possible, I think, it's not possible not possible that I opened my mouth and then *this*

Kenji is trying to say something to me, something that sounds like *we have to get out of here, hurry, we have to go now—*

But I'm numb, I'm dim, I'm unable to move one foot in front of the other and someone is dragging me, forcing me to move and I hear explosions

And suddenly my mind sharpens.

I gasp and spin around, searching for Kenji but he's gone. His shirt is soaked in blood and he's being dragged off in the distance, his eyes half closed and

Warner is on his knees, his hands cuffed behind his back

Castle is unconscious on the floor, blood running freely from his chest

Winston is still screaming, even as someone drags him away

Brendan is dead

Lily, Ian, Alia, dead

And I'm trying to reconnect my mind, trying to work my way through the shock seizing my body and my head is spinning, *spinning*, and I see Nazeera out of the corner of my eye with her head in her hands and someone touches me and I jump

I jerk back

"What's happening?" I say to no one. "What's going on?"

"You've done beautiful work here, darling. You've really made us proud. The Reestablishment is so grateful for the sacrifices you've made."

"Who are you?" I say, searching for the voice.

And then I see them, a man and a woman kneeling in front of me, and it's only then that I realize I'm lying on the ground, paralyzed. My arms and legs are bound by pulsing, electric wires. I try to fight against them and I can't.

My powers have been extinguished.

I look up at these strangers, eyes wide and terrified. "Who are you?" I say again, still raging against my restraints. "What do you want from me?"

"I'm the supreme commander of Oceania," the woman says to me, smiling. "Your father and I have come to take you home."

WARNER

JULIETTE

Why don't you just kill yourself? someone at school asked me once.

I think it was the kind of question intended to be cruel, but it was the first time I'd ever contemplated the possibility. I didn't know what to say. Maybe I was crazy to consider it, but I'd always hoped that if I were a good enough girl—if I did everything right, if I said the right things or said nothing at all—I thought my parents would change their minds. I thought they would finally listen when I tried to talk. I thought they would give me a chance. I thought they might finally love me.

I always had that ~~stupid~~ hope.

—AN EXCERPT FROM JULIETTE'S JOURNALS IN THE ASYLUM

When I open my eyes, I see stars.

Dozens of them. Little plastic stars stuck to the ceiling. They glow, faintly, in the dim light, and I sit up, head pounding, as I try to orient myself. There's a window on my right; a sheer, gauzy curtain filters sunset oranges and blues into the room at odd angles. I'm sitting on a small bed. I look up, look around.

Everything is pink.

Pink blanket, pink pillows. Pink rug on the floor.

I get to my feet and spin around, confused, to find that there's another, identical bed in here, but its sheets are purple. The pillows are purple.

The room is divided by an imaginary line, each half a mirror image of the other. Two desks; one pink, one purple. Two chairs; one pink, one purple. Two dressers, two mirrors. Pink, purple. Painted flowers on the walls. A small table and chairs off to one side. A rack of fluffy costume dresses. A box of tiaras on the floor. A little chalkboard easel in the corner. A bin under the window, full to the brim with dolls and stuffed animals.

This is a child's bedroom.

I feel my heart racing. My skin goes hot and cold.

I can still feel a loss inside of me—an inherent knowledge that my powers aren't working—and I realize only then that there are glowing, electric cuffs clamped around my wrists and ankles. I yank at them, use every bit of my strength to tear them open, and they don't budge.

I'm growing more panicked by the moment.

I run to the window, desperate for some sense of place—for some explanation of where I am, for proof that this isn't some kind of hallucination—and I'm disappointed; the view out the window only confuses me. I see a stunning vista. Endless, rolling hills. Mountains in the distance. A massive, glittering lake reflecting the colors of the sunset. It's *beautiful.*

I step back, feeling suddenly more terrified.

My eyes move instead to the pink desk and chair, scanning their surfaces for clues. There are only stacks of colorful notebooks. A porcelain cup full of markers and glitter pens. Several pages of fluorescent stickers.

My hand shakes as I pull open the desk drawer.

Inside are stacks of old letters and Polaroids.

At first, I can only stare at them. My heartbeats echo in my head, throbbing so hard I can almost feel them in my throat. My breaths come in faster, the inhalations shallow. I feel my head spin and I blink once, twice, forcing myself to be steady. To be brave.

Slowly, very slowly, I pick up the stack of letters.

All I have to do is look at the mailing addresses to know that these letters predate The Reestablishment. They've all been sent to the attention of Evie and Maximillian Sommers. To a street in Glenorchy, New Zealand.

New Zealand.

And then I remember, with a sudden gasp, the faces of the man and woman who carried me out of the symposium.

I'm the supreme commander of Oceania, she'd said. *Your father and I have come to take you home.*

I close my eyes and stars explode in the blackness behind my eyelids, leaving me faint. Breathless. I blink my eyes open. My fingers feel loose, clumsy as I open the letter at the top of the stack.

The note is brief. It's dated twelve years ago.

M & E—
All is well. We've found her a suitable family. No sign of powers yet, but we'll keep a close eye on her. Still, I must advise you to put her out of your mind. She and Emmaline have had their memories expunged. They no longer ask about you. This will be my last update.
P. Anderson.

P. Anderson.

Paris Anderson. Warner's father.

I look around the bedroom with new eyes, feeling a terrible chill creep up my spine as the impossible pieces of this new insanity come together in my mind.

Vomit threatens. I swallow it back.

I'm staring now at the stack of Polaroids, untouched,

inside the open desk drawer. I think I've lost feeling in parts of my face. Still, I force myself to pick up the stack.

The first is a picture of two little girls in matching yellow dresses. They're both brown-haired and a little skinny, holding hands in a garden path. One of them looks at the camera, the other one looks at her feet.

I flip the photo over.

Ella's first day of school

The stack of photos falls out of my trembling hands, scattering as they go. My every instinct is shrieking at me, sounding alarm bells, begging me to run.

Get out, I try to scream at myself. *Get out of here.*

But my curiosity won't let me go.

A few of the photos have landed face-up on the desk, and I can't stop staring at them, my heart pounding in my ears. Carefully, I pick them up.

Three little brown-haired girls stand next to bikes that are slightly too big for them. They're all looking at each other, laughing at something.

I flip the photo over.

Ella, Emmaline, and Nazeera. No more training wheels.

I gasp, the sound choking me as it leaves my chest. I feel my lungs squeeze and I reach out, catch the desk with one hand to steady myself. I feel like I'm floating, unhinged.

Caught in a nightmare.

I flip through the photos with a desperation now, my mind working faster than my hands as I fumble, trying and failing to make sense of what I'm seeing.

The next photo is of a little girl holding the hand of an older man.

Emmaline and Papa, it says on the back.

Another photo, this one of both girls climbing a tree.

The day Ella twisted her ankle

Another one, blurred faces, cupcakes and candles—

Emmaline's 5th birthday

Another, this time a picture of a handsome couple—

Paris and Leila, visiting for Christmas

And I freeze

stunned

feel the air leave my body.

I'm holding only one photo now, and I have to force myself, beg myself to look at it, the square Polaroid shaking in my trembling hand.

It's a picture of a little boy standing next to a little girl. She's sitting in a stairwell. He looks at her as she eats a piece of cake.

I flip it over.

Aaron and Ella

is all it says.

I trip backward, stumbling, and collapse onto the floor. My whole body is seizing, shaking with terror, with confusion, with impossibility.

Suddenly, as if on cue, there's a knock at my door. A woman—the woman from before; an older version of the woman in the pictures—pops her head inside, smiles at me and says, “Ella, honey, don’t you want to come outside? Your dinner is getting cold.”

And I’m certain I’m going to be sick.

The room tilts around me.
I see spots
feel myself sway
and then—
all at once

The world goes black.

Lose yourself in the exhilarating return to the #1 global bestselling Shatter Me universe, set ten years after the fall of The Reestablishment.

SHATTER ME: SERIES TWO

BOOK ONE

ROSABELLE

CHAPTER 1

When I open the cupboard, the shelves are empty.

This is no surprise, of course; the shelves have been empty for weeks. It's for Clara's sake that I make a show of opening them every morning, pretending there might be more than the same skittering cockroach living inside.

I close the cabinet door, then turn to face her. Clara never leaves the bed unless I carry her; today she's sitting up and staring out the icy window, her pale eyes made paler by the blast of early morning light. Her hand trembles as she twitches the threadbare curtain, and a blue glare briefly illuminates the glass.

"We're out of bread," I announce. "I'm heading out."

Some days Clara lets me leave without asking questions. Other days she asks me how I pay for the food I bring home. Today she says, "I dreamed of Mama last night."

I keep my face impassive. "Again?"

Clara turns toward me, so gaunt her eyes appear sunken in her face. "She wasn't well, Rosa. She was suffering."

I step into my boots, shaking my head as I move into a shaft of light. "It was only a dream," I say to her. "The dead don't suffer."

Clara looks away again. "You always say that."

"And you stare at her photograph too much," I say, knotting my laces. My right hand doesn't shake today, and I experience a rush of relief as I straighten, then a flash of terror as I note the dwindling fire in the hearth—and the disappearing pile of firewood beside it. I force the terror down. "Besides," I add, "you hardly knew her."

"Well, you hardly speak of her," Clara counters with a sigh.

Through the window I glimpse a redheaded woodpecker and watch, transfixed, as it hammers its beak into a mossy trunk. It's been just over a decade since the fall of The Reestablishment—just over a decade since we've lived here, on Ark Island—and I, too, wish I could bash my head over and over against a hard surface every day. I take a sharp breath, ignoring the ever-present ache of hunger.

It's still strange to see the birds.

They fill the sky with sound and color, rattling roofs and branches. All around us evergreens spiral skyward, never surrendering to the seasons. It's always damp here; viridescent; cold. Lakes shimmer unprovoked. Distant mountain ranges seem painted in watercolors, layers of teeth made translucent by fog. The warm and well-fed have been known to call this land beautiful.

"I won't be long," I say, buttoning myself into Papa's old coat. Years ago I cut off the military insignias with a dull blade, earning myself a scar in the process. "I'll see about rebuilding the fire when I get back."

"Okay," Clara says quietly. Then: "Sebastian came by yesterday."

I stiffen.

Very slowly I reanimate, wrapping my mother's tattered scarf too tightly around my neck. I was allowed to work at the mill yesterday, and by the time I got home Clara had been asleep.

"He came to deliver the mail," she says.

"The mail," I echo. "He came all this way just to deliver the mail."

Clara nods, then reaches under her pillow to retrieve a folded newspaper and a thick, unmarked envelope, both of which she holds out in offering. I tuck the two into my coat pocket without glancing at either.

"Thank you," I say softly. I imagine, for a moment, how it might feel to slit Sebastian's throat.

Clara tilts her head at me. "He said you missed last week's meeting."

"You were sick."

"I told him that."

I look toward the door. "You don't need to tell him anything."

"He still wants to marry you, Rosa."

I lift my head sharply. "How do you know about that?"

"Would it be so terrible?" She ignores my question, shivering violently. "Don't you like him? I thought you liked him."

I turn to face our little kitchen, the small stove, the rickety table and chairs we never use. The wooden plaque hanging above the sink.

Our society
REESTABLISHED
Our future
REDEFINED

My eyes unfocus.

I was ten when I came home to find a black bear tearing through the last of our food. Clara was three; Mama had been dead three days. I don't remember killing the bear or burying what remained of my mother.

I remember the blood.

I remember the weeks it took to scrub the floorboards. The bars of Clara's crib. The ceiling. Mama's last words to me had been *close your eyes, Rosa,* except that she'd closed her eyes and I'd kept mine open. She put the gun in her mouth just hours after we heard that Papa would no longer be executed for war crimes. He'd traded all of us in for a half-life, selling secrets to the enemy in exchange for a slow rot in prison. I used to think Mama killed herself because she couldn't withstand the shame. Now I'm certain it was because she knew she'd be forced to pay for Papa's treason.

Maybe she thought they'd spare her children.

I grab the bear pelt from its hook and drape it around Clara's trembling limbs. She hates the pelt. She says the bear's pain still lingers in the cottage, that it makes her retch even after all these years. So when she allows the fur to settle on her shoulders without protest, I know the situation is dire.

"If you married Sebastian, things would be better," Clara says, suppressing another shiver. She pauses to cough, and the hacking sound drives a hole through my head. "They'd lift the sanctions. You wouldn't have to pretend we have food in our cupboards every morning."

Slowly, I meet her eyes.

I remember when Clara was born, when I'd looked at her and wondered whether Mama had given birth to a doll. Only later did I realize I must've looked just as strange when I was born: all ghost and glass. I study her often when she sleeps, or when the illness overtakes her so completely she slips into a coma. At thirteen, she's tender and optimistic; nothing like I was at her age. Still, despite the seven years between us, she and I are physically similar: shockingly pale; hair so blond it's nearly white; eyes a disorienting shade of cold. Staring at Clara is like staring into the past, at what I used to be, who I could've been.

I was soft once, too.

"I really think he loves you," she says, her eyes brightening with feeling. "You should've heard the way he talked about you— Rosa, wait—"

I don't say goodbye to my sister.

I reach for the automatic rifle tucked away in the entry, pulling the strap over my head before tugging a battered balaclava over my face. I step into the cold, and thick flakes catch in my eyelashes just as the front door slams shut behind me, the sound briefly drowning out his voice. It's my only explanation for being startled.

"Rosabelle," he says, cutting in front of me with a smile. "Still dead inside?"

ROSABELLE

CHAPTER 2

I sidestep Lieutenant Soledad, absently running my hand along the cold weapon slung across my chest. Soledad is no longer a lieutenant the way he once was; the title is a relic of another time. In this newly imagined world he's the head of our island's security, which makes him nothing more than a glorified busybody. And a tyrant.

I nod at familiar faces as they pass, their eyes anxiously tracking between myself and Soledad, who's fallen into step beside me. Snow is beginning to stick to the ground; spirals of smoke curl away from stacked chimneys, smudging the skies like errant brushstrokes. I adjust the balaclava on my face; the wool is old and itchy. I am impatient.

"I thought our appointment was for tomorrow," I say flatly.

"I thought I'd surprise you," he says. "Impromptu interrogations often yield interesting results."

I come to a halt, turning to face him.

I remember when Soledad was young and fit and full of bravado—when he served under my father, the chief commander and regent of Sector 52. Now he's somehow barrel-chested but soft; stooped. His skin is waxy, his hair thinning. He wears the stale air of another time, the only lingering evidence of that epoch imprinted on his face. A soft blue glow pulses at his temples, his dark eyes occasionally brightening, then dimming.

Unbidden, my right arm trembles.

Quietly I change course for the day, feeling the pressure of a single, physical key tucked inside in the false pocket sewn into Papa's old coat. The only lock I own is bolted to the shed camouflaged in the wilds beyond the cottage—which I meant to visit first, and which I'll now have to avoid. No one in the pit knows about the lock because the lock is illegal; the homes in the pit are meant to be borderless. Our minds, too, are meant to be open at all times for inspection. It was the way of our parents, the way of The Reestablishment.

Surveillance is security, Papa used to say. *Only criminals need privacy.*

I glance at Soledad, who still wears his old military fatigues, the front pocket adorned with the tricolored emblem of a buried era. He lost an arm during the post-revolution skirmishes and wears his prosthetic proudly, one sleeve rolled up to reveal the silver gleam of muscular machinery.

"So," he says. "We can set up here, or we can head back to central. Your choice."

I cast a furtive glance around the pit, which comprises a cluster of cottages, square windows aglow in the gray morning light. People scurry along, heads down, avoiding eye contact with Soledad, who's never paid the pit a visit without doing some damage. Those who live here have been sanctioned—cut off from the community for any number of infractions—but no one has lived here longer than Clara and me, who've never known another home on the island. In the chaotic weeks after our supreme commanders were slaughtered, Papa sent us here with Mama, promising to follow as soon as he could. It turned out Papa had stayed behind on purpose, voluntarily surrendering to the rebels. As a reward, we were sanctioned upon arrival.

"Do we have to do this now?" I ask, thinking of Clara, shivering and starved. "I'd rather keep our appointment for tomorrow."

"Why, you have plans this morning?" He says this like it's a joke. "You're not allowed a shift at the mill today."

A sharp pang of hunger cuts through me then, nearly taking my breath away. "Just some things to do."

Soledad grabs my chin and I suppress a flinch, steadying myself as he forces me to look at him. He stares into my eyes for a long beat before letting go, and I kill the flare of revulsion in my chest, compelling my racing heart to slow.

I remind myself that I am dead inside.

"So strange not to know what you're thinking," he says, a notch forming between his brows. "All these years and I still haven't gotten used to it. Makes it hard to believe you're always telling the truth."

Another slight tremor moves through my right hand. I'm the only person here unconnected to the Nexus. Even Clara was brought online before Papa was arrested. Just before the end, all civilians under the directive of The Reestablishment had been connected to the neural network, a program quickly dismantled by the new regime. Soledad and the others like to remind us that the reason we lost the war was because the rebels hadn't been chipped.

I have no acceptable excuse.

"Pity we can't seem to get you online again," Soledad says finally. "Things might've been easier for you."

Memories flare to life: cold metal; muted screams; drug-induced nightmares. With Mama dead, there was no one to beg them to stop. No one who cared whether their experiments would eventually kill me.

"I couldn't agree more," I lie.

Soledad shifts his weight. Blue veins of light pulse through his metal arm, silver fingers flashing as they flex and curl. "So," he says. "Why'd you miss the meeting last week?"

Just like that, an unofficial interrogation has begun. Here, in the freezing cold. While my neighbors watch.

Clara, I realize, can probably see us from the window.

There's a sudden chorus of shouts and my heart stutters, steadying only when I spot Zadie's twin boys, Jonah and Micah, tackling each other in the snow. One of them punches the other in the gut, this accomplishment punctuated by peals of laughter. I catch the drifting scent of breakfast meat from a nearby cottage and my knees nearly give out.

I return my eyes to Soledad. "Clara was sick."

"Coma?"

"No." I look away. "She spent most of the night throwing up."

"Food?"

"Blood," I clarify.

"Right." Soledad laughs. He sizes me up through Papa's overlarge coat. "That makes more sense, considering the fact that you're both starving."

"We're not starving." Another lie.

A fresh circus of sound short-circuits my nervous system. A murder of crows lands heavily on a nearby roof, eerie calls clamoring, wings flapping. I'm watching them, fascinated a moment by an iridescent sheen of black feathers when two earsplitting shots ring out.

I stiffen on impulse—then force myself to thaw, my fingers to unclench, my pulse to slow.

"Fucking birds," Soledad mutters.

He walks over to the duo of fallen bodies, then stomps on their small, hollow bones, smearing blood and feathers into the snow. I blink, exhaling softly into the cold. I've been dead inside for years, I remind myself.

Most people here hate the birds for what they represent. The birds mean that The Reestablishment has been dethroned, that the project has all but failed. The New Republic and its traitorous leaders—the children of our fallen supreme commanders—have been a ripe source of hatred for as long as I can remember.

Clara, I realize, will have questions about the gunshots.

"I've got real work for you, if you're interested," says Soledad, now wiping his boots on a clean patch of ground.

I look up. Realization is swift. "You didn't come here for an interrogation."

Soledad smiles at me, but his eyes are unreadable. "Never misses a thing, this one. I've always hated that about you."

"How many this time?" I ask, my heart beginning a traitorous rhythm.

"We've got four altogether. Three have been processed already. New one came through last night and he's definitely—" Soledad's eyes brighten, glazing over in an inhuman shade of blue. Suddenly he whips around, marches over to the twins still grappling in snow, grabs one of them—Micah—by the scruff of his neck, and shoves him, angrily, to the ground. "You've just lost your rations for the week."

Jonah darts forward. "But— We were only playing around—"

"He was going to take your eye out," Soledad barks, then jerks his head in a familiar motion.

Micah screams.

Jonah stills, but his eyes are fixed on his brother, who's lying on the ground, now silent and twitching violently. There's the slam of a door, a sudden cry, and his mother, Zadie, comes running. Soledad shakes his head in disgust, and Micah is released from his paralysis. With some effort, the boy revives in his mother's arms.

“Sorry, sir,” says Micah, his chest heaving. “I didn’t mean—”

Soledad directs his next words to Zadie. “If you can’t get these two idiots to stop acting like animals, you’ll spend another year in the pit. Is that clear?”

Heads appear, then disappear, in neighboring windows.

Zadie nods, mumbling something inarticulate, then grabs her boys and bolts.

In the quiet aftermath Soledad returns to my side, scanning me for a reaction, but I’m careful, as always, to betray no emotion. It’s the only way I’ve survived here, where I’m surveilled not only by the system but also through the eyes of everyone I encounter—even my own sister.

Surveillance is security, Rosa.

Only criminals need privacy.

Only criminals need privacy.

For so many years I used to believe everything my father said.

Those were the years when Soledad was a friend to our family; the years we lived in a warm, comfortable home, when food was abundant, when Nanny would dress me in silks before braiding my hair. I’d sneak downstairs during my mother’s dinner parties just to hear the sound of her laughter.

“How many more before you’ll lift the sanctions?” I ask, ripping the balaclava off my head. I feel the static of my hair; the compression of my chest. Brisk wind batters my face but the icy air is welcome against my heated skin.

Soledad shakes his head. "I can't answer that. Your father is still alive, still feeding secrets to the enemy. For as long as we can't know your mind, you'll always be a question mark." He shrugs, then looks away. "We all make sacrifices for the security of our nation, Rosabelle. For the security of our future. This is your sacrifice—and it may never end."

He returns his eyes to me.

"Look," he says. "You can kill them all at once or one at a time. I'll let you decide. When you're done, I'll see about getting Clara some medicine."

"And food," I say too quickly, then pause, taking a moment to compose my face. "And firewood."

"All at once, then," he says, narrowing his eyes.

"All at once," I agree. "And right now."

Soledad raises his eyebrows. "You sure? One of them won't stop screaming. She had a bad reaction to the sedative."

I feel unseasonably warm. Overdressed. I distract myself by stuffing the balaclava into Papa's coat pocket, and the thick envelope from earlier kisses me with a paper cut. The pain focuses my thoughts.

It's not necessary to kill them like this.

We have among our ranks some of the best medics and scientists in the world; we possess far more advanced and humane ways to kill the rare spies who manage to breach Ark Island.

Of course, murdering them isn't meant to be humane.

"Do you care how I kill them?" I ask, and my voice is mercifully steady.

The electric hum of the helicopter pulls my attention skyward. Clara will see it. She'll know what it means.

"I don't care how you do it." Soledad smiles now; a real smile. "You've always been creative."

Can't get enough of the SHATTER ME world?

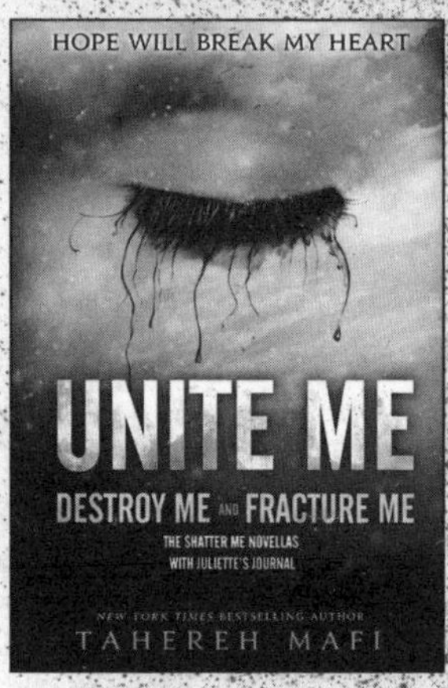

Read the digital editions of the Series One novellas: *DESTROY ME*, *FRACTURE ME*, *SHADOW ME*, *REVEAL ME*, and *BELIEVE ME*.

STORYTIDE
An Imprint of HarperCollins*Publishers*

epicreads.com